I0709063

About the Author

Lexie Winston has been an astronaut, rock star, princess and time traveller. In her dreams. But none of the dreams have lived up to what becoming an author has been like. She gets to live in a world of pure imagination, and her heroines get to do the things she's always wished she could.

When not writing books, Lexie is a mother of two gorgeous teenagers and the wife to a patient and understanding man. They live in Western Australia and are lorded over by two unruly and needy toy poodles. She loves camping, reading and if her Kindle was stolen, her world would explode.

And you can find all links at

www.lexiewinston.com

Trust Broken

BROKEN PROMISES
BOOK THREE

LEXIE WINSTON

Also by Lexie Winston

The Collectors Division

(Paranormal Reverse Harem Series)

Guardian

Guardian's Blood

Guardian Ascending

Collector's Division Omnibus

Neighpalm Industries Collective

(Enemies to Lovers Reverse Harem)

Abandoned Girl

Broken Girl

Tormented Girl

Wanted Girl

Cherished Girl

Loved Girl

Superficial Girl - Jacinta's Story Part 1

Superficial Girl - Jacinta's Story Part 2

Neighpalm Industries Collective 1-3

Neighpalm Industries Collective 4-6

Seductive Sins Collection

(Reverse Harem Series)

Glorious Gluttony

Gangs, Guns, and Glory

Glory Glory Hellelujah

Crowning Glory

What's the Story, Morning Glory?

(Seductive Sins Omnibus)

Galaxy Circus

(Sci-Fi Reverse Harem Series)

Apprentice

Stagehand

Whisperer

Mama - Galaxy Circus Novella

Performer

Ringmaster

Interlude

Spectacle

Ovation

A Night Most Wicked - Galaxy Circus Novella

Broken Promises

(Dark Poly Romance Series)

Secrets Kept

Lies Untold

Trust Broken

M.I.T.H.O.S

(Contemporary RH)

Spies Like Me

Spies Like Us

Storm View Stories

(Contemporary Standalone RH)

Ice Me Out

Kingdoms Series

(Paranormal RH)

Kingdom of Aramis Duet

Unwilling Queen

Ardent Queen

First published by Neighpalm Publishing in 2025

Copyright © Neighpalm Publishing 2025
The moral right of the author has been asserted.
All rights reserved. This publication (or any part of it) may not be reproduced or transmitted, copied, stored, distributed or otherwise made available by any person or entity, in any form (electronic, digital, optical, mechanical) or by any means (photocopying, recording, scanning or otherwise) without prior written permission from the publisher.
This is a work of fiction. Names, characters, businesses, places, events and incidents are either the products of the author's imagination or used in a fictitious manner. Any resemblance to actual persons, living or dead, or actual events is purely coincidental.

Trust Broken - Broken Promises Series 3

Mobi format: 978-1-7636228-8-3
Print: 978-1-7638409-7-3

Cover design by Breakout Designs
Editing by Elemental Editing

Content Warning

This books contains scenes of a sensitive nature and readers are advised to continue at their own risk. These scenes include and are not limited to
Drug Use
Violence
Non Con
Dub Con
Blood and Knife Play

The Broken Promises series will contain MM and FF and is considered a poly romance as opposed to a traditional reverse harem romance.

Chapter One

"She called the club, and they came and got me. We have to go. Our dorm room is on fire."

I gape as I try to compute everything that just happened. Tristan's words finally penetrate my mind as he reaches up to release Colton from the restraints.

"Your dorm room is on fire?" I ask and hurry to grab my coat, pulling it tight around my body. I look for my favorite knife, which I tossed somewhere—there's no way I'm leaving that behind—all while trying to wrap my head around how I've been cutting Colton and their dorm room is on fire.

Shit, Gio and Vienna!

"Is Vienna here? What about Gio? Was he with Casey?" My heart races at the thought of my brother and my new friends being trapped in a fire.

"No, she stayed home tonight. She has a book she wanted to read, and Xavier stayed with her. Hurry," Colton urges as Tristan struggles to release the cuffs. I grab my knife out of a wall and hurry back, slicing through the leather like butter. Tristan blinks, looking between the knife and Colton.

"Fuck, she cuts you with that?"

"Not now, Tris," Colton snaps as he grabs his clothes from a chair and gets dressed.

"I sent my car away," I say, remembering that I came in the limo and sent it back to the fortress. I pull out a phone and send an SOS message to Sage. He can bring my car and meet us at the university.

"Ride with us," Tristan grabs my hands and drags me out of the room. I clasp the edges of my coat to ensure they stay closed. I don't need anyone else seeing my tattoo and putting two and two together. Fuck, I can't believe I forgot to cover it, and speaking of tattoos...

"Where's your tattoo?" I ask Colton, remembering the rose he has over his heart that most definitely wasn't anywhere I could see it, and I could see a whole lot of skin.

He continues moving through the club at a clipped pace. My heels click on the concrete floor as Tristan and I keep up with him. "You aren't the only one good at using makeup," he mutters tersely. I almost snap back, but then I remember his other two partners are in danger, and I decide to let it slide this time.

We pass the club's changing room, but I pull him to a stop and gesture to my fur coat. "I can't run around dressed like this. I have a change of clothes in my locker." I drag them both into the changing rooms, heading for the one assigned to me. I always keep spare clothes in case I need to work after I finish a session here. Thankfully, the area is clear of people. I drop my coat, leaving me just in my straps as I dig around in my locker for clothes.

"Holy shit," Tristan mutters, and when I look over my shoulder, he's staring at me and biting his knuckle. "I understand why you decided to keep coming back, even before knowing who it was," he tells Colton.

Colton just scoffs. "The package was just the window dressing. What the girl can do with a knife makes me so fucking hard."

I can't stop the smirk that crosses my lips as I pull a pair of black cargo pants on over my sexy lingerie. I find a long-sleeved, black shirt and shrug into it, then I search for a pair of shoes but come up empty. Fuck, I must have forgotten to return a spare pair last time I needed them. Crap. I'll keep the heels on for now. I shove my feet back into them and wince at how uncomfortable they are. These are my play heels, not my work ones, and they are a lot less sensible than I would normally wear.

I dig around in my coat pockets, shove my gun down the back of my pants, and slip my knife into the holster sewn into the pockets, then I pull the fur coat back on. I won't leave it here for it to suddenly go missing out of my locker.

"Okay, let's go." I spin around, and Colton stands up, having taken the time to tie the laces on his own boots while I was changing. Both of them are wearing tight leather pants and boots. Tristan has on a long-sleeved, silk button-up, and Colton is wearing a mesh long-sleeve T-shirt. Both look like they've been clubbing, so they don't appear suspicious at all. If you don't look too closely at my outfit, it could pass as club wear as well, especially with the heels.

None of us stop at the discrete reception desk on our way out. I have a membership, and they will charge my account directly. I'm assuming Colton and Tristan are the same. I'm annoyed and sad that I didn't get to play with my sub tonight, even more so now that I know it's Colton. I'm not sure how I feel about making him bleed anymore though. It will be a conversation we will need to have before we go much further, but that's for another time.

A black Maserati's lights turn on when Tristan points the fob at it, then he gets into the driver's side while I slide into the back and Colton gets in the passenger seat. Tristan peels out of the Black Rose's parking lot like a bat out of hell.

My phone starts to ring, and I look down at it, seeing Sage's name on the screen. "Hey," I answer, grabbing hold of the door as Tristan smoothly slides the car around a corner at top speed. Holy crap, he can drive as well as Sage can.

"Are you okay?" I can hear how worried Sage is. I've never sent him an SOS message before.

"Yeah, I'm fine. I'm with Tristan and Colton, and

we're heading to the college. Their dorm is on fire. Can you meet us there?"

"Tris and Colt? What are you doing with them? I thought you were going to the Black Rose tonight." He doesn't sound upset, just curious.

"Funny story. Turns out Colton is my new favorite male sub," I murmur so neither of the guys in the front can hear, but they are both talking about the fire and not paying any attention to me.

"Huh," Sage grunts. "They seem to be turning up everywhere we go. Is this fate at play or something else?" he muses, echoing something I was wondering myself.

"We can worry about it later. Right now, my focus is on Gio and if this attack on their dorm is an accident or a deliberate attack on him." I look out the window and see smoke billowing into the air, and the red and blue lights from the fire trucks reflecting off the surrounding trees. The Black Rose isn't far from school, so we made good time with Tristan driving.

"It's been a while since there were any outward attacks on either of you. I was beginning to wonder if our enemies had given up," Sage remarks as I hear him change gears in the background. He's pushing the car as fast as he can. I hope there are no police between Banbridge and Suncity.

As we pull into a parking lot not far from the dorm, I can already tell most of them are here. Lots of people are milling about just outside of a taped off area, and there are police officers trying to keep everyone back. The fire seems to be contained to the top floor where Gio and the others had their apartments, but that isn't making it easier to fight. There are two big trucks with ladders against the walls and firefighters aiming large streams of water into the windows.

"Got to go, see you soon," I tell him without waiting for a response. "Fuck, that doesn't look suspicious at all," I grumble as I watch from inside the car. It's instantly going to be branded as arson. I consider my options as I watch Tristan and Colton hurry across the expanse of grass between the car and the apartment. They left as soon as the car stopped moving, not paying attention to me in their concern for their partners, but I know the minute I get out, all eyes will be on me, especially the suspicious eyes of the police. A few of them are on our payroll, but not all of them. Even though I literally just arrived, I will become the number one suspect. Actually, Gio will probably be number one, but I will be a close second. Where is my brother?

I peer through the crowd, my heart racing as I try to catch sight of him. I follow the direction I saw Tristan and Colton go, and I can see them just inside the barrier. Colton's arm is around a robe-clad, redheaded female. Vienna's okay. I heave a sigh of relief. I hadn't realized I was holding my breath. My gaze moves, and I find Xavier with Tristan standing next to him, waving his hands as he talks animatedly to him. I wonder if they are talking about the fire or if he's telling him about finding me and Colton together in the room.

My suspicions are soon confirmed as both of them turn toward the car, and Tristan points in my direction. There's still no sign of Gio as the four of them duck under the tape and head my way. My heart starts to pound furiously as my anxiety rises. Where is my brother? Was he injured? My gaze moves to a couple of ambulances parked behind the fire trucks. I see people sitting in them and being treated for smoke inhalation, but I can't make out any features.

I don't wait for them to get to me before throwing the door open. "Where's Gio?" I ask as they reach me.

Vienna's face is stained with tear tracks, and she coughs pitifully, her whole body supported by Colton. "You need to get yourself checked out," I tell her. "Why hasn't she been seen by a paramedic?" I snap, looking at Xavier and raising an eyebrow.

He arches an unamused eyebrow at me. "Easy, Tori." He holds up his hands like he's trying to placate a feral animal. "We're headed there now. It's where Gio and Casey are. She was coughing really badly, so he took her straight over. Vienna and I had to speak to the fire chief about the fire," he explains, but I don't bother waiting to hear anything else, hurrying over toward the ambulances.

I kicked off the ridiculous heels before I got out of the car, so the grass is damp and cold against my bare feet. I also left my fur coat behind, because getting the scent of smoke out of it would have been a nightmare.

I don't wait for the others, my suspicious nature starting to rear its ugly head. Sage is right. These four seem to be everywhere we go. I mean, I know they are Gio's friends, but the Black Rose is not Gio's scene. That's a me thing, and I kind of feel like they've ruined it for me. I liked the anonymity of it, and I can't get that back now. Even though Colton was becoming my favorite sub, I'm not sure we can ever return to what it was before we discovered one another's identities.

I'm actually completely thrown off balance by these four, which hasn't happened to me in a long time. I'm not an overly emotional person. Even before everything that occurred with Stacey and losing Dad, I didn't have a lot of friends and couldn't understand how people thought being popular and social was so important. Sure, I love my brother, Uncle Mickey, Aunt Carla, and my dad, and I'm pretty sure Sage has wiggled his way into my heart, but I've never been particularly emotional. That may be because I was raised with no motherly influence. Penelope certainly wasn't loving, but my head is spinning, and I am completely overwhelmed. I'm so fucking angry with my brother and so busy with the business that I didn't think there was room in my life for anything else. Now, I have all these conflicting emotions. I'm certainly attracted to the four of them and really tempted by their offer, but I can't help feeling like something is off. Every time I interact with them, something niggles at the back of my brain, warning me not to let my guard down.

I sigh as I approach the ambulance. I hear my brother shouts something, but it's not intelligible. My body is tight with tension, and my anger starts to simmer again. I didn't get to make anyone bleed tonight, so I'm walking on thin ice as I refrain from pulling my gun out and blowing Gio's brains all over the back of the ambulance.

I'm going to have to stop using the Black Rose in Suncity, and that makes me even madder. I know there is another in Vegas, but this one was conveniently close. I guess I can combine work and pleasure, though, and check on all our own holdings there. Ugh, my subs were so well trained. I hate the idea of having to train new ones.

I approach the row of ambulances and peer into the first one. There are a couple of pajama-clad teenagers being treated, but neither of them is my brother or Casey. I move on to the next one, and when I look inside, I scowl at what I find. Stacey and another female are there with oxygen masks over their faces. I don't recognize the girl as someone we went to school with, but I don't bother stopping because I don't really care if she chokes or suffocates.

Thankfully, she doesn't see me, so there are no snide remarks or flirty comments for the boys who are following me, keeping Vienna between them. I duck around a policeman, keeping my head turned so nobody recognizes me, and peer into the final ambulance. It's there I finally locate my brother and his girlfriend. Gio is coughing with a mask over his face while a paramedic listens to his chest with a stethoscope. Casey is wringing her hands, her face covered with tears as she watches. Seeing him makes some of the tension leave my body now that I know he is relatively unharmed. I guess I should feel a small amount of relief about Casey too, but I don't. In fact, it probably would have benefitted me if she had perished in the fire, but that's not something I will ever voice aloud.

I open my mouth to say something, but Casey starts to sob, and I wait for her to finish.

"Our apartments. Where are we going to go? I don't want to go home and have to live with him again, Gio. You know how I feel about that. The others will like it even less."

Huh, that's certainly interesting information. I need to dig deeper. It seems my brother is keeping even more secrets. The relief I felt at seeing him safe slowly ebbs away, replaced by the usual annoyance as the others catch up to me.

"Casey," Vienna calls with relief, and Gio lifts his head, catching sight of us just as the paramedic steps away from him.

"You're going to be fine. Take it easy for a couple of days, nothing strenuous, and drink plenty of fluids. If your throat continues to be irritated, use some throat lozenges, and if the cough docsn't go away, see your doctor," the medic tells him as Gio slips his arm around Casey and pulls her close, whispering words of reassurance.

I stand back and listen as the paramedic checks

over Vienna at Xavier's insistence. "What are we going to do now? I don't want to go back to that house," Vienna mutters. Those are the same words Casey spoke. Xavier quickly shakes his head, shushing her, but Gio must have heard her.

"It's okay, you don't have to. We'll help them out, won't we, Tori?" Gio looks at me with his eyebrows raised, but I can see the cold steel in his eyes, as if he's daring me to contradict him.

I don't know exactly what he's suggesting, but it better not be what I think it is.

"Tori," Sage yells, causing me to turn my attention to him, ignoring what Gio just suggested. I find him hurrying toward us from the direction of the parking lot, and I smother a sigh of relief. I was feeling very vulnerable now that most of these guys know my secret fetish, and the fact that Gio obviously doesn't have my back over his new friends. Hopefully, Sage is still on my side and hasn't been seduced by these admittedly distracting people.

Chapter Two

"Fuck, is everyone okay?" Sage looks around the group, grabbing Vienna's hand and giving it a little squeeze as she assures him she's okay.

"My eyes hurt, and so does my throat, but Xavier got us out as soon as the window smashed."

"The window was smashed?" Sage focuses on that comment.

"Yeah, a flaming projectile came through the window. It definitely looks like it was an attack on me, but they must not have been sure which dorm room was mine, so they took out both just in case," Gio growls.

Well, shit, look at that, there is some fire left in him after all. Pardon the pun, but that's a hell of a shot considering they were up so high. They must have had some kind of launcher.

"I'll check all the security cameras as soon as I can get my laptop..." Colton winces and looks back at the fire. Crap, of course all their belongings are in the fire. My annoyance at my brother slides away, and it's replaced by sympathy for their situation. They just lost everything—or everything they had with them. I'm assuming they have things at their usual place of residence, but that's a whole other story, judging by the two girls' reactions. Damn it, I really need to dig deeper into their history. I'll talk to Sage about it. I hate that I've let this slide, but with all my other responsibilities, it didn't seem so urgent. I'm thinking maybe that should change now.

"Oh my god, I'm so sorry. All your stuff," I say awkwardly, especially since a few days ago, I was committing arson.

"Well, actually, I have backups in a fireproof safe, but I'll have to wait until the firefighters give us the all clear, but apart from them and some important documents, I'm guessing we lost everything else."

Casey sobs, and the other four exchange a loaded glance that I can't even begin to read.

Gio opens his mouth to speak, and I brace myself for what's about to come out. "Don't you worry about a thing. Tori and I are going to make sure you're okay," he tells Casey then looks at the others. Before he can say anything else, I pull out my phone and swipe my finger across it.

"Sure, I'll message the Lucky Diamond and organize for you to have rooms there. I'll open accounts in the restaurants and stores until you can get to the mall to replace your belongings. We also have family accounts with a lot of the major stores at the malls, so I'll have your names added to them. We will help you get back on your feet in no time," I reassure them, but to be honest, I'm secretly pleased that Gio will have to move home now and distance himself from them. He's getting attached, and I was starting to catch feelings that are confusing and uncomfortable. I've held everyone at arm's length for a long time. I only just started letting Sage in, and I'm not ready to expand that circle of trust any further just yet.

I don't think they are lacking in money. Hell, Tristan drives a Maserati, but it also sounds like their relationship with their guardian isn't as rosy as it could be. If I can help with that, then I'm happy to. God only knows our relationship with the step-monster isn't peachy. The only reason I haven't had her killed yet is because it would be too obvious.

I realize there's an awkward silence and look up from my phone. They are all staring at me with various expressions. Gio looks furious, while Casey and Vienna both have pink cheeks like they are embarrassed, and the guys just look angry. Sage winces like I did something wrong. Shit, did I do the wrong thing? I'm really not good at this peopling thing. This is why I prefer to use my guns and knives to get things done.

"We can take care of ourselves," Xavier growls. "We have enough money. We don't fucking need yours."

Oh shit, I insulted them. That was not my intention, but I won't show him I'm affected by his anger. I pop my phone back into my pocket and shrug, feigning disinterest.

"Okay, whatever, I was just trying to help. The offer is there, and the rooms are waiting if that's what you choose to do."

Gio shakes his head and glares at me. "Tori, I meant they can come stay at our place. They don't need to go to the fucking hotel. What are you think‐ing?" My brother sounds pissed, and I just stare at him, unflinching in the wake of his anger.

Oh no, he did not just invite these mostly strangers to come live in our house, our sanctuary. It's the one place where I feel comfortable enough not to carry a weapon around with me. It's the only place where I can go to sleep without worrying someone is going to stab me in the chest while I'm sleeping. He is going too fucking far. I was okay with them staying that one night, but I am not willing to make it a permanent thing.

"No." I shake my head, my focus on my brother. I don't even look at the others' reactions at my refusal. I feel Sage step up behind me, his body heat reassuring me of his support. Gio drops his arm from around Casey, steps down out of the ambulance, and squares up to me. I'm not wearing my heels, so I'm consider‐ably shorter than him and have to look up, which makes me wild with anger. His expression is thunder‐ous. It's the most amount of anger I've seen him show in months, and he's directing it at me. I feel betrayed, but I hold my ground. There's no way I am letting this motherfucker know that he hurt me.

"Tori, I'm not asking. They will be staying with us, and I don't want to hear anything from you about it. Now should I advise Ben and Suzy, or would you like to?"

I grit my teeth and shake my head, determined not to let him steamroll me, acting like he's in charge when he hasn't shown any interest in months.

"No Gio. It's not happening. It's my house too, and it's the one place where I don't have to worry about being anyone but myself. I feel safe there, and I will not let you ruin that for me." The hard glint in his eyes softens ever so slightly, but I can tell by the stubborn set of his jaw that I am not changing his mind. I also doubt I'm going to like what is going to come out of his mouth next.

"Am I or am I not still the head of the Russo family?" His tone is flat, and the small amount of softness I saw in his eyes disappears. He gets a dead look in his gaze, and I know he's finally channeling his inner monster. The sick part of me gets a thrill, and my heart starts to race with excitement. Are we finally going to have this out? This probably isn't the best of times with all the witnesses, but I am practically frothing at the mouth to pit my skills against my brother's.

I scoff, my fingers flexing with the urge to grab my knife and shove it into his gut, but I push it down. "Only when it fucking suits you. You've been too busy playing happy family and busy college student.

As far as I'm concerned, you are head in name only. I'm the one who runs the business, and just because I have a pair of tits and nothing hanging between my legs, I'm not considered good enough. Well, fuck you, Gio, and fuck all the other assholes who get in my way."

How dare he suddenly start throwing his weight around now when it finally suits his fucking agenda. I've been holding this business together for months, taking out the trash and eliminating the competition and threats while he's been sneaking around with a girl and sulking because he couldn't go to college like he planned.

There's an awkward silence as Gio and I have it out, but I don't have any fucks to give for their feelings. My brother is trying to steamroll me, and no pretty face is going to change how I feel.

"But I am still the official head, and it will stay that way. None of our people would ever follow a girl," he sneers, but I think if he took a good look at the business, what he would see would shock him. Our people respect me and recognize what a great job I have done running the Russo family business. I have expanded and improved on various income streams, and we are making more money than we ever have. I am also passing that on to all our members, even the small ones. They love me, and so do their wives and girlfriends. Gio needs to watch his back. I have support, and frankly, getting him permanently out of the way would be in my best interest, but the stupid fucker is so blind to everything going on that he can't see the fox in the henhouse.

"Unless I put a bullet in your skull. Be very careful, Gio, because you will never hear me coming," I warn him quietly, and it's his turn to scoff.

"Please, no one will ever accept you as head of the Russo family. Not only are you a girl, but a dyke on top of that, and you've proven to be unstable. You're just lucky that your bloodlust is a good trait for an enforcer. Otherwise, you would have been married off to secure an alliance just like Dad planned." And just like that, Gio breaks my heart and destroys any kind of trust I had left for him. How could he say that? He knows Dad never wanted that for me. He even told me himself. How could he throw that in my face now? Does he know something I don't?

I'm not quick enough to smother my emotions, and I must show some outward display of how much his words hurt me, because the anger in his eyes fades, replaced with a small amount of panic, but it's too late.

"Screw you, Gio," I spit and turn around, not even waiting for a reply. I just stalk back across the grass toward my car. I sense Sage keeping up with me, and while I'm grateful he chose to come with me, I'm thankful he keeps quiet. We're on the road and heading back to the fortress before he even thinks of breaking the silence. I've been stewing in my anger, half wanting to ask him to turn around so I can take care of my brother once and for all, but I know I would regret it if I did something like that while I was mad.

"Are you okay?" he asks quietly. "Do you want to talk about what just happened, or should I take your mind off everything?" he suggests, and his hand slides onto my knee and gives it a squeeze. I know he's trying to distract me, but in the mood I'm in, it could be dangerous for him, and I know he doesn't like pain.

"No. I'm really not. You should probably stay far away from me for a little while. I'm afraid I don't have the kind of control I normally do, and I wouldn't want to accidentally hurt you."

"What can I do? How can I fix this for you? You didn't get to cut anyone at the club?" he asks, and I shake my head.

"No, I hadn't even started the session when we were interrupted, and I discovered that my new favorite sub was Colton. I can't believe I did the things I did to him." I blush as I remember our last session. The memory of his blood and cum still haunts me, and at times, I find myself craving the taste. The possibilities that come to mind now that I know I was enjoying Colton are limitless, but I need to resist. The good thing about the club was the anonymity involved, though I can't deny having someone to cut at my beck and call is tempting. I don't like that they now have one more thing they know about me that others don't.

Sage shakes his head. "I can't believe they keep turning up at places we frequent coincidentally." He puts his hand back on the wheel as I tap my fingers against the door, twitchy as fuck from my confrontation with Gio.

"Hmm," I muse, staring outside. "I had the same thought, but how did they know I was a member of that club? It's anonymous, and the rest of it is Gio's doing." I growl my brother's name.

"I really thought you were going to pull your gun out and pop a cap in his ass when he implied you weren't good for anything but an arranged marriage," Sage says carefully, and when I turn my head, he's glancing between me and the road, a worried frown creasing his brow.

I grunt. "The only thing that stopped me was there were so many police officers around. Gio can thank the local police department for the fact that he is still breathing. He's lost sight of what is important, and I don't think he's fit to be the head of the Russo family anymore. I can't believe he implied I'm only good for marriage. He knows how I feel about that and that Dad didn't want that for me."

Sage is silent, and when I look at him, he's frowning, his eyes on the road as he purses his lips.

"What, you don't agree?"

He sighs loudly. "I don't disagree that he's not focused on the business, but has he really lost sight of what's important? It seems like maybe he's putting his happiness first, and isn't that what matters?"

"Please," I scoff. "Our happiness was never going to matter. Remember the family motto, Sage." I tap the tattoo on my body. "Blood, honor, and valor.

None of that implies we need to be happy. Family first, and that doesn't mean flesh and blood family, but the organization. Gio has forgotten that."

"Maybe, or maybe he's just realized there are more important things in life," Sage replies quietly.

"What the fuck is wrong with you?" I demand. "You're in a weird mood. If you really feel like that, why don't you turn the car the fuck around, and I'll leave you to play happy family with them while I get on with business. I'm sure they will be thrilled to have you." I'm pissed at his words, but deep down, I know it probably has to do with the fact that he isn't wrong. That isn't something I'm going to admit to at the moment though. I'm also jealous. Does he want to be with them more than he wants to be with me? They can probably give him a more normal relationship, even though there are four of them, which is more than I will ever be able to.

"Nothing," he says quietly before shaking his head and grinning at me with a wink. "Just playing devil's advocate. Now what are we going to do about Gio and your raging bloodlust? I think fratricide might still be a bit extreme, even for you. You'd end up regretting it once your bloodlust cooled." The tension in the car lowers at his playfulness, but my body is still wound tightly as can be.

"Don't be so sure," I mutter as he pulls into the fortress gates. "I need to get out of town for a few days. I can't be anywhere near him, otherwise we may come to blows. Hopefully he'll come to his senses, and he'll see that bringing them home would not be in anyone's best interest." Sage looks at me doubtfully. Pfft, who am I kidding? I don't even believe the words coming out of my mouth. "Sure, we moved the chemistry lab, but we still have your weed warehouse underground, and shipments of arms and ammunition come through on a regular basis. It isn't something we could hide from people living in the house twenty-four seven. They would end up wondering where you, Suzy, Ben, and I keep disappearing to. He will realize that, right?"

Sage mutters something under his breath that I don't hear. Ugh, Gio is such a fucking asshole. If I hang around, I'll probably end up doing something I will regret.

"Pack a bag. We aren't staying. We will head up to Seattle to check out the Lucky Diamond and Kitty Kat, then we'll make our way back down the coast. I want to know how many places Lorenzo has gotten his hooks into. We'll be subtle and blend in. We aren't as familiar in the other places as we are in San Jose and Vegas, so let's see if we can figure out anything more about the trafficking ring we can share with the agent. It would also help if we could figure out what happened to his sister. Before we go, though, we will check out the club here. Arrange to send Candy to San Jose to fill in for Stella and promote Lacey."

Sage grimaces. "I'll call Sam and Dean and let them know we're on the move."

"Have Sam tell the pilots to submit a number of flight plans. I don't want anyone too certain on where we are going. I'd like to keep these trips on the down-low as much as possible."

"How about we send the main jet to Cancun or something? Make it look like you're taking a few days in the sun, and then charter something under one of our aliases," Sage suggests.

"And who says you're just a pretty face?" I blow him a kiss, forgiving him for everything. I need someone in my corner, and being mad at him for pointing out the possible truth is not going to help.

His eyebrows draw inward in confusion. "People say I'm just a pretty face? I'm a fucking genius," he grumbles under his breath as the gates open after he waves at the guard who pokes his head out to have a look.

I smile for the first time tonight. I'm truly grateful to have Sage in my life.

Chapter Three

"When we get to Vegas, I might pay a trip to the Black Rose there. It may have to be my new regular club. I'm not sure I can go back to the one here anymore. Maybe they will have a sub who enjoys blood play." It isn't a common kink, so I'm not holding my breath. "We can stay at our hotel and see if Lorenzo or anyone associated with him or any of our enemies have become frequent visitors recently. I will need to set up a meeting with him when we return. We need to put our double cross into play. The sooner he is out of my hair, the more I can relax."

"Are you sure you don't want to keep going to the Black Rose here? Hell, maybe you can finally make use of the playroom you installed in the house."

My head swings around as I gape at him in surprise. "You know about that?" I ask, slightly concerned that he knows about the work I had done on the room on the other end of the hallway. I thought

I was pretty subtle. It was an unused storage room that was hidden behind a bookshelf. It was so dusty when Suzy showed it to me, I figured everyone else had forgotten it existed. She was the one who helped me sneak the contractors in to do what I wanted to it.

He shrugs and smirks. "Suzy isn't very subtle. I'm pretty sure she was deliberately banging around when she was cleaning the room loud enough for me to stick my head out and see what she was doing. She tried to play it down, but I'm certain she was scheming an attempt to get us together."

"When was this?" I ask, biting my lip.

"At least a month ago. That's how long it's been finished, right? I was kind of surprised. Until recently, you liked to keep your sex life far away from the house."

He sounds hurt and curious, and he's right, I've never brought anyone to the house and never planned to. I have no idea why I had the room built. Maybe subconsciously I was hoping Sage and I would use it one day, even though I know he isn't into cutting.

"Yes, well, I mean, I started wondering if maybe you and I could be more, and then I was too worried to mess up the dynamics of our relationship, and then I was too scared to ask you to join me in the room because, well, you know..." I trail off, knowing I'm rambling, caught off guard by his question. I also won't ever forget the assault he suffered under people who were supposed to be his safe place—kind of exactly like what Stacey did to me. How can I ask him to play with me when it might trigger past trauma?

"I mean, it isn't just a wet playroom. I kind of got them to put a little of everything in there. I used the same contractors the Black Rose club owners did." The words tumble nervously out of my mouth, and for the first time in a long time, I actually feel my age, like a nervous teenager talking to her crush. "There are all sorts of toys in there, and I don't know..." I'm completely out of my depth. It's a new experience not to be completely sure about something. I'm so flustered I hadn't even noticed we're parked and the car is turned off. How long have we been sitting here?

"Oh, I know. I worked out the mechanism and poked around. I really liked the look of that black strap-on you had in there, hoping maybe one day you might use it on me," he says casually as he opens the car door and gets out.

My mouth drops open, and I'm speechless as I watch him walk around the front of the car to my side and open the door for me. He holds out a hand, and I take it, still completely flustered. The concrete is cold on my bare feet as I step out of the car. I guess my heels and fur coat are still in Tristan's car. My anger surges again. Damn it, that was my favorite fur, and it certainly wasn't cheap. I'm going to have to get another one now.

"Tori?" Sage drags my attention back to him. The moment I'm standing next to the car, he slams my door shut and pushes me against it, crowding me with his body. Without my heels on, I have to look up at him, and the wicked glint I see in his eyes as well as the small smirk on his lush lips have my heart rate speeding up again. "Don't overthink it. You and me? I'm all in, and I couldn't care less if I ever saw the others again. While they are sexy and fun, it almost seems kind of convenient. You know what I mean? All of them are bi, and you and I are both bi. It kind of feels manufactured, like they were put in our path."

My thoughts race as I try to wrap my head around what he just said, but he leans in and peppers kisses on my temple, down my cheekbones, and across my lips then back up the other side, as one of his hands slips under my shirt and caresses my breast. His fingers pause when he feels the strappy underwear I have on, but he quickly keeps going. He rolls a nipple between two fingers and grinds his thigh against my core. He's trying to distract me from everything that happened tonight, and it's working.

I struggle to untangle my tongue to reply to his comment. "Yes, but I first met them before all of this. Well, not before Stacey, but before I knew about Dad and the family and his death. They were going to be Gio's college roommates back then. Vienna and Colton were supposed to be in my high school class, but I never ended up attending my senior year. I home-schooled instead. Hell, I met them before I met you." I grab his shirt and give him a playful shove away from me. "I can't concentrate when you're so close, smelling so good, and doing things that make me ache," I mumble as he arches an eyebrow. The grin that spreads across his lips is like sunshine.

He grabs my hand and tugs me toward the elevators. "Come on. We need to pack and let Suzy and Ben know we're leaving for a while. I'll call the henchmen as well and get them moving. Why don't you take a long, hot shower? We have time for that. Wash the smoke out of your hair. You'll feel better afterwards."

The elevator doors open, and we step in. Sage leans forward to scan his eye in the retinal scanner before pressing one of the buttons. The doors close, and the elevator starts to move, bypassing the ground floor and taking us directly to the level our bedrooms are on. My heart still beats swiftly, and I'm feeling a little light-headed from the small bit of attention he gave me. I bet an orgasm would help right now.

"Are you going to join me?" I ask him as we stop moving and the doors start to open. His eyes widen in surprise, and there's a brief moment of hesitation, like his brain is trying to make sense of what I just said, but then he pushes off the wall, snatches my hand, and drags me down the hallway to my room. A small, inelegant snort of laughter escapes my mouth, but I have to hurry to keep up with him so I don't fall over.

Instead of going to my bedroom door, he pushes open the one on the right and tugs me into his room. The curtains are pulled closed, and the night shutters are down, making his room impenetrable to any ambient light from outside, but he has no trouble navigating the darkness with only the dim hallway illumination assisting us.

He stops suddenly, and as my eyes adjust to the darkness, I see the shadow of his huge bed. He spins around and slides his hands onto my hips, gripping my shirt and pulling it up over my head, before returning to my pants and helping me out of those. He steps away, leaving me standing in just my underwear. I hear him move away from me, but before I can ask him what he's doing, a low light switches on next to the bed. He stalks back to me, and I see the heat and desire in his eyes as they roam over my lingerie.

"Holy fuck, that's how you dress when you're at the club? How does Colton not bust a nut just by looking at you?" His hands slide onto my mostly naked hips, apart from a few strings of underwear, and I feel my nipples pebble at the contact as my core throbs. He just stands there, staring down at me, his fingers running lightly over my skin as he drinks in the sight.

"You are so fucking gorgeous, Tori," he murmurs as he leans forward, placing one hand in the middle of my back while the other one still rests on my waist, dragging me toward him. He kisses me slowly, like he's trying to memorize my taste. I shudder and kiss him back, tangling my tongue with his. I feel his hard cock pressing against my belly, so I slide my hand down to palm it through his jeans.

He moans and pulls away, sliding his hand higher to the clasps on my bra. The fabric falls down my arms, revealing my tight, heavy breasts to him. He leans forward and captures my nipple with his mouth, sucking hard while reaching up to palm the other one, his rough palms scraping delightfully against my skin. I moan and thrust my breasts forward, wanting to feel more friction. He drags his teeth over the nipple in his mouth, and I gasp before he soothes the slight pinch with his tongue.

I run my hands through his curls, tugging slightly, and the vibrations of his groan send spikes of pleasure from my breasts directly to my pussy.

I push him away, and he drops to his knees, peeling the rest of the straps down my body as I toss the bra to the side, leaving me naked and slick with arousal. He leans in and nuzzles my clit, pressing a kiss to it before flicking his tongue through my folds and tasting the wetness there.

I step back. "Shower now," I demand and spin, not waiting for him. In the bathroom, I turn on the faucet and wait for the water to heat. I hear Sage divesting himself of his clothes behind me as steam starts to fill the room. Before I can step in, Sage catches me and carries me into the stream. Hot water cascades over both of us, my back pressed to his front as his hands span my waist and stomach, holding me tightly against his lean body. His erection presses against my ass as the glass surrounding the shower fogs with the heat.

Water streams down both our bodies, our breaths coming in harsh pants. Sage steps forward before spinning me around. He presses me against the tiled wall, the cool surface making me shiver in surprise as he claims my mouth again.

Our kiss continues as he braces one hand against the wall and slides the other down my body, circling my clit twice before he parts my folds and slides a finger deep into my aching core. I moan, and my head falls back against the tiles as he slides it in and out while sweeping his thumb over my clit.

Breaking the kiss, he slides his mouth to my neck, where he sucks before biting down hard. A slice of pain spikes through my body, creating a sharp contrast with the pleasure he's wringing from my pussy, driving my desire higher.

Dropping to his knees, he throws one of my legs over my shoulder, cups my ass cheeks, and buries his face in my cunt. His tongue plunges in, licking broad strokes from my entrance to my clit before he sucks the throbbing nub. I cry out, unable to control the volume, my wet hair flying around as I grind into his face, chasing more of the delicious torture.

"Sage, I want you now." I tug his hair, and he release me, lowering my leg down to the ground and rising to his feet. I have to brace myself, because my knees buckle slightly now that he's no longer supporting me, but in a flash, he scoops me up, sliding his arms under my legs, and he lines himself up before thrusting smoothly until he's fully seated, and I'm gasping for more.

He presses his forehead to mine, staring deep into my eyes as he slowly pulls out before slamming back in.

My mouth drops open on a silent scream as my walls clench around him, and the wet slapping of skin fills the enclosed space. Our breaths heave, and the grunts and groans from us create a musical accompaniment to the sounds of falling water, a symphony of our attraction.

"Harder," I beg, gripping his shoulders and meeting each of his thrusts. My core ripples with every movement, sending me closer to an orgasm. He obeys, and our mouths smash together as his pelvis slides across my slit with each hard plunge. My body shutters, my cunt gripping him like a vise as I shout his name before biting his shoulder. He stiffens, and his hips jerk once more before he follows me into oblivion, flooding my core with his hot cum, each pulse painting me with his seed.

We stay still, just breathing in the moment, until the water starts to run cool. As it does, I push him away, and he lowers me to the ground, pulling his semi-hard cock from me. I groan at the loss as our combined fluids slide down my leg. He grabs a loofah and begins to wash me before the warm water runs out. Neither of us talk, and the silence says so much.

Chapter Four

"Has Colton found anything interesting about the people working for us? You went to see him this afternoon, didn't you?" Sage asks, running his finger up and down my spine in a way that makes goosebumps erupt on my skin. I shiver and snuggle closer to him, throwing my leg over his, enjoying the way his body heat seeps into me. I rub my face against his pec, not wanting to meet his eyes or answer his question. Will he see what I did with Vienna as cheating, or will he be okay with it? I know he expressed being okay with it in the past, but I don't know if he will still feel the same way when faced with the reality of it.

He chuckles. "Who would have guessed Tori Russo is as cuddly as a kitten when she's fully fucked." We moved to his bed after the intense sex session in the shower.

I hiss at his words, which makes him pull me closer and press a kiss to the top of my head, still chuckling.

"I did go to see them this afternoon, but I kind of got sidetracked," I admit, knowing I need to be honest about it.

His finger pauses on my spine, and I feel him inhale slightly. "Oh?" His voice is neutral, and I wince and close my eyes, not wanting to look at him when he rejects me.

"Yeah, Vienna kind of ambushed me, and we fooled around a little. When Colton returned, I forgot to ask him what he found about the trafficked women, and he didn't offer up anything. Both of us kind of had our minds on other things."

"Oh, and what were those other things? What did you and Vienna get up to?" His voice is still neutral, and my stomach rolls in distress.

"Oh, um, so we kind of went down on each other," I admit, and there's a loaded pause before he asks.

"Sixty-nine?"

"Yeah, and Colton kind of walked in and found us lying naked together."

He squirms underneath me before groaning loudly. "Fuck, that sounds so hot. I wish I had been there."

My eyes pop open, and I see his other hand gripping his rapidly hardening cock. "You don't care? You're not upset?"

He scoffs and rolls over, shuffling down the bed a

little so we're face-to-face. "Tori, it would be hypocritical of me to be jealous when I know you watched me make out with Xavier and Tristan in the hot tub the other night. You also know I did a bit more with Tristan previous to that." I remember watching them and thinking how good they looked, and that I'd like to be between them. I'd also love to know how much further he and Tristan went. In fact, I would love a play-by-play, but I'm not ready to admit that yet. He's looking at me with affection in his eyes and no small amount of lust. "I don't have any problems with you fooling around with any four of them, as long as it's only them and I have the same permissions from you. Are you going to be upset if I fool around with Vienna?"

An image of Sage pressed between me and Vienna fills my head. The idea of me fucking his ass while he fucks her has me squeezing my legs together. "Uh, no, can I play too?"

He smiles. "Of course, but there will be times when you aren't there and I'm with her, or I'm not there and you're with them. Is that going to be an issue?"

He's insistent, so I take the moment to consider his question. Will I be upset if he and Vienna fuck when I am otherwise occupied and can't be involved? There's a small twinge of jealousy, but it's not at the thought of the two of them being together—it's at the thought that I would be too busy to join them. The pressure and responsibilities of the Russo family that have fallen onto my shoulders in the wake of my father's death and Gio's apathy are enormous, and I resent that my life has become so complicated, but I am also proud that I have the ability to step up and make sure the Russo name stays feared.

"No, of course not. I'll be jealous because I can't be there playing too, but not at the two of you together. In fact, it makes me happy that if business takes me away from you for whatever reason that you will have others to keep you occupied."

I don't voice that who I am makes me a huge target, and I could die at any time. I'm just glad that if I am taken out that someone will be around to comfort him.

That reminds me, I need to speak to Gio about the line of succession. Neither of us have children. I probably won't ever have any. I can't imagine bringing a child into this kind of life. Gio may want them one day, but until then, we need to make sure if anything were to happen to either of us that Sage becomes the head of the Russo family. It doesn't matter if he carries Russo blood or not. Dad gave him our name, and that is enough.

"Then that's settled. You and I are solid, and if we want to play occasionally with our new friends, neither of us are going to be upset," Sage says, tucking a lock of my hair behind my ear and giving me that gentle smile that I love so much. It's full of acceptance and love, and it makes me feel all warm and gooey inside. Ah hell, when did I become such a sap?

"Come on. Let's get moving. We've wasted enough time. I bet Gio will be home soon, and I can't look at him without wanting to shove my Glock into his mouth and pull the trigger," I say, pressing a kiss to Sage's lush lips. "But thank you, I needed this. It wasn't bloodshed, but it did help a little."

Sage groans. "Fuck, it's such a turn on when you get all stabby. Are you sure you don't want to stay here and fool around a little more and take care of this?" He rubs his hard cock against my thigh, and I bite my lip as I consider attempting to give him my first blow job.

"As tempting as that is, we better not. I'm serious about running into Gio, and I'm almost certain he will bring them all back here tonight, even though I told him there are rooms for them at the Lucky Diamond. He won't want to let Casey out of his sight when she's had such a close call."

I press a kiss to the middle of his chest then roll away before I cave. I slide off his bed and pad across the room, gathering the clothes he tore off me in his haste.

"I'll meet you downstairs in fifteen?" I suggest, and he nods absently, his eyes glued to my naked ass as I open the door and walk across the hall into my own room. There's still a smile on my face as I contemplate dressing and packing.

When I arrive downstairs after packing a bag for our trip, I find Sage in the kitchen talking to a bleary-eyed Suzy in a robe and Ben, who's wearing a pair of sweatpants and nothing else.

"What's going on? We didn't wake you, did we?" I blush, thinking about how loud Sage and I were while we were fucking. I wasn't even thinking about anyone being around. Did they hear us?

"Gio called and told us what happened. He's heading back with those friends of his, and he wanted to make sure the rooms they stayed in last time were ready," Ben explains, and I feel my cheeks heat even more. I look at Sage with wide-eyed panic.

He must be able to read my mind, because he just chuckles and shakes his head. "They haven't been up there to check yet. They only just came out while I was making us coffee to go." He points at the machine, which has my travel mug sitting under it.

I sigh with relief, and my cheeks stop flaming, but then I realize what he said, and I growl.

"One night, and then they need to leave. I arranged for them to have suites at the Lucky Diamond."

Ben's eyes widen at the aggression in my tone, and Suzy's lips purse in disappointment.

"They just lost everything, Tori. Have some compassion."

"They haven't lost everything. They have a home they can go to but choose not to," I snap at her, and when she flinches, I instantly feel guilty. "Shit, Suzy, I'm sorry. It's just that this is the only place where I can relax, and if there are strangers here, that isn't going to be easy." I hate that my bad mood is causing me to lash out at my family.

The hurt in her eyes fades, and she nods. "Yes, but Tori, maybe they don't have to be strangers. Being an island in the middle of a sea can get lonely. You're going to have to let people in eventually. Remember, we talked about this." She nods between me and Sage, reminding me of the previous advice she gave me.

I shake my head. "We don't know enough about them. They seem to be everywhere, and I can't be sure that isn't a coincidence or something more sinister. I want to keep them at arm's length until I can do a deep dive into their backgrounds, and I have no one I trust to do that at the moment."

Ben nods, looking thoughtful. "She isn't wrong, my little crepe." He puts his arms around his wife's shoulders and places a kiss on top of her head. "You always want to see the best in everybody, but you know in our line of work that can't be how it is. What about the Irish? Maeve's family has no reason to lie or protect them. Why don't you ask if their tech wizard can dig into them a little?" Ben suggests.

"That's actually smart. I'll contact Mickey and have him ask her to facilitate it for us. Do we know their last name?" I look at Sage, who frowns and shakes his head.

"No, I don't think we do. We need that to do thorough background checks."

"Leave that to me. I will do a little digging while

they are here. I'm sure none of them will be going to school tomorrow, and I will fuss over them like a mother hen," Suzy assures me, and Ben snorts with laughter.

"Suzy is a master manipulator and will have the information out of them before they even know they've been interrogated."

"Okay, thanks, that would be great. Send me a message or an email, and I'll make sure Mickey gets it."

"How long will you be gone?" Suzy asks, looking at the bag at my feet with a frown. "That seems like a lot of packing for a night or two."

I shrug. "We will head up to Seattle and make our way back down. I'm going to make discreet inquiries at all our locations, so don't share where we are. Sage had the pilots take the jet to Cancun. As far as anyone is concerned, we're on the beach drinking mai tais," I instruct them.

"Even Gio?" Ben asks carefully.

"Especially Gio. He doesn't get to know anything, and I very much doubt he will ask, but if he does, assure him everything is being handled. We have no big shipments of ammunitions or drugs due over the next couple of weeks. It's just business as normal through the rest of our holdings."

"Be careful, Tori. You were attacked the other night, and now Gio was targeted. It looks like someone is gunning for the Russo family again," Ben cautions, and I frown.

"It does seem that way, and there aren't many

players left for us to point a finger at. We took care of a lot of them just after Dad and Carla were killed. I have a suspicious feeling that this is internal. I was only targeted after I found out about the Kitty Kat up in San Jose. I would place money on my attack being Lorenzo's work. As for tonight, I would suggest the same. When Gio was living here, there was no way for Lorenzo to get at him, especially at night when this place locks down, but his college apartment doesn't have those kinds of protections, and anyone could have breached it. I'm just surprised they used the method they did instead of straight up sending an assassin to take him out in his sleep."

Sage leans against the counter and crosses his arms. "You know, you're right. It seems a little random, to be honest, especially bombing both rooms like they did. You think they would have done their research first to figure out which one Gio was in."

"So maybe Gio wasn't the target?" Suzy suggests, and I gape at her in surprise. She shrugs. "Well, I mean, they are family, aren't they, and they were spread out over those two rooms. Gio rooms with Xavier and Tristan, right? And the other three room together. I'm just saying maybe one of them was the target."

"Suzy isn't wrong. We know absolutely nothing about them. It's why I want an independent background check ran on them. Gio had one done back when he was originally going to room with them, but that was completed by one of the guys we disposed of after Dad died. Turned out he was being paid on the side to leak information to a third party, which we weren't able to get out of him. No matter what I did to him, he took that information to his grave."

"That's pretty loyal," Ben comments offhandedly, but Sage shakes his head.

"Not really. He knew Tori was going to kill him, and she had already tortured him quite badly. It was a giant fuck you to her." Sage grimaces, probably remembering the bloody swathe I cut through our family as I weeded out those who were loyal and those who had been turned to the dark side.

"Okay, so that is our main focus. You find out their surname, and I'll put Mickey and Maeve on it. It will give them something to do. I think Mickey is going stir crazy at the lake cabin. He wants to help more, but he needs to remain comatose a little longer. Sage and I will let you know how we get on."

"I booked us in small chain motels, so no one should recognize us. We'll go to the various businesses undercover and make sure Lorenzo isn't using the Kitty Kats as a breeding ground for his sex trafficking venture."

"He was very unhappy when I took over the Kitty Kat clubs back when I first joined the business, but I only thought it was a bunch of sleazy asshole managers. I wonder if women were disappearing even then. I should go back through all our records. If only Carla was still around, she would know any details." A stab of sadness ripples through me at the thought of my dearly departed pseudo aunt. I still miss her and

Dad on a visceral level, I just learned to shove it deep down. Family men don't show their grief in public, and I am being held to those standards despite my gender, especially because there are still people who want me to return to the kitchen, barefoot and pregnant, and submissive to a man who is in charge.

At that annoying thought, I grab my coffee off the machine, and Sage and I say our goodbyes to Suzy and Ben before escaping.

Chapter Five

"Let's pay a little visit to the club here first. I want to send Candy up to San Jose to cover for Stella, and I can't put it off any longer." I grimace as Sage pulls my car out of the underground garage, and we leave the estate.

I see him wince out of the corner of my eye. "Fuck, that's going to be messy. You know that's going to go over like a lead brick," he warns unnecessarily.

I blow out a huff of air. "Oh, I have no doubt. Why do you think I've had Sam and Dean do anything with that club? I dreaded going there because Candy made a huge ass scene every time, and putting a bullet in the head of an ex didn't really appeal to me."

"When was the last time anyone went there?" Sage frowns, keeping his eyes on the road as he maneuvers the car to the Kitty Kat club.

I purse my lips as I try to remember the last time either of the boys went there. "I haven't been there for about a month, but I went there in the morning so I didn't have to run into Candy. I'm not sure when the guys were there last, to be honest. You know the two of them have something going on with Lacey, right?"

"Yeah, I do, but they go to her place, or she comes to theirs."

I gape at him. "They have a place?"

Sage chuckles and runs a hand through his hair, keeping the other on the steering wheel. "Yeah, babe, they aren't robots who come when you summon them. They have lives too. Haven't you noticed the few houses at the back of the estate? They live in one of those. They are accessed from the back street though, no direct access from our place."

I feel my cheeks heat in embarrassment. Of course I know about the houses at the back of the estate, I just thought they were empty.

"I hadn't really thought about it at all," I mumble, and he shakes his head, a smile of amusement on his face.

"You are so fucking adorable."

"I have a lot of other shit on my mind, so sorry if I don't really think about my henchmen's lives," I snap defensively, still feeling guilty about the fact that I don't know anywhere near as much as I should about the men paid to put themselves between me and a bullet.

"Hey, easy." He slides the hand closest to me onto my knee, giving it a squeeze. "It's okay. I know, and they know too. They know you love them, even if you don't show it."

I wrinkle my nose at the sentiment. "I don't love them. They are an unfortunate necessity," I grumble, and he gives my knee another squeeze.

"Okay, keep telling yourself what you need to hear, but you can't hide it from me, Tori Russo. I know you care about them. You're secretly a big ball of marshmallow, all squishy and sweet." I grimace at his description, wondering if he even knows me at all. I'm not squishy and sweet. I'm a hard ass, ball busting bitch. "That's why you assigned them that specific job. It allowed them to see Lacey without needing an excuse."

I shift uncomfortably in my seat, hating that he's pointing out my somewhat flawed sentimental nature. "That's not true. I want them at the top of their game, and if a few orgasms with a pretty woman can help them focus when they are with me, then I support it." I cross my arms stubbornly as we pull up to the parking lot behind the building reserved for staff. I grimace when I see Candy's beat-up Honda Civic in the lot, knowing things are about to get dramatic.

I sigh before steeling my spine and climbing out of the car. I look down at myself and wince. I didn't really dress mob boss appropriate this evening, wanting to keep a low profile on the plane. I'm wearing leggings, knee-high leather boots, and a slouchy, off the shoulder sweater. It doesn't really inspire fear in anyone who looks at me. I look at Sage who is dressed somewhat similarly. He has on a pair of ripped jeans that do wonderful things for his ass and is wearing a hoodie with a band logo on the front and a pair of combat boots. We look like a couple of college students ready for winter break.

I grab my gun out of the glove box and tuck it into the back of my pants before pulling the sweater down over the top. We aren't going to be able to carry weapons on the plane, and we made other arrangements for when we arrive in Seattle, so I'm not wearing my usual holster. It's thrown into my bag for the following days. I pass Sage his as well, and he tucks it into the back of his jeans before gesturing to the back door.

"After you."

Bracing myself, I adopt my mafia boss resting bitch face and head for the back door, punching in the code on the scanner next to it. It beeps and turns green, and I watch the door open to allow us entry. We walk into a dimly lit hallway, which leads to the front of the club. I pass by the girls' dressing room, but slow down as I catch sight of Lacey.

"Hey, Lace, how are things?" I lean against the doorframe, smiling at the gorgeous dancer. I don't know her very well, but if my boys are interested in her, then I should probably make an effort to be polite. *Take that, Suzy. I can be friendly.*

She startles and looks up in surprise. "Ms. Russo, I didn't know you were coming in tonight." She looks nervously over my shoulder before returning her gaze to me. "Does Candy or Melissa know you're here?"

A prickle of warning trickles down my spine, and I push off the frame, becoming more alert. "Melissa? Who the fuck is Melissa?" I ask the girl who stands up and crosses her arms, glaring at me. My eyebrows jump in surprise. The girl has a backbone. Maybe I do approve of her and my boys being together.

"Melissa, you know, the girl you hired to shadow Candy instead of me? Francis and Nico said I should just speak to you about why you replaced me. What did I do wrong? I thought you were happy with my performance." Her last words are filled with such sadness that I almost flinch.

I blink, confused by everything that just came out of her mouth. Sage pushes me aside and steps into the room. "Hey, Lace," he says before looking at me and noting my confusion.

"Francis and Nico are Sam and Dean," he mutters out of the side of his mouth.

Oh my fucking god. How could I forget those aren't actually their names? I shake my head and turn my attention back to the girl. "I'm super happy with your work. You are an excellent stripper, and you've picked up management like it was meant for you, or so the boys have told me. I have no complaints at all despite your personal relationship with the boys. They would have told me if you were bad at it," I reply, not pulling my punches.

Her lips purse, and I watch her struggle with the information I just shared. "So why did you hire someone else? Candy told me I was to stick to stripping and the new hire was learning the ropes."

I growl and turn to Sage. I bet Lorenzo has his hooks in Candy. I could see the bitch jumping at the opportunity to undermine me. Damn it, I was sure she didn't have the guts to betray me. "And this is why I can't have nice things," I whine to Sage, who just watches me with amusement in his eyes.

"Well, I guess our flight to Seattle will be delayed. It looks like you have to clean house again."

"Lacey, are there any more new hires apart from Melissa? Or any unusual patrons who have seemed a little sketchier than normal?" I ask her.

She tips her head to the side as she thinks before she shakes her head. "No, not really, but Lorenzo has been here quite a lot, and he, Candy, and Melissa all disappear into the basement for long periods of time. We just assumed they are all fucking in the rooms down there." She shrugs her shoulders and shudders at the thought of fucking Lorenzo. I don't blame her. My father was a handsome man, but Lorenzo is a pale imitation who's weaselly and greasy looking.

"The basement? This place has a basement?" I look at Sage, and he appears as surprised as I feel. "How did we not know this place had a basement? What rooms are down there?" I hate being blindsided by things I should have known. It irritates me.

"They are left over from when the Russo family used to run skin auctions." Lacey frowns, screwing up her nose in disgust, and I'm surprised at her knowledge. I think I remember hearing Sam and Dean say that her family has been associated with the Russos for generations. "I've heard rumors that tunnels run under the city to the port. They say this place was left over from Prohibition, and that they used to use them to transport bootlegged liquor to avoid authorities. They converted some of the rooms below to bedrooms and allowed buyers to try before they bought." She pales at the thought, and I don't blame her. I can't imagine the kinds of atrocities that may have taken place below our feet.

Sage and I exchange a loaded look. Well, this is certainly new information, and it's very fucking helpful. I can tell he's thinking the same thing I am, and maybe this sweet little stripper just assisted us way more than she could possibly know.

I grasp her hand and give it a squeeze. "Lacey, I was going to transfer Candy up to San Jose to cover for Stella while she recovers from a car accident we were all in a few days ago, and I was going to promote you to manager here. Is that something you are interested in?"

Her eyes widen, and I see the interest in them before they dull again, and she shakes her head, pulling her hand out of mine. "There's no way Candy will go, and if she hears you want me to replace her, then she will kill me." She sounds terrified, and I see her glance around the room like she's expecting Candy to jump out and shove a knife between her ribs.

I growl, annoyed as fuck that I haven't paid enough attention to what's going on here. I let my personal shit get in the way of family business. Fuck, this is just too much for one person to handle. My anger at Gio flares again. If he was pulling his weight, then none of my responsibilities would have slipped under the cracks.

"I promise Candy and Melissa will be no problem. Are there any other issues? Are any of the girls giving you a hard time or any of the security?" I ask, wanting to make sure Lorenzo hasn't interfered anywhere else.

"No, Ms. Russo, we have a good team here. We're like family, looking out for one another."

I let out a small sigh of relief. At least this one seems to be okay, except for the suspicious movements of Candy, Melissa, and Lorenzo. It will make everything a little easier now that I know we don't have a whole slew of new people to get rid of.

I nod. "Okay, good. Let's pretend this conversation never happened and just go about business as usual until I can take out the trash, alright?" I ask the girl, and she mimes zipping her lips.

"As far as I'm concerned, I haven't seen you." She looks up at the camera in the corner of the room. "But that doesn't mean Candy doesn't already know."

I close my eyes and count to five in my head. Fuck, the cameras, but I feel Sage put his hand on my shoulder and give it a squeeze.

"Remember, all cameras immediately start a recorded loop that shows business as usual as soon as you or I put our entrance codes into the door. We had it set up when you first took over so nothing we did was caught on camera. Nobody knows we are here or that this conversation took place."

I feel my body relax minutely, and I kick myself for forgetting. I was worried that Candy and Melissa, whoever she is, would have scurried like rats from a sinking ship as soon as they noticed me here. Now I'm hoping I have something on my camera in my office that may clue me into their actions.

"We're just going to head up to my office and get to the bottom of all this. Have you seen Lorenzo here tonight?"

She shakes her head. "No, he hurried out of here like a bat out of hell a couple of nights ago and hasn't been back since."

I'd bet every last dollar I have, and it's not an insignificant amount, that it was the same night I took apart his operation in San Jose.

"Okay, thanks. Consider tonight your last night of working the floor. Tomorrow, you'll be a manager. Unless you want to continue to take your clothes off for fun, I don't expect to see you on the stage again. Hire a couple of new girls if you need to, because Candy won't be available anymore either," I say through gritted teeth, and while her eyes widen, she jumps on the spot with excitement, clapping her hands.

"Oh, I'm going to need to go shopping for a more appropriate wardrobe."

Sage pulls out his wallet and grabs a card, handing it to her. "This is where we send our management to shop for more professional outfits. Go buy yourself whatever you need on us."

I smile as she squeals and throws her arms around his neck, but that quickly drops as my stomach rolls when she gives him a kiss on the lips, and I grind my teeth, my insecurities wreaking havoc with my mind. Surely a sweet girl like Lacey is more Sage's type. She would be able to offer him more than I can. Before I can let those insidious thoughts gain any ground, though, she releases him then flings herself at me. I can't react fast enough to stop her before she smacks a kiss against my own lips. Well, okay then.

"Thank you. You have no idea how much this means to me." She starts skipping toward the door. "I can't wait to tell Nico and Francis." She stops and turns around, one hand grasping the doorframe, and she nibbles her lip with concern as she meets my eyes. "I didn't want to say anything before, but Candy's using drugs. You know how we have a few party favors here for people who want them?"

I nod, knowing that's part of our supply chain.

"Well, I'm pretty sure she's been helping herself to that. It didn't start until Melissa arrived, and I think both of them use the free supply that nobody tracks. I know I should have come to you and told you, but she always looked out for us girls and protected us before you took over. I can see now that was a mistake. If I said something, maybe she wouldn't have gone down the dark path she's taken. Please don't kill her. I'm pretty sure she was in love with you, and you broke her heart."

I start to shake my head to argue, annoyed because I never gave her any indication that I was in it for something permanent, but Lacey stops me.

"I know you never promised her commitment, you aren't to blame, but sometimes you can't help who you fall in love with." Her eyes soften, and I wonder if she's talking about my henchmen. "She needs help. Get her that and then transfer her out of town like you planned. Give her a chance, like you've given so many others that go down that slippery slope, for me." She doesn't wait for my answer, disappearing down the corridor and out into the club. I'm assuming she's going to work the floor, since she wasn't dressed to perform.

"Yikes, that was heavy," Sage grumbles, breaking the almost painful silence she left us in. Uneasy swirls of guilt roll around my stomach as I wonder if I really caused the previously loyal and strong stripper's downfall. "Pfft, don't let any guilt get into your head. Not everybody who gets their heart broken becomes bitter and turns to drugs. She's allowing herself to be manipulated. Don't blame yourself for her weakness. Look at what happened to you. You became stronger and fiercer when you were broken."

I scoff with dark amusement. "Yeah, I get off on killing people and blood. Not sure that's any better. Come on, let's get this over with." Rolling my shoulders back, I take a deep breath before blowing it out again and putting myself in the right headspace. I block all the messy emotions that have been rolling through me and allow the cold, emotionless Tori to come forward. It used to be my constant state before Sage wiggled his way into my heart. Now, he's making me feel all kinds of uncomfortable things, but I don't regret any of it. I just refuse to let anyone else worm their way in.

Chapter Six

We leave and head farther down the corridor to the steps that lead up to the office. "Sage, poke your head out and see if Joe and Bill are out there, and if they can give us a hand in taking out the trash." After our initial run-in that first day with Carla, Joe and Bill have proven their loyalty, and I'm a little surprised neither of them said anything to me about the new hire, but I guess I did leave all the decision-making to Candy, so they probably thought I knew. I would have appreciated a heads-up about Lorenzo hanging around again. I hope he hasn't gotten his hooks back into them. I would have to kill them. They don't get a third chance. They are lucky they even got a second chance, but that was Carla's call.

Both men follow Sage through the door separating the front of the house with the staff areas, and when they see me, I see the caution in their eyes.

"Candy told us we would both lose our jobs if we

said anything to you," Joe says quickly, knowing he fucked up again. He's slightly pale and sweaty, which gives me a small amount of joy. At least someone still knows who's boss around here.

"And you should have known the possibility of losing your lives was a bigger threat," I growl at him but spin and stalk up the stairs.

"Candy's going through a rough patch," Bill says, making excuses for her. "She was at an all-time low when Lorenzo showed up and started paying attention to her. We tried to warn her it was a bad idea and you wouldn't be happy."

"Yeah, but that just seemed to make her happier," Joe mutters.

"Do you both know she's using?" I ask, not looking back at them. There is a silent pause before Bill huffs out, "Yes."

"We told her that nothing good would come from stealing from you, but she claimed you owed her that and more. She has seemed happier since Melissa was brought on."

Joe scoffs. "Only because she's higher than a kite, and Melissa knows how to manipulate her. Hell, you really did a number on her, boss."

I stop, spin around, and glare at them.

"When I want your input and advice, I'll fucking tell you. I never promised her a white picket fence or any kind of fucking future. She was a convenient way for me to get my rocks off and nothing else, so unless you want me to put a bullet between those fucking lips, stop flapping them."

Sage winces and mutters under his breath as the two men realize they've gone too far. They both pale even further, and I storm even faster up the steps. I'm done with this shit. This is why I don't like to be nice to people. They think it means more than it does and start taking liberties and giving opinions.

At the top of the stairs, I let my annoyance fuel me as I open the door to the office and stride in. What I find really shouldn't surprise me, but it kind of does. I stop, feeling Sage bump into my back, then I hear Bill and Joe mutter behind him, but my focus is on the sight in front of me.

Hardcore metal music blares through the speakers of the office, causing my head to pound, and Candy is strung up in a sex swing, bound, gagged, and naked. A busty, dark-haired female wearing a dominatrix outfit, complete with strap-on, does a line of coke off her mound before swirling her fingers through the powder and shoving them deep inside her pussy. Candy moans and rolls her eyes as her head falls back, her hair almost hanging to the floor as the girl removes her fingers and smacks her clit.

"Such a good bitch for me," the girl croons, and I don't even think she notices she has an audience—Candy certainly doesn't.

"Holy shit, she looks a lot like you," Sage mutters into my ear, and I slide my gaze over to see him cock his head and watch as the girl notches the huge strap-on at

Candy's hole then push forward. "A Temu version of you, but I'm getting so many fucking ideas." I roll my eyes, annoyed at him.

"Not now," I snap and step farther into the room, pissed that neither of them have noticed us, but that's not actually the case, I realize, as the girl turns her head and glares at me.

"Who the fuck are you?" she asks, not stopping her thrusts as she grabs hold of Candy's hips to stop her from swinging, using her momentum to pull her harder down the plastic cock.

I can tell by the gleam in her eyes that she knows exactly who I am, but this poor girl thinks she has more power than she does, and she's going to get over herself very quickly.

Candy is lost in the haze of her drug fueled fuck and doesn't even notice the intrusion as I slide my hand into the back of my pants and pull out my gun.

"I'm the fucking angel of death, and I've come to collect your soul," I tell the girl who rolls her eyes and scoffs.

"Oh please, bitch, you're nothing but a puppet playing at mafia queen. Lorenzo is going to put you in your place, and you'll be nothing but a hole to be used and abused, a puppet on someone else's strings." She sounds gleeful as she keeps pumping her hips, the drugs making her lips loose. "Poor little deluded mafia princess with daddy issues," she rambles before laughing loudly, her pupils glassy with drug infused glee.

Flicking the safety off, I lift my gun and put a bullet through the bitch's head. The gunshot echoes through the room with a loud bang, and I hear Sage groan with annoyance behind me.

Blood splatters the wall behind the girl, and Candy screams as her lover falls on top of her. The harness swings back and forth uncontrollably as Candy starts to struggle with the weight of the dead body lying on her.

"Now who's a puppet on a string, bitch?" A smile crosses my lips as I watch blood drip onto the floor in a kind of avant-garde pattern. Candy thrashes and screams and tries to get the lifeless shell off her, but it's to no avail.

"I'll call the cleanup crew," Sage mutters and pushes past me to go to the desk. The room falls silent, apart from Candy's frantic noises, when he switches off the sound system. He pulls a burner cell out of one of the desk drawers and arranges for this girl's body to be collected.

I wave a hand, and Bill and Joe step forward. They pull the corpse off Candy, and it slumps to the floor, then they extract Candy from the swing. She's hysterical and sobbing, but when I approach, she calms down and glares at me with hatred.

"You'll pay for this. Lorenzo is going to make you suffer, and I hope I'm there to see it."

I feel my hand twitch on the gun and consider putting a bullet in her brain just to be done with her. It would really solve the problem, but there's a small part of me, one hidden deep inside, that whispers this is all my fault. I'm the one who drove her to seek comfort in drugs and meaningless sex and be manipulated by Lorenzo. Lorenzo knew exactly how to manipulate her by bringing in a Tori look-alike to get her right where he wanted her.

Instead of doing what I normally would, I tuck the gun back into the waistband of my pants and give Joe and Bill a nod. They hurry her out of the room without another word. They know where to take her to sober up and will make sure she is cleaned up before she goes. Am I worried she's going to blab about what I did? Maybe, but if the cops come looking, there will be no proof of what she claims, and we can blame her ramblings on a drug-induced psychosis, especially since they will take her directly to rehab.

The door closes behind them, leaving me, Sage, and the dead girl's body with a round bullet hole in her forehead. I turn my back on the sight, feeling the calmest I have in a while, and take a seat behind my desk. Grabbing the decorative jade tiger paper weight off the bookshelf behind the desk, I pull out the SD card and plug it into the laptop on the desk, then I power it up.

Sage throws himself into one of the chairs on the other side, putting his boots up on the desk, his eyebrows raised in surprise. "You have another camera in here?" he asks, and I nod.

"Yeah, I don't trust anyone, and I have cameras in all the offices that aren't connected to the normal system, so if anyone turns the surveillance off, I still have eyes on what's going on."

He whistles under his breath. "My girl is so freaking smart. It's sexy as fuck," he tells me, giving me a wink and adjusting his cock. I'm pretty sure he's been hard since we walked in. Sage is such a man-whore, but even I can admit what the two of them were doing was hot as fuck. Now that some of my anger has cleared, I can acknowledge that seeing the two of them—one with dark hair and the other with red—gave me ideas of doing the same thing to Vienna. I would love to have her at my mercy, naked, restrained, and dripping for me. When my eyes meet Sage's, I can see he's clearly having the same thoughts.

"Hmm," he hums, sliding a finger across his lips. "I can see that swing in your room getting a lot of use in the future."

I shrug in acknowledgement, and his lips spread into a wicked grin as he adjusts himself again, but I don't have time to think about that right now. I pull up the folder of the last few days. Thankfully the camera is motion activated, so it switches off when no one is in the room, and it has the capacity to store a lot of footage. I scroll back through the files until the day of our accident and click on one. Sage gets out of his chair and comes around to stand next to me as we watch them.

Candy and Melissa walk into the office, followed by my weasel of an uncle, Lorenzo. He's wearing a suit and has his hair slicked back with way too much product, so it makes it look greasy. He waves at the couch and tells the girls, "I want to watch the two of you fuck while I do business."

Melissa wraps an arm around his waist and whispers something in his ear, and he goes to the desk drawer, snapping his fingers at Candy.

She pulls the master set of keys out of the tight pocket of her cutoff shorts and tosses them to him. He unlocks the drawer we keep the drugs in and tosses them a bag of blow before taking a seat in my chair.

Melissa lines up some coke on the coffee table while Candy shimmies out of her clothes. She's lost weight and looks rough. She has the lean, sucked in look of a drug addict, and her clothes aren't the classy ones that she first wore when I promoted her to management. She looks like she's been shopping at the thrift store. The shorts are ragged and worn, and the shirt is faded and stretched. Only her underwear looks like it might be newish.

"What happened to her?" I mutter, and Sage puts a hand on my shoulder, giving it a squeeze. The girls do a couple of lines, giggling and talking about nothing much before they start making out. Melissa palms Candy's naked breasts, and Lorenzo watches for a while, but he soon loses interest and grabs his phone. He starts speaking to someone, and I lose interest in the girls as well and tune into his conversation.

"Yeah, the next shipment is due to arrive in two weeks, as well as the stock we still have in holding. We will deliver all the stock to the docks on schedule." The words are all innocent enough, except for the fact that we don't ship anything overseas that needs to be at the docks.

The conversation goes on a little longer, but they don't mention a time or a date, so we have nothing to go on, and then he hangs up. By now, Melissa and Candy are fucking noisily, writhing against one another, their bodies shiny with some sort of oil they dribbled all over themselves.

"Get over here and suck my cock," he demands, standing up and dropping his pants. He fists his dick, and I grimace, feeling a little nauseous at the sight, but Melissa grabs Candy by the hair and drags her over before forcing her mouth down on it, holding her there until she starts struggling.

"Oh yeah. Fuck, she feels so good. You know what I love, babe." He slaps Melissa on the ass, and I see Candy struggling to move. Melissa finally releases her, and Candy's head pops up. She gasps for breath, her pretty face ravaged with tears, snot, and saliva. She's shaking and gulping for air, but Melissa just slaps her face.

"You fucking slut. When we tell you to suck his cock, you do it right." She forces Candy down again, and Lorenzo groans his enjoyment.

"I want to fucking wreck her ass. Lube it up for me, will you?" he says, his eyelids lowered and his mouth open as he thrusts into the back of Candy's throat.

Melissa gets down on the floor and parts Candy's

butt cheeks, burying her face in them to tongue her hole. Candy starts to squirm, but Lorenzo slaps one of her tits, so she stops moving. Just as Melissa spits on her fingers and starts probing Candy's asshole, Lorenzo's phone rings again. He picks it up and answers.

"Yeah?" he grunts, listening to whoever is on the other end. All of a sudden, his eyes pop open, and he violently shoves Candy off his cock. She falls back into Melissa, and they both tumble to the ground. "She fucking what? Damn it, that bitch. I want her taken out. I don't care how you do it, but she needs to die tonight," he shouts, holding his phone with his shoulder as he tucks his dick into his pants and fastens them.

Sage points at the screen. "I'm going to guess he just found out about the San Jose club."

I chuckle. "Ah, I love making Lorenzo sweat. I think we've seen enough for now. I'll take this with me and see what other information we can get, but how about we head down to the basement and see what we can find before we leave?"

I'm super curious about the tunnels now, especially if they lead to the dock. I turn off the computer, grab a fresh SD card out of the bottom drawer, and insert it into the tiger before returning it to its spot on the bookcase.

"I bet the only fucking you see on that now are Sam, Dean, and Lacey." Sage chuckles as there's a knock on the door. I grimace, not sure that I need to see any of that. I'll make Sage watch them if we ever need to.

Sage lets our cleanup crew in. No words are exchanged, but polite nods are given to the both of us before they get on with their job. They know what they need to do. We head downstairs in search of Lacey to ask where the basement entrance is.

Chapter Seven

The basement is exactly what Lacey said it is—a large space set up much like the room upstairs, with a bar, tables, chairs, and booths all facing a stage. It shows signs of having been used in the recent past. Sticky drink rings still line a couple of tables, and the scents of smoke and stale beer fill the air instead of dust and mildew, which should be present if this place was unused. A couple of condom wrappers litter the floor, and there's a sheen of white powder on a table as well.

I guess Lacey was right, and they were coming down here to fuck, but has anything else happened down here?

Sage and I bypass the large area and approach a single door on the far side of the room. He pulls out his gun and gestures for me to move behind him before grasping the doorknob and pushing it open.

The door swings open with a creaky groan, and I peer over his shoulder. All I can see is a dark corridor. I look around for a light switch and find one just inside the door. I reach over Sage and flick it on.

Dull, incandescent bulbs dangle from the roof, lighting up the inside of a nondescript concrete corridor with five doors on either side before they stop, and the concrete walls continue to a dead end probably about fifty feet away. I look down, noting the dusty floor has been disturbed, and there are a number of footprints in the thick layer of dust and debris. I wrinkle my nose at the sight of rat droppings as well.

"Let's take a look, shall we?" Sage suggests, and I nod and follow him in, his gun still raised in front of him. We reach the first door, and again, he gestures for me to stand behind him while he opens it. I roll my eyes but don't argue with him. Sometimes, I need to let him lead, and I'm surprisingly okay with that.

He pushes it open, and we peer into the darkness. I wrinkle my nose at the stale air that billows out. I don't think this one has been used in a while, but I reach in and turn the light on so we can see what we're working with.

The same dull lightbulb illuminates the room, which is basically nothing but an old rusty bed with a moldy mattress that I'm pretty sure the rats have been living in.

"I guess Lacey was right, a space to try the merchandise," Sage says bitterly as I look around the room to see if I can find anything else, but there's nothing, and you couldn't pay me to check under the bed. I turn the switch off, and we do the same to all nine remaining bedrooms. It's not until the last one that we find signs of use. The rest of them were the same as the first—empty save for a rusty bed that had seen better days—but I gape at the last one and feel a shiver run down my spine.

Instead of a rusty bed, this one is full of equipment that wouldn't be looked at twice in a sex dungeon. There's a St. Andrew's cross and a thick metal pipe running across the roof with chains dangling from it. There's also a hook, which makes my skin crawl, a set of stocks, and a number of tools on a side table that wouldn't be out of place in my torture rooms. Worst of all, there's a drain in the floor, and instead of a bed, there's a rack.

"I don't know whether to be turned on or terrified," Sage mutters, and I shiver.

"You know both torture and bondage revs my engine, but none of this is turning me on. If what they say is true, then no one who was in this room wanted or deserved to be here." My stomach rolls, but there is a thick layer of dust covering everything, so I assume no one has had the unfortunate pleasure of being in this room in the recent past.

I flick the light off, and we pull the doors closed. "I don't know the exact timeline, but the Russos gave up the skin trade when my grandmother asked my grandfather to stop it, and he was so in love with her, he was happy to grant her that wish. It must have been at least thirty or forty years ago now. These rooms don't look like they've been touched."

"No, but the footprints continue down here." Sage points farther down the corridor, where there looks to be a dead end, but the light is not bright enough to tell for sure.

"Come on, let's have a look." This time, I take the lead. I don't bother with my gun. If there was anyone here, we already would have come across them. "I'm going to get Sam and Dean to set up some cameras down here. I want eyes on this place all the time. If what Lacey said is true, and these lead to the wharf, then I bet they are going to use them to transport women. Agent Garcia said he thinks that's where they are being transported out of."

As we get farther down the corridor, I notice it isn't a dead end, but two tunnels that branch off in opposite directions. We stop, and I look both ways and listen.

These tunnels are a lot wider, and they turn pitch black a few steps from where we stand, so it's impossible to see anything.

"Look at that." Sage points at something on the ground, and I crouch down to get a better look.

"Holy crap, those look like train tracks." I stare at the metal rods inlaid into the dirt floor.

"A trolley possibly. It's at least twenty miles from here to the port. I bet they had a faster way of moving things than just walking. I wonder where the other tunnel leads." Sage takes his phone out and turns on the flashlight, trying to see deeper into both tunnels, but it doesn't penetrate the darkness at all.

"Let's get some of our men down here to explore. We have a two week time frame to break it all down. I'll give the agent a call and let him know what we discovered, but we won't let them know any details regarding the shipment until we're closer to the time. I don't trust them not to poke around more than they promised they would."

Sage lifts his phone and sends a message. He soon gets a reply, and he looks up at the ceiling.

"Sam and Dean are already here," he tells me.

"Good, then they can get started right away. It won't take long until Lorenzo finds out Melissa is dead and Candy is in rehab. He'll probably put a hit out on her. That's what I would do. She knows too much now."

We start retracing our steps.

"He won't be able to find her. Bill and Joe will hand her off to our contact, and they will make sure she's enrolled in rehab in another state under an assumed name. If she reaches out to him, then that's on her, and if she ends up dead, then that's no one's fault but her own," he says, trying to reassure me, but I don't need it.

"I really don't care what happens to Candy. She's lucky she's still breathing. The only reason I didn't kill her was because of the drugs, but she won't get another chance. If she comes at me again, I'll put a bullet in her head as quickly as I shot Melissa."

"What are we going to tell the staff? Lorenzo will probably ask around."

I shrug my shoulders. "I don't care, as long as Lorenzo doesn't find out we know about the tunnels down here. Tell them I popped her in a jealous rage. It fits the brand, and no one would find it hard to believe."

"The staff here are loyal to you," he tells me, and I scoff.

"Candy wasn't, but hopefully she's the exception."

He wraps an arm around my shoulders and presses a kiss to my head. "Nothing more vicious than a woman scorned." He chuckles as I give him side-eye.

"And don't you forget it." He throws his head back and laughs.

"Oh, I can assure you, Ms. Russo, that I won't ever forget how deadly you are, but I'm like a junky, and I love the thrill of making you mad."

I roll my eyes but can't help smiling. Sage is so damn happy all the time, and it's hard not to be affected by it. He's like living ecstasy, making me happy and horny with just one wink and a grin.

When we get upstairs, I find Lacey, Sam, and Dean in a booth having a drink. Sam lifts his glass and gives me a nod. "Hey, boss."

"Lacey, can you give us a moment?" I ask, and she quickly climbs over Dean and slides out of the booth.

"I'll just go and check on the next act then. I saw Joe and Bill walking Candy out through the back, and although most of the girls know what they are doing, it won't hurt for them to know who is in charge now."

She proudly struts off, and I watch with bemused

amusement. "Oh, I think she's going to do just fine." I sit down, and one of the topless waitresses comes over and takes our drink order, flirting shamelessly with the guys before she leans in and whispers in my ear.

"Let me know if you'd like a lap dance, Ms. Russo. I'd love to see to your needs." She smells fresh and fruity, and in the past, I wouldn't have hesitated to take her up on her offer, but things are different now. I give her a small smile, and she stands and gives me a wink before sashaying back to the bar, her rounded ass cheeks shaking delightfully in her thong.

"Ugh," Sage groans, biting his fist. "Please let me watch."

I shake my head and ignore him before telling the guys exactly what we found. I give them their instructions, warning them only to use our most trusted employees and to be careful.

"I want to know where both of those tunnels go, and I want cameras installed ASAP. I also want you to do a deep dive into the operations here. I want to ensure Melissa and Lorenzo didn't mess with this business as well and corrupt any of the other staff like they did in San Jose. Get the forensic accountant in also. I want the books checked and the place swept for bugs and cameras that don't belong to us. We also need to put a tail on Lorenzo. We haven't had one on him for a while now, but it seems it's needed again. I want to know where he goes and who he sees, and while we're at it, put one on Penelope too." I look at Sage. "Am I missing anything?"

"Nope, I think you got it all."

The waitress returns with our drinks and wears a disappointed little pout when I send her on her way. Sage's pout matches hers, and I elbow him in the side.

"Cut it out. I thought we decided we were going to try this thing with the others and be monogamous within the group," I hiss into his ear, not wanting Sam and Dean to hear. I trust them with my life, but just like I don't need to know what they do with Lacey or each other, they don't need insight into my sexual activities.

"Oh, I know, but I've had a raging hard-on since we were upstairs, and I was thinking about you and Vienna in that swing instead of those two bitches. I'm only human," he whines, and I can't stop the chuckle that escapes my lips.

"You would think we hadn't fucked each other's brains out only a few hours ago."

"What can I say, I have a high sex drive," he replies and slides my hand that's resting on his thigh to the bulge in his pants. I give it a little caress before removing it, tossing my drink back, and standing up.

"Okay, we have a plane to catch. Keep in touch, and I want to know the minute you find anything, okay?"

Sage groans but follows my lead.

"Do you want us to tell Gio?" Dean asks cautiously, and I shake my head.

"As far as I'm concerned, Gio doesn't get to learn anything about what's going on. If he asks you for any information, send him to me, but I doubt he will since he's too busy playing happy family," I say, unable to stop the bitterness in my voice.

"Oh, and Tori." Sam stops me as I turn to leave. "Thanks for trusting Lacey. You have no idea how happy she is."

"Why didn't either of you tell me that there was a new girl here?" I ask, voicing something that has been bothering me. I see them all the time, and they obviously knew about Melissa if they told Lacey to talk to me about it.

"We were going to, but Candy threatened her and told us if we said anything to you that Lacey would disappear, and neither of us were going to risk it. I'm sorry if that seems disloyal, but Candy was nasty to Lacey, and we figured it was probably for the best anyway. She was always so miserable working with Candy." Sam looks down at his hands, and I can see he's visibly shaken by the thought of Lacey being hurt. I guess she means more to them than having a good time.

"We were going to tell you in San Jose back at the hotel, but then you got into that accident, and it slipped our minds," Dean adds. "I swear if we had known Lorenzo was involved, I would have told you immediately, but Lacey never mentioned him coming and going."

"Candy probably threatened her too," Sage says, crossing his arms.

I sigh and glare at my henchmen. "No more

secrets. No matter how little and insignificant you think the information might be, I need to know, even if you think you're wasting my time, okay?" I tell them, unable to be mad about them protecting their girl. They are family, and that's how family is supposed to be. How can I be angry at them?

They both promise, and with that, Sage and I leave.

"You did good," he tells me, squeezing my hand in the car. I get a little rush of pleasure at his praise.

"Well, it isn't like I can put a bullet in my henchmen. Then I would have to train new ones and find a new manager for my strip club. I don't have time for that shit with everything else going on," I say gruffly, shaking off his hand and looking out the window.

"Sure, my little marshmallow. You keep telling yourself that." Sage puts music on and starts singing along to Taylor Swift, making little dance moves up as he goes. I can't help the smile that spreads across my lips as I lean my head back and enjoy the ride.

We actually don't charter another plane, instead flying commercially with a couple of fake IDs we have for occasions such as this. I wrinkle my nose as we board the plane, and Sage laughs at me.

"Come on, princess, it will be an adventure. You're so spoiled."

Thankfully he booked us business class, and as he takes my cabin bag from me and puts it in the overhead storage, I take a seat.

"The flight isn't even that long," he tells me, sitting beside me. "You can cope with it."

I stick my tongue out at him, and his eyes heat.

"Want to join the mile high club?" he asks, and I almost gag.

"Not in a public bathroom, I don't. Save it for the next time we use the jet." He pouts, but I don't pay attention. Instead, I watch in horror as a family with four small children board the flight. I clutch the armrests and chant under my breath, "Please don't be in business, please don't be in business."

One of the children is a toddler who is already losing their shit, with tears rolling down their face and snot bubbling from their nose as they shake their tiny fists on their harassed looking father's back.

Sage scoffs with amusement. "You really don't like kids, do you?"

I turn my attention from the family, exhaling with relief as they keep moving past us. "Um, I haven't really been around them, but I mean, they are smelly and loud, and you have to actually look after them, like feeding and bathing them. I don't have time for that shit."

His mouth turns down a little. "There's more to them than that. The mind of a child can be a wondrous place." He glances away from me, reaches for the in-flight menu, and studies it. I frown, wondering exactly what kind of experience he has with children. As far as I know, he had a pretty crappy childhood, and only my father rescuing him improved his life. Shit, I wonder if he had or has any siblings? Where are they now if he did? He wouldn't be the kind of person who would leave them behind. Now I feel guilty that I haven't shown more interest in his life.

I reach out, placing my hand on his arm to gain his attention. "Are you okay? Have you been around kids before? You sound like you have experience." Look at me go, being all empathetic and shit. See? I can do this relationship stuff.

"I had a little sister. There was ten years between us. She was a surprise to my parents. They called her a mistake, but I loved her, and I practically raised her since my mother didn't give a shit about her once she gave birth."

"Why did she? Why didn't she just terminate the pregnancy?" I ask, curious to know more about the man I am so in love with.

"She couldn't afford to. All their spare money went to drugs. I don't even know if she was my dad's child since Mom regularly took johns to keep the money rolling in. They didn't care enough to name her. They told me to do it because she was now my responsibility. They were going to get money from the government for her, and that was all that mattered." He pauses, seeming to gather his thoughts.

"Sissy was special. Mom used drugs during her entire pregnancy, so she was born early and went through withdrawals. They didn't expect her to survive, and I was the only one sad about that, but she did, and when she eventually came home, she didn't like to be put down. I would wear her in a harness on my chest so her crying wouldn't upset my parents."

"How old were you? What about school? What did you do?" I pepper him with questions, absolutely horrified at the complete opposites of our childhoods. Despite my father being the head of one of the most ruthless mafia families on the west coast, he still went out of his way to make sure that Gio and I had a fairly normal upbringing.

"I missed a lot for the first six months after Sissy was born, but child protective services paid us a visit and scared the shit out of Mom and Dad. They got her into a subsidized childcare program—not that either of them held down full-time or regular work—but Sissy was a sickly kid, and one day, when she was about four, she came home from child care and had caught another cold. I tried to get my parents to take her to the doctors, but they refused to spend the money, insisting she'd get over it in time. The cold turned to pneumonia, and by the time they got her to the hospital for treatment, it was too late. Her lungs were already underdeveloped from being a preemie. She didn't survive." A tear rolls down his cheek, and my heart aches for this beautiful man. If his parents weren't already dead, I would chase them down and make them guests in one of my basements.

"That's when the small amount of affection I still had for my parents died and my usefulness to them changed. I was fourteen, and I became a new means of income for them. I ran away a few times, but the police kept bringing me back to them, even when I told them what they were doing to me. They just didn't care."

My temper burns hot, and I add the police to the list of people I want to destroy in Sage's name. I grab his hand and give it a squeeze, but I allow him a moment of silence while he relives his past. The plane door closes, then it taxis out onto the runway and lines up for takeoff by the time he takes a deep breath and wipes a few stray tears from his cheeks.

"Sissy, despite being sick, was such a bright spark. I don't know how two druggy assholes like my parents managed to produce two above average intelligent kids, but she was quick-witted and funny and had a way about her that made you smile and laugh. So yeah, I can see the appeal of children. They make life interesting."

I scoff and roll my eyes. "Because our life isn't interesting enough."

We fall into an awkward silence, the noise of takeoff making it difficult to maintain a normal volumed conversation, but by the time we even out and the seatbelt sign goes off, Sage hasn't given up.

He shakes his head, and I see pity in his eyes. "But not in the same way. There are innocence and joy in children that is sorely missing from our lives, Tori. I also understand why you think children do not belong in your life, but your dad seemed to make it work."

Jesus, Sage is insistent. Does he want me to have a baby? Because that is not going to fucking happen. I would make a terrible mother. Is our relationship doomed before it has even really started?

"Did he though? Gio and I are both so messed up. Gio because he wants and craves a normal life, which is just not going to be possible, and look at me. Blood and violence get me off. That's not normal."

The flight attendant blanches when she hears my

words, but she quickly assumes a professional expression and offers us a glass of champagne. I take one in each hand, and although she can't stop the raised eyebrows, she doesn't say a word. I down one quickly before returning it to the tray, and I place the second next to me. Sage takes one and politely thanks the flight attendant before dismissing her by turning back to me.

"Tori, you may be a little bent, but I don't think you're completely broken. I think you just need a group of people around you to show you that you are loved and capable of love—a group of people who don't want anything from you except to be with you."

I think back to what Suzy and Ben told me when they encouraged the same thing. Maybe I do, and maybe the others can be that for me, but background checks need to come first.

I don't argue with him, nor do I agree, and Sage knows me well enough to drop it.

The flight is uneventful, and we hire a car on the other end. It's nothing as flashy as we usually drive, and Sage grumbles at the handling and acceleration, but we make it to our hotel in one piece. Again, to keep with the theme of staying under the radar, we check in under our aliases, and the hotel is a solid three star, unlike our usual five star tastes. When we get to the room, there is only one bed—a very big bed that could probably sleep more than just the two of us, but we both kind of pause for a moment and stare at it.

After contemplating sharing a bed with Sage and deciding I'm excited by it, I find him looking at me with concern and biting his lip nervously like he's waiting for me to lose my shit. Instead, I toss my backpack on the right side.

"Dibs, and I hope you don't snore," I say lightly before sitting on the bed and groaning at the lack of bounce. "Ugh, it's a bit harder than I like it." I bend down, unzip my boots, and pull them off. I went for comfy, casual, and discrete clothes for this trip, but I strip them all off until I'm down to a pair of panties. I stretch out and look over to find him grinning.

"That's not what you usually say." He winks playfully before dropping his own carry on. He then grabs the other bags from outside the door and drags them inside, leaving them out of the way before joining me on the bed. He toes off his shoes then quickly strips down to his briefs, exposing all his delightfully naked skin to my closely watching eyes before he puts his hands behind his head and closes his eyes. "Oof, you're right, it isn't great. Luckily we're only here for a night or two."

I yawn, stretching and rolling to snuggle into his body. One of his arms wraps around me, pulling me tightly against him like he's trying to mold my body into his. The heat of his skin sinks into mine, making me feel sleepy and content. It's still morning, but I don't want to head out until later tonight once the club opens. For now, catching up on sleep sounds like a pretty solid idea, since both of us are running on empty. "Love you," I mumble into his chest before pressing a kiss to his pec. His hand tightens on my hip, and I hear him gasp slightly.

"I will never tire of hearing you say that," he replies as I drift off to sleep, feeling safe and comfortable and loved for the first time in a very long time.

———

We sleep soundly all day, and when I finally wake, we're no longer wrapped in each other's arms. I'm turned away from him on my stomach, my arm hanging over the side of the bed. I frown and turn my head to find Sage spread out like a fucking champion, taking up every spare inch of the mattress. "Well, that's just fucking great," I grumble as I slide my legs off and sit up. "I should have guessed you'd be a bed hog." He doesn't move, but his breath blows a stray curl that has fallen across his mouth. He wrinkles his nose as it falls back down, tickling his cheek. It's so fucking adorable that I smile, making it hard to stay annoyed with him. I lean over and push it behind his ear, and his frown smooths out as his mouth drops open in a quiet snore.

Rolling my eyes, I get up and head for the shower, groaning at all the aches and pains in my body. Damn it, I must have slept cramped up in that tiny space for a while. How did I not wake up when we shifted?

I remove my panties and turn the shower on,

waiting for it to steam up the tiny bathroom before stepping in. At least this hotel has hot running water. I moan in relief as the water washes over my body, easing some of the aches. As my body wakes up, so does my mind. I start running over a list of things that I need to do in my head, ignoring all the other issues niggling in the back of my mind.

First, coffee and food, but then I have to speak to Mickey. I need to set him on that task of getting all the information he can about Vienna and the guys. If they are going to live in my house, I want to know everything I can about them. Then, I need to do some shopping. I want to buy a wig and an outfit so when someone looks at me, they won't see Victoria Russo, enforcer for the Russo family, but just another girl out for a good time with her boyfriend. Sage probably needs a disguise too. He isn't as recognizable as me, but the two of us have become quite prominent back home, and I wouldn't put it past Lorenzo to pass our photos around to anyone in his pocket. I need to touch base with the manager of the Kitty Kat club here in Seattle as well. Fuck, what was her name again? She was an old friend of Carla's, so I'm pretty sure this town is safe from Lorenzo's interference, but it doesn't hurt to check. It's also a long way for them to be trafficking women to the cartels, since there is a higher chance of them being caught between here and the Mexican border, but I want to warn her just in case.

I'm so lost in thought that I don't hear the shower curtain open, and it's not until two hands encircle my waist and Sage nuzzles my neck that I realize I'm no longer alone.

"Hmm, you smell so good," he murmurs, breathing in deeply. I frown. I haven't even washed myself. I've basically been standing here, letting the water wash over me.

"Are you going to hog the shower too?" I ask, grumbling halfheartedly as his hands rub my shoulders, working out some of the kinks.

He chuckles, and I feel his hard cock brush against my ass as he deepens his ministrations on my shoulders.

"Sorry, babe. You should realize by now that I like my sleep, and I'm not used to actually having someone in my bed. Usually, I kick them to the curb before anyone can get too comfortable," he admits unashamedly.

I turn around and glare at him. "Well, you better get used to it. I'm not waking up every morning feeling like a pretzel." I stab a finger into his naked chest, but he just grabs it and smiles goofily as he presses a kiss to the tip.

"For you, anything," he promises before we proceed to wash each other, just enjoying running our hands over each other's naked bodies. He washes my hair, and I return the favor, and his groans of enjoyment have my core clenching and my nipples pebbling with desire, but I have things to do, and my own pleasure is going to have to wait.

Once we get out, dry off, and dress, I place the call

to Mickey. He puts me on speaker, and I tell him and Maeve what I need. They assure me they will get to it quickly.

As I hang up, a call comes in, and my screen shows it's Gio. I decline the call, sending him to voicemail, and we head out in search of disguises.

Chapter Nine

Our week is a whirlwind of flights, undercover work, and dodging calls from my brother. I don't even bother to listen to the dozens of messages that have filled up my voicemail, but it seems that the only other clubs that were compromised were the ones in Tucson, Arizona and San Antonio, Texas, which makes sense, both are close to the Mexican border. I didn't interfere with either club, not wanting to show my hand to Lorenzo. I want to make sure he is out of the way before I go in and dismantle the operations there. I also don't have enough trusted staff to put in place. I tasked Lacey with discretely interviewing new staff for both locations. She has flourished and is taking to the roll like a boss girl. I think I'll probably offer her the job to oversee all locations to free up more of my time, but first, I need to deal with my uncle.

I didn't get a chance to check out the Black Rose in Vegas, and by the time we arrive at Suncity, I'm pissed off and just a little murderous. I consider heading home, but when I spoke to Suzy earlier in the week, she confirmed Gio moved his friends into the house. I decided a night at the Lucky Diamond to get my emotions in check would be beneficial.

Thankfully she had gotten their last name, so Maeve's Irish connections are busy doing a deep dive into their background.

"Ugh, it's good to be home," Sage says as he throws himself onto one of the couches in the presidential suite of the hotel. "I'm itching to get my hands on my plants."

Sage has been so patient. A couple of times, he had to distract me from my murderous tendencies and did so by fucking my brains out. I'm not sure why I didn't explore men as a sexual outlet earlier. I let Stacey get all up in my head when I could have been enjoying all the pleasures a male body has to offer.

"We will head home tomorrow. I just needed to catch up on a few things here before I get distracted by Gio and all his drama again," I murmur, pouring us both a drink from the wet bar and joining him on the couch.

I pass him his drink as he puts his arm around my shoulders and pulls me into his side. "What are you going to do about Gio?" he asks and I give him a small shrug of my shoulders.

"Not much I can do, is there? Short of killing them, I'm just going to have to accept they are now living in our house."

"You would kill them?" he asks without judgment.

"I mean, sure, if they were a danger to us. I'm still waiting to hear back from Mickey and Maeve."

"But don't you have feelings for them?" he asks, and I turn to look at him when I hear the concern in his voice.

"Feelings of attraction. The four of them are sexy, and Vienna does this thing with her tongue that makes me see stars, but not anything deeper. I barely know them," I reply, studying his expression for his reaction. His lips turn down in disappointment. "Did you catch feelings already?" I ask, unable to hide the surprise in my voice. He shrugs and avoids meeting my eyes as he takes a sip of his drink.

"They are okay," he hedges, but my heart sinks. Ah shit. Sage is such a fucking softy, and he already caught feelings. I can tell.

"Well, don't let me stop you if you want to spend more time with them," I say, standing up and downing the rest of my drink. There's a rush of jealousy inside me, and I don't like how it feels. Who am I to demand anything of him? I'm not the most emotionally available, and I can tell he needs more than I'm giving him at the moment.

All of this shit is getting to me. I need to put some distance between me and Sage before I inevitably put my foot in my mouth by saying something to upset him. "Why don't you get some sleep or even head out, and I'll meet you back at the house tomorrow? I'll probably be busy for the rest of the day, and I don't want to stop you from returning to your plants or the others." I try to hide the hurt in my voice, so it comes out harsher than I wanted it to. I hoped to sound like I didn't care, but from the wince on his face, I don't think I succeed. "I'll catch up with you later," I tell him, not waiting for a reply before leaving the suite and heading to my office.

My heart races, and my palms sweat as I move through my hotel. It's early morning, and I would love to climb into bed, but I have some work I want to get done in my office. I didn't get any sleep on the flight from Texas, too busy mulling over everything we discovered on our little tour. There is only a week until the merchandise Lorenzo was talking about is moved, and I need to find out everything Sam and Dean discovered. They are coming in to brief me later, but I want to go over the previous week's operations of the hotel and casino. I don't have time for the abundance of annoying emotions that are plaguing my body. I have to lock that shit down and focus on the most important task at hand, and that is keeping control of the Russo family and making sure Lorenzo pays for attempting a hostile takeover.

A few staff members say, "Good morning," and I give them a polite nod in return, but I don't stop like I usually do. When I enter the office area, the secretary that looks after both me and Bryce isn't in yet, and I let out a small sigh of relief. I don't really have the mental capacity for small talk this morning. Taking a seat at my desk, I begin catching up on reports from the previous week. I'm going to be busy with other family stuff for a while, and I don't want to get behind on the legitimate part of our businesses.

I'm deep in concentration when my door bangs open, and when I look up at the clock, I realize I've been hard at work for three hours. My lips purse in annoyance when I catch sight of Penelope at the door, but then I do a double take when she tows a small child in behind her.

"Who the fuck trusted you with a small human?" I ask dryly, leaning back in my chair as she waltzes into my office, gently tugging the small child with her.

The little girl with curly strawberry blond hair skips happily next to her and climbs up into one of the chairs in front of my desk while Penelope elegantly lowers herself into the other.

"You said a swear word," she lisps, her eyes wide with amazement. "Grandfather says ladies aren't supposed to swear." I blink, not sure if I'm surprised at her comprehension or her conversational skills despite the lisp. Aren't children mute until they are in school?

"Tori, watch your language," Penelope scolds with no heat in her tone, and I become suspicious. What does she want now? "Addison is Mario's grandchild, and he asked me to take care of her today while her nanny is indisposed." Her nose wrinkles at the words, and when I turn my attention from the freckled faced child to my ex-stepmother, I'm surprised at what I see. Penelope looks tired. She has big circles under her eyes and looks like she may have lost some weight. There are also lines around her mouth and eyes, which indicate she's not attending her ritual Botox appointments. I watch as she pulls her phone out of her handbag and hands it to the small child who claps her hands with joy.

"Thanks, Penny. Grandfather never lets me play games." The words rush out of her mouth with excitement as she takes the phone and focuses her full attention on the screen. My mouth almost falls open in shock as Penelope reaches out and brushes a ringlet back from the child's face, her eyes softening with what looks like some kind of maternal emotion. I clear my throat to get her attention.

"And he trusted her with you. Let's be real, you aren't exactly a maternal candidate of the year."

She huffs out a breath of annoyance, but her eyes loose the softness and become a little more wary. "When your dad and I got together, you were already old enough not to need or want a mother figure. I thought it would be best if I kept my distance."

Distance? I scoff. What explains her downright pettiness?

"But Addi is still a baby, and to be honest, that woman who calls herself a nanny is nasty. Look at the bruises on poor Addi's arm. Someone has been squeezing her too tightly." Penelope lowers her voice and nods in the direction of the child's arm, and I see a shadow of bruises on her upper arm that is fully on display in the sleeveless dress she wears.

I feel a rush of anger at the sight but control my

expression so Penelope doesn't suspect I have a soft spot. I study the girl a little closer. The dress she's wearing is old-fashioned as fuck, paired with a pair of pristine white socks with frilly lace around the top and shiny black leather Mary Janes. She looks like little orphan Annie after Daddy Warbucks had gotten his hooks into her.

"Where are her parents? Does Mario know about the nanny?" I ask, and when Penelope's eyes sparkle, I realize I've fallen into her trap. Showing too much interest in the small human is going to bite me in the ass. I stifle a groan, though, not wanting to let her know she won.

She waves her hand. "Mario is fucking the nanny, so I don't think he cares." My eyebrows jump at her breezy response. I thought she was fucking Mario, but she doesn't seem too concerned. She sees my response and scowls. "Mario is into some shit that I don't want to do." She shudders. "And if he's doing that with the nanny, then I don't have to," she snaps, looking at the child to make sure she isn't paying attention, but the little girl is completely in her own world. From the noises on the phone, I'm assuming she's playing some kind of game.

I keep my face blank, but I'm gathering all this information against Mario Mancusio just in case I ever need it. Who would have thought Penelope would be an asset? I'm still kind of suspicious of her behavior though. What does she want, and why is she sharing this information so freely? Is she trying her hand at playing both sides, because that shit won't fly with me.

"As for her parents, well, they aren't in her life at this stage... or not very often." Her tone has me looking a little closer at her. She sounds kind of concerned, but before I can make anything of it, she shakes her head and slaps her hands on her knees and stands up. "Anyway, Mario has a thing tonight, and I'm attending with him. I have an appointment in the salon to get my nails done because I can't possibly go with this." She raises her hands and shows me what I think looks like a fairly decent manicure. "Mario expects me to present a certain degree of perfection, and these just won't do. Be a dear and watch Addi for me while I'm gone. It shouldn't take too long."

Excuse me, what the actual fuck? I can't believe her audacity, and I am so stunned that I haven't replied by the time she extracts her phone from Addison and breezes from the room. My mouth is still wide open when the little girl giggles and points at me.

"You look like a fish." She opens her mouth and closes it a couple times in what I think is an imitation of a goldfish.

"Fuck." I lean back in my chair, blowing out a breath as my poor brain tries to catch up.

"That's another bad word. What's your name?" I'm Addi," she says, swinging her legs back and forth while holding onto the armrests. "You're really pretty." She looks around my office, her pretty green eyes wide.

"Do you have any food? I'm hungry. Also, where's the bathroom? I have to potty."

Potty? Fuck, does she wear a diaper? Am I going to have to change it? I stab the intercom with my finger.

"Susan!" I shout. "Susan, get in here." I can't hide the panic in my voice, but the door doesn't burst open, and our secretary doesn't appear. "Fuck!"

The little girl crosses her legs and winces. "Please, I have to go bad."

In a panic, I push my chair back and jump to my feet, hurrying over to the door to my bathroom and wrenching it open. She slides off her chair and rushes over to me, her hands clasped between her legs. She hurries to the toilet and pulls her underwear down to the floor before climbing onto the seat. I turn around, giving her my back as she does her business. I don't turn until it flushes, and when I do, her underwear has been pulled up again, and she's holding out her hands.

I step back and put my hands up, not wanting her to touch me.

"You have to help me wash them. I can't reach," she tells me, staring at me like I'm stupid, and I glance from her to the sink.

"Lift me up," she orders, waving her arms in front of her. Wrinkling my nose, I go over and bend down, putting my hands under the child's armpits, then I lift her to the sink. She leans forward and turns on the tap before using the pump soap and rubbing her hands together. She makes bubbles and claps her hands together twice before she washes them under the running water, then she turns her head and looks at me.

"I'm done now," she explains, and I frown. She looks down at the floor, and I realize I am still holding her. I lower her and step back like my pants are on fire.

She moves over and dries her hands on one of the towels on the rack before looking at me again.

"What?" I ask, and she frowns, putting her hands on her hips and looking up at me like I'm an unruly toddler who could use a nap.

"You're grumpy."

"Well, you're short," I retort. Not my finest moment, I admit, but what the fuck am I supposed to do with her now? We're at a stalemate when I hear my office open, and I say a prayer to those watching over me, hoping it's Penelope realizing it was a bad idea to leave a child with me.

I hurry out of the bathroom but screech to a halt when I see Bryce standing there, holding a gun.

"I heard you screaming. Is everything okay?" He looks around the room, and I see his shoulders relax when he realizes there isn't any imminent danger.

"Put that thing away," I hiss, and he tucks it into the holster at the small of his back just as Addison comes out of the bathroom.

"Oh my god!" Bryce practically clutches his invisible pearls. "Who the fuck let you around a child?" he asks, looking between me and the small being.

I groan and go back to my chair, slumping into it. "Penelope blindsided me. This is her latest squeeze's grandchild, and she had a manicure appointment."

"Hi, I'm Addi." The little girl skips over to Bryce and holds out her hand like she wants him to shake it.

He slowly reaches forward, a charmed smile appearing on his lips. "I'm Bryce."

"Nice to meet ya," she says and starts walking around the room, poking around the things on my office shelves.

"What do I do with her?" I ask him desperately, and he begins to chuckle.

"Oh my god, look at you. You're completely panicked. I've seen you face some of the toughest SOBs without even blinking, and a small female child turns you into a quivering mess. I have to get a pic.' He reaches into his pocket to pull out his phone, but I growl, and he freezes.

"Not a fucking word to anyone if you value your life."

He nods slowly but doesn't stop grinning like a complete fool.

"So what do I do with her?" I ask again, and he shrugs, but before he can answer, she does.

"Can I have something to eat? I'm so hungry." She turns to look at me, and there's a twinkle of something in her eyes.

I look at Bryce again, not sure if I should feed her or if she's like a gremlin and shouldn't be fed at certain times.

He shrugs. "Sure, what do you want? We can get the kitchen to bring you something."

She claps her hands and bounces on the spot. "Can I have those chicken things that are nice and crunchy and fries? My grandfather says that ladies shouldn't eat fried food if they want to keep their figures, but my mommy got them for me once, and they were delicious." Her face drops, and she looks at the floor. "Grandfather wasn't happy with her, and Mommy cried."

I stare at her. There is so much to unpack with that whole thing. What in the ever loving Stepford wives crap is that? "Crunchy chicken things?"

I look to Bryce for help, and I can see him trying to process it.

"Chicken fingers?" he asks the little girl who lifts her head and nods enthusiastically.

"Yes, the fingers of chickens. I really want those." She bats her eyelashes at him, and I can see him melt. He's a complete goner for the pretty little thing.

I scoff and reach for the phone. "Nice little bit of manipulation there, kid." I put in the order to the kitchen, adding a strawberry milkshake for her and my own lunch order before looking at Bryce with narrowed eyes. "What do you want?"

He shakes his head and opens his mouth to give me some kind of excuse, but I growl again, and he sighs before rattling off his order, knowing he isn't leaving me alone with this kid. They assure me it will be up in twenty minutes, so I hang up and look around for something I can distract her with.

She picks up a pack of cards from the table and sits on the floor. "Can we play Go Fish?" she asks me before turning her attention back to Bryce, instinctively knowing he's the pushover.

He sighs and toes of his shoes before hiking his suit pants up and sitting down on the carpet across from her. "We can play a few rounds before lunch gets here. Come on, Tori, it's better with more than two players."

The smirk he gives me is mischievous, and I consider getting up and kicking him with the pointy toe of my heel, but the little girl clasps her hands together like she's praying and looks at me.

"Pretty please."

I catch sight of the bruises on her arms and blow out a breath, knowing I have already lost this battle. I toe off my own shoes, leaving them under the desk, and join them on the floor. Bryce is shuffling the cards like the pro I know he is.

"Do you know how to play Go Fish, Tori?" Addi asks as Bryce deals us each seven cards.

I scoff and pick up my hand, fanning them out to see what I have—all singles, unfortunately. "Of course I do. I'm going to wipe the floor with you."

"Tori," Bryce scolds, but if he thinks I'm going to let the little girl win, he is dreaming. I watch as she struggles to hold all the cards in her hands. She picks them up one at a time and holds them in a pile, turning each over to look at it. I sigh and shuffle over.

"If you are going to play cards, you need to know how to hold them properly." I show her how to fan them out, which is a little tricky with such small hands, but she eventually gets the hang of it, and she looks proudly at me before glaring.

"You looked at my cards. That's cheating."

I wave my hand and move back to my spot. "You're right, that isn't fair, is it?" I toss my crappy hand into the middle and gesture for the others to do the same. "We can redeal." She grins and nods as Bryce shuffles and redeals.

"What is the prize?" she asks with a gleam in her eye, and Bryce chuckles.

"How about whoever wins the most hands can have a cookie from the restaurant?"

She purses her lips and taps a finger on the side of her mouth like she's thinking about it, and I suspect this little girl is not as clueless as we first thought. "Make it a banana split and you've got a deal."

Bryce bursts out with laughter and holds out his hand, and the two of them shake. "You've got yourself a deal."

Chapter Ten

Addison thoroughly thrashes both of us. I'm not sure Bryce was trying all that hard, but I was, and I still lost to a four-year-old. Talk about fucking humbling.

She's sitting on the other side of my desk, devouring her banana split with chocolate sauce smeared across her face, when Penelope finally returns.

She leans against the doorframe and smiles, something that looks genuine, unlike the usual smiles I am used to. "Well, look at that, she survived. I knew there was some good in you, Victoria Russo." That almost sounds like a compliment from the woman who I thought despised me.

I frown, utterly confused and still highly suspicious of this woman. "Don't ever ask me to do this again, Penelope. I'm too fucking busy for any of this crap, not to mention it's not exactly the safest place for a child."

I glare at her, and she pushes off the doorframe and comes inside, sighing. "No, but neither is her life in general. Thankfully Mario keeps her separated from his life most of the time. He has her and the nanny in a townhouse away from his main residence, but it means that I can't keep an eye on her all the time."

My eyes just about bug out of my head at her sharing this information. She basically just told me about a weak link in Mario's defenses, but would I stoop so low as to use a child against the man? I glance at the girl, her riotous head of curls sticking up all over the place from bouncing around when she won at Go Fish. When she looks up at me, she smiles with such an air of innocence and joy, I know that there is no way I could do anything to harm this child despite what it might gain me.

"Well, that's not my problem," I tell her, and I see her frown and sigh with disappointment. What did she expect? For me to add kidnapping to my repertoire? It's not like that's something I could hide, unlike bodies, which are easy to dispose of. Kidnapping someone without torturing and killing them is complicated, and what the hell would I do with a four-year-old?

She walks into my bathroom and returns with a washcloth then proceeds to clean Addison's hands and face. "Come on, sweetie, we need to go home. Miss Macy will be waiting for you," she tells her, and the smile on Addison's face drops, and tears well in her eyes.

"But I don't want to go home. I hate Miss Macy." She crosses her arms and pushes out her bottom lip in a pout that would give Sage a run for his money. "I want my mommy." Tears start to trickle down her cheeks, and I clench my fists and grit my teeth. She is not my problem. I raise an eyebrow at Penelope and nod at the girl.

"You deal with this, I have places to be." I stand up and move around my desk. I've had enough. Today has been a lot, and I'm ready to go home and smoke some weed with Sage and forget about all of this, especially because I have an urge to put a bullet in Miss Macy's head, and that would probably go over like a lead balloon.

Addison jumps off the chair and rushes at me, and I freeze. Fuck, what do I do? Before I can make a decision, she wraps her little bruised arms around my legs and presses her tearstained cheeks to my belly.

"I love you, Tori, please don't make me go."

I gulp and look around, holding my arms up like I have a weapon pointed at me.

"Help!" I plead with Penelope for the first time ever.

Her eyes have something like regret and sympathy in them, but she nods her head and untangles Addison's arms from around me. "Come on, sweetie. Tori has things to do. Let's go home, and I'll read you a story before I have to leave," she promises as she gently drags her from my office, Addison's sobs echoing behind them. She pauses at the doorway and looks back over her shoulder. "Be careful, Tori. As much as we don't get along, I loved your father, and he wouldn't want anything to happen to you or Gio."

With that parting comment, she leaves, and I frown, not sure what to make of it.

"Well, fuck," I grumble as Bryce appears in my doorway.

"Aw, did the big bad mafia princess grow a heart?" he teases, and I glare at him.

"Fuck you. I just didn't want her to go back to an abusive household, but there's nothing I can do."

"I don't know. Killing her nanny and grandfather sounds pretty good," he replies. "Addi told us enough stories about both of them to warrant it."

"Her grandfather is Mario Maricuso," I tell him, and his eyes widen.

"Oh shit. Yeah, now it sounds even better."

"But then what do we do with her? You want to take her in? Because I'm not qualified, nor do I have the desire to look after a small human," I ask him, and he frowns.

"Where are her parents? I didn't think Mario had children."

"Penelope said they are not around at the moment, and she all but confirmed he did a while ago." We still haven't been able to get any more info. "Fuck, I should have grilled the kid. I can't believe I didn't make the most of what I had. I'm ready to kick my own ass."

Bryce shakes his head and smiles. "Seriously, you would feel good pumping a kid for info?"

I shrug nonchalantly. "I mean, sure, why not? I could have bribed her. She seemed amenable to gifts."

He scoffs and shakes his head. "Sure, you big old softy," he teases, and I flip him off before grabbing the keys to my car.

"I'm heading out. If you see Sam and Dean, tell them I'll catch up with them tomorrow. I have a headache, and I'm exhausted from this week. I need some peace and quiet."

He waves a hand in acknowledgment as he heads back to his own office, and I walk to the elevator, going down to the parking garage.

A piece of paper sitting under my wipers flutters in the small breeze that blows through the parking garage, and I look around to see if the person who left it is still here, but no one is close by. I can hear muffled voices farther away, but they aren't trying to stay concealed or anything, so I doubt they left the note. I pull it out and glance at what's written on it—nothing but an address. I flip it over to see if there is anything else on the other side, but it's blank.

Suspicious, but I am too tired and emotionally drained to worry about it now, so I tuck it into my pocket. I'll google the address tomorrow once I've caught up on some much needed rest.

My thoughts are a chaotic mess as my body goes into autopilot, taking me from Suncity back to my home. I have so many balls in the air that keeping them afloat is becoming nearly impossible.

My hands clench around the steering wheel as I

think of the utter useless asshole my brother has become. I want to confront him, but to be honest, I'm exhausted, and I'm pretty sure nothing I would say would convince him to change. He's become so fucking selfish. I basically rely on Sam and Dean to be my right-hand men these days, even though they technically started as my protection detail. They've really stepped up, and I can rely on them to handle the things I need done. Tomorrow's meeting should shed more light on the Lorenzo situation. It would be nice if I had one less thing to worry about.

The gates open for me as I pull into the estate. They must have seen my car coming down the road, so I don't have to stop, but I wave at the guard booth as I drive through and into the underground parking. I take the elevator up to the main living area, thinking about the hot bubble bath I'm going to take after I've grabbed some food, but when I reach the kitchen, the sound of voices and laughter have me pausing.

Fuck, I forgot about our unwanted guests. I really don't have the energy to be social at the moment, but despite me not wanting them in my house, I still feel something for Vienna and her guys.

Cautiously, I push the door open to the kitchen and find Suzy and Vienna standing at the island, chatting and cutting vegetables together. The kitchen smells delicious. I don't know what they are making, but it has my stomach rumbling in anticipation. Before I can say anything, the door opposite me swings open, and Tristan practically bounces in. He presses a kiss to

Suzy's cheek before twirling Vienna around and dipping her, giving her a more thorough kiss before returning her to her previous position, snatching a piece of carrot, and popping it into his mouth. None of them have noticed me yet.

"Get away with you." Suzy flicks him with the tea towel that was resting on her shoulder, and he dances backward, taking a seat opposite them at the island. Vienna just smiles at him, her eyes filled with a love that makes my dead heart speed up a little. I'm envious, grumpy, and tired. Maybe I should just go straight to my room and bypass any social interaction today. I don't trust myself to be kind to anyone.

"I'm starving. How long until dinner is ready?" Tristan pushes back a lock of hair that has fallen over his eyes. He's wearing gray sweats and a tight white shirt that does nothing to hide how nice his body is, and his feet are bare, which does something to me. I don't want to look too closely at that something though.

"Another hour. Why don't you go find the others and harass them so we can get this finished?" Suzy tells him.

"Sage is back," Vienna says, and her eyes sparkle as he sits up, looking around the kitchen. "Not here, silly." She chuckles but then frowns. "Actually, I don't know where he went. He seemed to disappear, but then again, this house is so big, he could be anywhere."

Suzy starts to cut her vegetables faster and ignores the conversation. I'm guessing Sage went down to play with his plants, and we don't really want them asking any questions about that. Time to cause a distraction.

"Well, isn't this cozy," I comment, pushing the door fully open and stepping into the kitchen.

"Tori!" Suzy exclaims, dropping her knife and hurrying around to envelop me in a wave of French perfume and affection. "Be nice, I really like them," she growls into my ear before pulling away. "Why didn't you let us know you were returning? We haven't heard from you all week," she scolds before stepping back and looking me over. "You look exhausted, and have you lost weight?" She pulls me into another hug and whispers, "Seriously, I like them and think they could be just what you need."

"They could be what I need elsewhere," I hiss back, and she gives me a little shake and a look of disappointment before returning to what she was doing. My attention switches to the others in the kitchen.

"Hi." I wave awkwardly, feeling uncomfortable, which is exactly why I didn't want people in my safe space.

"Hey there, poppet," Tristan says, giving me a wink, but both of them are looking at me like I might explode at any moment.

Vienna bites her lip and looks down at the knife in her hand before looking back up, words rushing out of her mouth. "I know you wanted us to stay at the Lucky Diamond, and we told Gio we would have been happy to go there, but he insisted."

"It's okay, V, we can pack up and go now that Tori

is home. It's not a big deal." Tristan pushes off the stool he was slouching on. "I'll go let the others know."

Suzy glares at me and shakes her head, and I groan internally. She's going to give me hell if I make them go.

I wave a hand. "It's fine, you don't have to go. It's a huge place, and I'll be busy, so we probably won't see that much of each other, especially with all of you going to college as well."

Suzy is still glaring at me, and I glare back. What the fuck does she want me to say? Does she want me to beg them to stay? I'm not going to do that.

Vienna looks relieved, and I see her whole body sag with relief. Tristan is looking at me rather seriously, not something I've seen in his face before.

"Are you sure, Tori? We don't want to make you feel uncomfortable in your own home." Something about his words causes some of my own tension to release, and when I think about it, I do actually mean what I'm saying, not just for Suzy's sake. I just don't know if I want to mix my personal life with my professional one. After all, I am a killer, and they are college students. How much more different can we be?

"Seriously, you're fine. Please forgive me. I'm tired, and it's been a long ass week. I'm going to head up and have a bath if I have time before dinner is ready." I look at Suzy who gives me a nod, her eyes shining with pride.

"Of course. Dinner will be served in the dining room now that there are enough people not to make it look obnoxious," she tells me with a smile. "Can you let Sage know?" she asks, glancing downwards to share that he is, in fact, down in his grow warehouse.

"Will do. I'll see you guys at dinner?" I ask, and Vienna nods enthusiastically while Tristan gives me a wink.

I head upstairs to my room to run a bath and get my head on straight.

Chapter Eleven

By the time I get to the dining room, it is a chaotic, noisy affair. Everyone is there, including Suzy and Ben. Sage sees me and stands up, gesturing to the chair between him and Xavier. "Tori, I saved you a seat," he tells me, and I send him a grateful look before moving toward it, but I get waylaid by Gio on my way.

He pulls me into a big hug, and I stiffen. My bath may have relaxed my body, but I am still so fucking angry with my brother and how he has constantly been letting me down.

"Tori, I missed you," he tells me, pulling away and looking into my eyes. I don't hide how I'm feeling, glaring at him, and he has the decency to wince, but he doesn't say anything. "How was Cancun?"

"We didn't go to Cancun. We did some business up north and then headed south to check on some of our holdings," I murmur before pulling away and continuing to my seat, exchanging pleasantries with the others I haven't already run into. His eyes narrow, and I can see questions rolling around inside his brain. I move quickly away, hoping he won't bring anything up in front of our guests.

Sage squeezes my knee when I sit down, and Suzy starts to serve the delicious smelling casserole. Bread rolls and butter are also passed around, and I murmur my thanks to Xavier when he puts one on my plate.

"It's good to see you back," he says quietly, "and thank you for letting us stay. I know you weren't consulted, but the girls feel safer here than they do at a hotel."

"It's fine. I probably won't be around much anyway," I reply, spreading some butter on my roll and taking a bite before moaning. I love hot, fresh bread with butter, and I really am hungry.

"That would be a pity," he replies, surprising me, and I lift my head to find him looking at my lips with undisguised heat.

I struggle to swallow my bread before grabbing the glass of wine Ben poured me and taking a sip to wash it down. Holy fuck, he can be intense. Sage doesn't miss a thing and gives my knee another excited squeeze, all while carrying on a conversation with Tristan on his other side.

"So, Tori, how was your trip? Is everything okay with our holdings elsewhere?" Gio asks, and I can't stop my scowl as I look at him. I can't believe he wants to discuss things in front of our guests.

"I thought you went to Cancun." Casey frowns, looking at the others for confirmation.

"I guess Gio made a mistake," I say firmly, not inviting any questions. "Everything is fine. I dealt with a few problems, but nothing I couldn't handle," I answer evasively, not wanting to go into any details.

"I'm sure glad to be back in my own bed though." Sage changes the subject smoothly. "I think I have a permanent kink in my neck from sleeping on some pretty rough beds."

Gio frowns. "Our hotels don't have comfortable beds? I seem to remember them being pretty fucking comfortable when I stayed in them in other states."

I roll my eyes and stifle a sigh. "We didn't stay at any of our holdings. We were doing incognito spot checks. It would have been counterproductive to let them know we were observing," I reply vaguely.

"Oh, were you doing an undercover boss type thing?" Vienna asks, her eyes bright with excitement.

"Ah, yes, you could say that," I confirm. I mean, she's not wrong. We just weren't at our hotels.

Sage laughs. "We had disguises and everything. Nobody knows that Tori Russo was in town, keeping an eye on her establishments."

"And did you bust anyone doing anything wrong?" Casey catches on to Vienna's excitement and looks at me with wide eyes.

I shrug. "Nothing we couldn't handle."

Gio nods. "Good, let's get together tomorrow and

go over your findings. I have classes in the morning, but my afternoon is free."

I stare at my brother with confusion. What the fuck? Is he actually showing some interest in the family business again? My heart starts to pick up with excitement.

"Oh, we have that pottery class tomorrow afternoon." Casey puts her hand on my brother's arm, giving it a squeeze, and he grimaces before looking at me, and my heart sinks again. Of course he's going to let me down. I don't know why I dared to hope he was changing.

"Sorry. What about tomorrow night?"

"I'll have to check my schedule, and I'll get back to you," I say through clenched teeth.

"Easy tiger, your killer is showing," Sage whispers in my ear. "We don't need him. Take a breath and put down the knife."

I look down at the bread knife in my hand that I clench in a tight fist and slowly relax my fingers, placing it back on the table.

"How about we all watch a movie tonight?" Vienna says brightly, trying to ease the very noticeable tension.

"Sounds good," Gio agrees as Ben and Suzy beg off, claiming they want an early night.

"What about you, Tori?" Colton asks, and when I look at him across the table, his pretty blue eyes study me carefully, looking between me and the knife I placed on the table with something that looks like desperation.

"I'm going to pass. I want to go down to the shooting range and blow off some steam. I have entirely too much pent-up aggression and need to release some of it," I reply, wondering if it would be bad form to whisk him away to my secret room and do some damage to his pretty skin. I can't go back to the Black Rose now, but I also have a live-in sub, which I hadn't added to the plus column of them living with us. First, though, I need to kill some targets so I don't do too much damage to him.

"You have a range?" Tristan's eyes light up with excitement, looking around like it might appear. "I haven't seen it."

Although the range is in the basement below ground, there is a way to access it from the house that won't give away all the other facilities down there.

"Yeah, it's off the parking garage. You just need to put in an access code on the door. You're welcome to use it. There are a range of weapons down there to choose from and a few different target options. You should see Tori throw knives. It's kind of scary." Gio looks at me proudly, oblivious to the tension flowing through my body.

Sage groans next to me as I reach for the knife again. Fucking Gio and his big mouth. Now, instead of being alone, it looks like I'm going to have some company.

"I'd love to watch you shoot, I bet it's sexy as

fuck," Tristan teases me lightly, and I can't come up with a reason to deny him.

"Maybe Tori wants to go on her own, Tris," Colton suggests gently, but the way Tristan's joy fades from his eyes has me feeling guilty, so I shake my head.

"No, it's fine. You're welcome to join me as long as you don't get pissy when I kick your butt." I try for lighthearted, and Sage mutters, "Good girl," under his breath. The praise has me shivering slightly, and Xavier moves ever so slightly. His leg brushing against mine causes goosebumps to rise on my skin.

"You all better watch out. Tori could shoot the dick off a sparrow," Ben says, holding up his glass of wine in a toast, and all the tension, sexual or otherwise, seems to drain out of the room. The rest of dinner is more pleasant than I thought it would be. The others carry the conversation, allowing me to relax and enjoy having company around. I'm able to get out of my head for a little while, and I hadn't realized how much I needed that.

***

Our guests try to insist on cleaning up after dinner, but Ben and Suzy shoo them away. Casey and Gio have already disappeared when we all sort of drift into one of the living areas with large windows that overlook the landscaped pool and back-yard. It's the one Sage and I use most. It has a large, comfortable sectional and Sage's gaming system, which is connected to the hundred inch TV. The windows are currently covered by bulletproof shutters, which automatically lower when the sun sets. We can manually override this, but I haven't felt the need to since living here. If I want to swim at night, I use the indoor pool.

Vienna eyes the shutters warily but doesn't say anything as she sinks down onto the couch next to Colton. Sage bounds over to the gaming system and lifts up two controllers, tossing one into Colton's lap. "How are you at GTA?" he asks, sitting down and powering the system up.

"Fairly decent," he replies, picking up the controller as Vienna rolls her eyes.

"Fairly decent is a lie. He's extremely proficient," she tells Sage, whose eyes sparkle.

"Awesome, this will be fun."

"Isn't GTA a little too close to your real life to be enjoyable?" Tristan stands behind the couch, and his hands go down to Sage's shoulders, giving them a little squeeze. Sage moans and leans into the pressure.

"Oh yeah, right there," he mutters.

"I'm a legitimate businesswoman with legitimate businesses, thank you very much," I say primly, and all of them look at me with disbelief in their eyes.

I scoff and whirl around, leaving the room and heading toward the elevator. It's true, some of them are legit. I hear footsteps behind me, and when I glance over my shoulder, I find both Tristan and Xavier are following me.

"Coming to kill some things?" I ask bluntly, but neither of them flinch at the suggestion. In fact, Tristan gets a manic look in his eyes that reveals his excitement.

I push the button, and all three of us step into the elevator when it opens. I press the button for the garage, knowing I can't use the entrance from the bunker, and the car descends, a comfortable silence surrounding us. It barely takes moments before the doors open again, and I lead them over to a door in the side of the wall. I press the code into the keypad. It swings open and a light switches on, and the low hum of the ventilation system kicks in.

"Holy shit!" Tristan's voice echoes through the large area as he scopes out the setup. We have a couple of lanes, but an entire section is designed as a tactical obstacle course similar to what the military or special forces use to train their teams. All of it is soundproof and designed to catch any stray bullets.

Off to the side is the gun locker, and I key in another code and gesture for the guys to help themselves, while pulling my own gun from the waistband of my lounge pants.

"You were carrying that the whole time at dinner?" Xavier asks, studying me carefully while Tristan mutters excitedly about the array of guns.

I shrug, pulling the slide back to chamber the first round. I don't tend to keep one in there when I'm at home. "I'm usually armed no matter where I am." I reach into my top and pull a small knife out of the bra

I put on after my bath. "You can never be too careful, you know."

Tristan groans, and I find him looking at me with a whole heap of lust in his eyes. "That's so fucking sexy."

Xavier purses his lips. "Would you have had those if we hadn't been living in the house?"

"On me?" I clarify, and he nods. I shake my head. "No, probably not. I have weapons in easy reach all around the house, and I mostly don't feel the need to carry one with me while I am in my own home."

Tristan's desire bleeds away, and the two of them look at me with what feels like pity.

"We're really sorry we're invading your safe space. You shouldn't feel like you have to protect yourself in your own home, especially because it's a fortress," Xavier says gruffly, and I wave him off.

"It is what it is. Gio invited you, and I can't very well uninvite you. He wants you here, and what he wants goes." *For now.* I don't bother adding that last bit out loud though.

"I promise the four of us and Casey have no ulterior motives, and as soon as the dorms are rebuilt, we will leave. If at any stage you get sick of us, we will move into the Lucky Diamond like you said, no arguments," Xavier promises as Tristan chimes in, looking uncomfortable.

"But it might be at least a couple of months. The whole dorm was relocated because the top two levels have structural problems, and until they are fixed, they won't let anyone live there."

"It's fine, I promise, and if you start to piss me off, I'll just get rid of you." I smile, but the threat is very clear, and I can tell they understand when they exchange a glance.

"Well, in that case, we better do everything we can to stay on your good side." Tristan becomes all flirty again and winks at me. "Now why don't you show us what you can do with that thing?" He nods at the Glock in my hand and passes a similar one and a magazine to Xavier, who slams it home and pulls the slide back.

"Care to make this interesting?" he asks me as the three of us move toward one of the lanes.

Chapter Twelve

When we get to the lane, I place my gun on the ledge and use the switch on the side to bring the target forward. "Sure," I agree as I grab a fresh target sheet from under the bench. "What are the terms?"

They exchange a glance, and it's like they can communicate without words. I'm kind of envious, to be honest, that they have this capability.

"If you outshoot the two of us, then the four of us will leave tonight and stay at the Lucky Diamond, but we can't speak for Casey," Xavier says.

I keep my face blank as a rush of emotions runs through me, both excitement and disappointment, and I'm not sure which one is more prominent. Do I even want them to actually leave now? Fuck, I'm such a goddamn mess.

"Okay, and if you two outshoot me, what do you

get?" I ask, and it's Tristan who answers this time, his eyes sparkling.

"A kiss. One for each of us." He points between himself and Xavier.

"And you stop carrying your weapons on your person while we are in the house," Xavier adds. "I hate that you feel like you aren't safe in your own home, and we are responsible for that." Xavier's brow furrows with concern, and I feel a wave of warmth at the knowledge that he cares about me to some degree.

It would be nice not to carry my weapon constantly, and it isn't like there aren't plenty hidden around the house in case of an emergency. Although I don't know a lot about these people, I don't think they mean me any bodily harm—or at least I hope not. If they wanted to kill me, they've had plenty of opportunities to do so, and I think they'll find I'm not such an easy target.

"Okay. Sounds fair," I agree, feeling confident I have this in the bag. "What are the terms?"

"Five shots. Closest grouping to the bullseye is the winner, and since you have home court advantage, Xavier and I get to go first," Tristan replies, pulling on a pair of earmuffs and settling into a confident stance. Xavier and I both don our ear protection and stand back a little, giving him some room.

Both guys obviously have experience with handling a firearm and seem comfortable around them. I thought Tristan would be flashy and rapid fire his rounds into the target, but he's slow and methodical, taking his time and lining up each shot perfectly. The report echoes through the range in five controlled shots, the scent of gunpowder tickling my nose, with him taking his time between each round. When he's finished, he places the gun down on the ledge in front of him and takes off his earmuffs before flicking the switch to bring the target forward. I can already see he scored well—a close grouping around the nine ring with one even slicing halfway between the bullseye.

He releases the target from the clips and turns, waving it at me with a huge grin on his face. "Look at that, I'm on fire. It's going to be hard to beat that. Do you need some lip balm to get those lips ready for me? I can probably find some of Vienna's," he teases and does a little victory dance that involves a lot of hip thrusting, very similar to what Sage has done in the past. I giggle at the display. He's so carefree and joyful, and he reminds me so much of Sage. No wonder the two of them clicked.

"Settle down, Rambo, it's my turn," Xavier grumbles good-naturedly and grabs Tristan by the nape of his neck. "How about a kiss for good luck?" He doesn't wait for him to reply before smashing his mouth against Tristan's. The kiss is aggressive, and I can't drag my eyes away from them, watching as Xavier scrapes his teeth over Tristan's plump lip. My core throbs, and I squirm at the overt display of possession. Tristan groans, and when Xavier pulls away, he follows, not wanting to let him escape, but Xavier just shakes his head and grins, pushing him back. "Well, now I'm feeling very lucky."

Tristan leans back against the wall, his head thumping against it as he groans, his eyes heavy with lust. "You're going to be very lucky no matter if we win or not," he mutters under his breath before exhaling and running a hand through his hair, pushing back a lock that fell over one eye.

"Sure you don't want to rethink this bet?" Xavier teases me, grinning and winking. "I have this in the bag."

I cross my arms, keeping my face blank. "I think I'm okay," I deadpan, and he shrugs and steps up in front of the lane. He puts a new target on the system, and it rolls down the lane. Xavier picks up the same gun Tristan used and takes his stance, wrapping both hands around the grip.

"You know Xavier is a crack shot, right?" Tristan pushes off the wall to stand next to me as we watch Xavier take his turn. "A goddamn expert at just about everything he puts his hands on. You should see what he can do with a sniper rifle."

Xavier's first round reverberates through the range, and I look down the lane to see how he did. My eyebrows jump when I see he put it straight through the center. Damn, this may not be as big of a shutout as I thought it would be, but I have put in many hours in the range, shooting out my frustration when I haven't been able to get bloody. I still think I can beat them.

"Hmm, really?" I try to sound uninterested, but in truth, I'm fascinated, though not really unsurprised. Xavier is the strong silent type, but I bet there is a carefully curled ball of violence underneath all of his control. There's a sniper range at the lake house where Mickey and Maeve are hiding out, but I won't bring strangers there just because I want to see him in action. I wonder where the two of them got their skills from.

Xavier takes his shot four more times, and his groupings are even closer than Tristan's. I'm going to have to hit the bullseye every time if I want to win this thing—not that I can't do it, but I'm in two minds now with the bet. Dinner was kind of nice, and having them around isn't as bad as I thought it would be. It's nice to have company other than Gio, Sage, Suzy, and Ben. I wish this happened in a week's time so I knew for sure one way or another whether or not I want them in my space. I'll just have to do my best.

Xavier brings his target forward and takes it down before turning and raising an eyebrow at me. "Feeling worried yet?" he asks as he holds it out for me to inspect.

"Well, I can't say that's not impressive." I let my eyes run up and down his body suggestively, and his hand clenches the target. "Very impressive, but I'm pretty sure I can do a little better than that."

Tristan's mouth drops open in surprise, and Xavier scoffs, "To do better, you would have to put all five rounds through the same hole."

I shrug. "Yeah, and?" I load another target and

send it to the back of the lane before taking my position, gripping my weapon with both hands. I relax my shoulders and spread my feet.

"No fucking way," Tristan argues.

Closing one eye, I line up the bullseye, knowing this barrel has a small kick to the left. I compensate slightly and squeeze the trigger, and my first round goes through the center of the target before slamming into the backstop.

I don't wait too long before I take the next shot. This one goes through the same hole but slightly to the left, gouging a big center hole through the target. I feel both guys step closer to me, like they need to see the next shot better, but I don't let them distract me. My third shot finds the center again, and I smile, knowing I've got this in the bag.

But then, out of the corner of my eye, I see Tristan grab Xavier and kiss him. I take another moment to calm my racing heart, not wanting to be distracted. I don't even turn my head to get a better look, my focus on winning the bet.

"You were so sexy holding that gun. I can't wait to get down on my knees tonight and show you," Tristan says loudly. I'm pretty sure they are trying to distract me, so I do my best to ignore them, but now I have dirty visions of them living rent free in my head.

Just as I'm about to squeeze the trigger, Xavier replies, "You look so pretty on your knees when I'm skull fucking you." My whole body jolts, and I squeeze the trigger, and the fucking shot goes wide, completely missing the target and slamming into the backstop two lanes over.

"Fuck," I mutter as I feel a hand on my hip. I turn my head, and Tristan is smirking at me. "Well, Tori, that completely missed. Did something distract you? There's no coming back from that. Looks like Xavi wins."

I huff and put my gun down, propping my hands on my hips. "You play dirty," I grumble, and he winks at me.

"You have no idea how dirty I play. Time to pay up."

"Fine then, a kiss for each of you, right?" I ask. My palms get sweaty, and I wipe them on my lounge pants. I step up to Tristan and put my hands on his shoulders, planning on giving him a quick kiss on the lips, but he shakes his head and pushes me back against the ledge in the booth.

"Uh-uh, not so fast now. Xavi and I are in charge now." Gone is his playful flirtatiousness, and in its place is an intensity that I haven't seen in him before. "And we never specified which lips we were kissing you on." He bends and tugs my pants down, revealing the cotton panties I put on after my bath.

"What the hell?" I yelp and go to grab my pants, but Tristan grabs my hands and leans in to whisper in my ear.

"Be a good girl and pay your dues, and we will make sure you are taken care of." His words brush across my earlobe, and goosebumps erupt on my arms.

I consider just lifting a knee and nailing him in the balls, but if I'm being honest with myself, I want to see where this goes.

He lifts me onto the ledge, nudging both guns out of the way before peeling my panties off, leaving me half naked and exposed. I feel myself grow wet as both of them stare at my bare pussy. Tristan smirks and nibbles my neck, and I shudder at the sensation. "Now be a good girl and watch Xavi and I eat our prize."

Xavier drops to his feet and shuffles forward, dragging his tongue through my wet folds before groaning. "How does she taste, my love?" Tristan looks down at his boyfriend.

"Like heaven," Xavier growls before driving his tongue deep inside me.

"Well, don't hog all the room." Tristan grabs my head and kisses me hard, the dual sensations of them wreaking havoc with my senses, and I can't help the loud moan that escapes my mouth. Tristan pulls away and kneels next to Xavier, pushing my legs wider until I'm spread obscenely in front of them. "Let me have a taste." Instead of leaning in and sampling from the source, he grabs Xavier's hair and yanks him away. His face glistens with the evidence of my desire as Tristan runs his tongue over his lips before the two of them clash in an aggressive, steamy kiss.

I moan at the sight before me. "Holy fuck, that's hot."

"You're right, she is delicious," Tristan says, pulling

away and looking up at me, his eyes heavy with lust. "We're going to devour you."

They lean forward in sync, both of their tongues lapping at my folds. My eyes just about roll back in my head, and I almost lose my balance, so I reach out, running my hands through their hair and getting a good grip to keep me upright. Tristan moans as I tug, and it vibrates against my sensitive skin.

"So wet, and so good," he murmurs as I watch, enthralled at the sight before me. Tristan's and Xavier's lips brush together as Tristan moves toward my clit, rolling it beneath his tongue with just the right amount of pressure as Xavier thrusts his tongue inside me, fucking my pussy with wet, probing strokes.

"Oh God, that's so fucking good." The words spill from my mouth as the two of them push my pleasure even higher.

"So fucking wet and sweet," Xavier murmurs as he pulls away and replaces his tongue with two fingers. They share another kiss, my arousal glistening on their faces, and my core throbs, tightening around Xavier's fingers. "Oh, she likes that a lot." He smirks against Tristan's mouth, both of them looking up at me.

I feel like a fucking goddess with my worshipers at my feet. I yank on Tristan's head, putting him back where I want him, and his laughter rumbles over my clit, causing me to shiver and tighten even further. Xavier pumps his fingers in and out of my channel slowly, scissoring them wider to make room so that when Tristan quickly adds his, the burn isn't so intense.

I can barely keep my eyes open, but I don't want to miss a minute of the sight before me as both of their mouths return to my clit, kissing messily. Their tongues slide against each other and my swollen nub, the vibrations sending intense jolts to my pleasure center.

"God, don't stop," I beg, grinding down onto their fingers and mouths.

Xavier pulls away, moving his head below where their fingers disappear into my cunt, and I feel his tongue lap at my asshole. I freeze slightly before relaxing into the sensation.

"Good girl," he praises as he removes his fingers from my pussy. Tristan adds another, all while his tongue flicks my clit, the ring in it creating a delicious pressure.

Xavier probes my tight ring with his finger, and I groan loudly as he slips it into the first knuckle. "You're going to take me here one day, aren't you? I'm going to fuck this sexy ass while Tristan is buried deep inside your tight little cunt. You're going to take both of us like the good slut you are. Maybe I'll let Vienna lick your clit while Colton fucks your mouth. Sage can join too. Maybe he can fuck Tristan while he's fucking you."

"We'll be like a human pretzel, all of us joined together in the pursuit of getting you off," Tristan mumbles against my clit, the vibrations of his words humming against it.

It's all too much. My walls flutter around their invading digits, and when Tristan lightly nips my clit, it pushes me over the edge, and I come hard, screaming loudly as my pussy gushes all over their hands. Neither of them stop their assault, using their fingers and tongues to catch everything I give them until I'm a boneless mess.

When I finally come back to my senses, I look down and find the two of them kissing, their faces shiny with my release. It's intense and sexy, and I'm lost for words, but my brain starts to come back online, and my hearts begins to race for an entirely different reason.

Chapter Thirteen

I'm ashamed to admit that as soon as I recovered from that mind-blowing orgasm, I bolted from the range, my heart racing and my chest heaving. With my mind trying to make sense of what just happened, I stumble, trying to pull my pants back on while shoving my panties into the pocket. I'm in such a hurry, I leave my gun behind, but I'll grab it in the morning. The elevator can't come quick enough, but neither Tristan nor Xavier follow me, and I have to feel grateful for their restraint. I'm both mortified and tempted to go back and see what else might happen. When the elevator arrives, it makes up my mind for me. I step in, and the doors close just as the range door opens, and I see Tristan and Xavier step out.

Sage and I discussed this previously, but to be honest, I kind of thought it would never happen. Prior to Sage, I was very much inexperienced when it came to romantic entanglements and used sex with women as an outlet in the past, but never did I ever feel an emotional connection to any of them. What just happened was way beyond what I expected. It felt like it was on the same level of what Sage and I have, and that is disconcerting, because I know less than nothing about those two and only a small amount more about Vienna and Colton. Am I so much of a mess that I'm grabbing onto any form of affection with both hands, damning the consequences?

I bypass the ground level and take the elevator straight up to the level my bedroom is on. I have no desire to see them with my face flushed from pleasure, guilt, and regret. I rush down the hallway past Gio's room, grateful there aren't any sex noises coming from it, before thrusting open my bedroom door and hurrying into my bathroom. I'm breathing heavily when I brace my shaking hands on the sink and lift my head to look at myself. My curls are a mess from Tristan running his hands through them when he was kissing me, and my cheeks are red. My eyes glisten with tears, my emotions so close to the surface that they are about to erupt.

"Fuck, Fuck," I sob as I drop my head again, not wanting to look at myself. Instead, I leave the bathroom, strip off my clothes, climb into bed, and curl up on one side, trying to scrub the vision of Tristan and Xavier between my legs from my mind. It's almost impossible. Watching them kiss before they spread my legs so they could both eat me out is something I'm never going to forget. The feeling of Xavier's fingers thrusting deep into my channel while Tristan flicked his tongue across my clit was mesmerizing. Both of them looked like they couldn't get enough of me, and damn, I liked it a lot.

"Ugh!" I scream into my pillow and bang my fist against the mattress. "I am so fucked."

"Tori?" I hear my bedroom door open, and Sage steps into the dark room, his silhouette highlighted by the hallway light. "Are you okay?" I hear concern in his voice as he shuts the door behind him and walks over to the bed.

"Yeah," I mumble from behind the pillow.

"Did they do something you didn't want? Because I'll go back there and gut them." There is a hard promise in Sage's tone as he sits down. I pull the pillow off my face to look at him. My room is dark, only illuminated by the light I left on in the bathroom, but it's enough to make out his features. He's frowning, and I can see how tense his body is. If I don't reassure him, he will make good on his threat.

I huff out a breath and shake my head. "No, and that's the problem," I admit, and his body loses some tension, his shoulders relaxing. He stands up and peels off his jeans and shirt, leaving him in his briefs before he slides into my bed. He wraps his arms around me, spooning me from behind, before nuzzling my neck. "Hmm, you smell like Tris. So it was good? What's bothering you?"

I close my eyes, even though I'm not looking at

him, because I'm about to admit something I haven't ever admitted out loud before.

"You know, I kind of understand why Gio is the way he is. This is no life for a teenager. I don't want to manage this fucking organization. Sometimes I want to say fuck it and just let another family absorb the Russos, but then I think about my dad and how he died for this family, and he would be so disappointed in me, and I feel guilty as fuck."

"So you feel guilty for enjoying yourself with Tris and Xavi?"

"Yeah, and selfish and all sorts of self-loathing. I don't know how I'm going to face them in the morning. I ran out of the range like my ass was on fire." I roll my face into the pillow and groan. "They must think I'm an idiot."

"No, baby, they were worried they upset you. They told us about the bet and insisted I come and make sure you are alright. Vienna was yelling at them when I left."

"Are we doing the right thing?" I roll over and face Sage, wanting to see him when he answers my question. "Are we not just setting ourselves up for a whole heap of heart break and disappointment?"

He purses his lips before answering. "We could be, but life is boring without a little risk, and it would be pretty lonely going through life avoiding making connections because we are scared to. I know it's more difficult for you, having to always be conscious of people's motives, not to mention dangerous if you trust the wrong person, but that's no way to live. I don't want you to end up looking back and regretting your life, and if we are making a mistake, then at least we're doing it together." He squeezes me before giving me a kiss on the lips. I sigh and sink into his embrace, enjoying how his mostly naked body feels against mine.

"I want to do it again," I whisper into his chest, admitting how I feel out loud. "I want to experience everything the four of them have to offer."

"So you aren't kicking them out?" he asks, holding me tighter.

"No. Even if I'm making the biggest mistake of our lives, I'm going to enjoy it. I have so much stress in my professional life, having four other people for us to come home to might be nice for a change, right?" I ask, wanting to hear his opinion, because this involves more than just me. I know he said it before, but I need his solid reassurance. Sage has become my rock, and I won't jeopardize that.

"Four very sexy people," he growls in my ear. "You know I'm all in as long as you are happy. The minute that changes, I'll ask them to leave myself. I was going to tonight, but you seemed to enjoy dinner."

"It wasn't as uncomfortable as I thought it was going to be," I murmur, and he chuckles.

"I thought you were going to stab Gio with your knife when he asked what we had been up to."

"God, he's such an idiot. When did my intelligent,

business savvy brother become such a fucking moron?" I grumble.

"I think it happened right around the time he looked into a pair of pretty blue eyes and fell madly in love."

"I'm in love with you, but that hasn't turned me into an idiot." I lift my head to look at him, and he smiles, his eyes soft with love.

"I know, babe, but you're amazing. Women can multitask so much better than men. Even I can admit that." He winks, when it makes me laugh, I realize all the turmoil and guilt has seeped away. Just having him here to support and hold me while I'm being dramatic is fucking everything. I press a kiss above his heart and snuggle into him.

"I do love you, more and more each day," I murmur and close my eyes, knowing I'm going to need a good night's sleep to be at my best tomorrow morning.

"And I you." He presses a kiss to the top of my head, and we fall asleep wrapped in each other's arms.

Despite having fallen asleep holding one another, I wake to find myself just about dangling off the edge, again. I grumble as I toss the covers back and slide my feet to the floor. This is becoming an issue. Sage is spread out just like he was every day this week, and I've just about had enough of it. He can sleep in his own damn bed until he learns to share. I use the bathroom before putting on my workout gear and heading to the gym. I need to let Lorn and Castiel know I'm back and ready to train again. It's been a few weeks since I've had a session, and I feel like a good workout.

When I get to the gym, I freeze in the doorway. Xavier is lifting weights, and I'm not quite sure how to face him after I ran from him last night. My nose wrinkles at the smell of sweat and gym equipment. No matter how often the room is cleaned, it just doesn't lose that scent. Xavier hasn't noticed me yet or is pretending not to, and I appreciate the effort if that's the case. I decide to warm up on the treadmill and head straight for it, my shoes silent on the mats in the middle of the room for sparring.

Various machines are situated on either side, all designed to keep a person in peak condition if they deign to use them, and mirrors line all the walls. Out of the corner of my eye, I see Xavier tracking my path with his own eyes, but he still doesn't say a word. Stepping up onto the machine, I put my earbuds in and program the treadmill to a speed that won't allow for easy conversation. Selecting a playlist from my phone, I start to move my feet in time with the moving belt. This program starts off slow and gets faster, lowering and raising the incline to make the workout more strenuous. It's perfect for my needs, and for the next twenty minutes, I focus on keeping my breathing even and not falling off the damn machine with a misstep. It's pure bliss. All other thoughts drift away as I focus on the air in my chest and the burn in my muscles.

When my workout tapers off to a cool down walk, I'm breathing heavily, and my skin has a sheen of sweat on it. It's been a while since I worked out, and I'm paying for it. Thank goodness my trainers aren't here to see the sorry state I'm in.

I feel rather than see Xavier approach me. It's like my body is attuned to his, and goosebumps erupt on my arms that have nothing to do with the air conditioner blowing across my sweaty skin.

"Hey, I was wondering if you wanted to spar." I pull the emergency stop button on the machine, and it responds instantly. I turn to face Xavier, the machine putting me eye to eye with him. His face is carefully blank, but I can see the worry in his eyes, like he's approaching a skittish kitten and is hoping it doesn't lash out with its claws.

I take a big breath and exhale, trying to get my heart rate under control after the hard workout. "Ah, yeah, sure, that would be good. I haven't called my trainers yet to let them know I'm back in town."

He holds out a hand to assist me down, and I take it. My hand looks so dainty in his large one, and his fingers are strong but comforting. Back on solid ground, I toe off my shoes and socks and leave them next to the machine, then I move to the basket of padded fingerless gloves for protection for my hands. I don't have time for broken knuckles or fingers, and even though we won't be sparring full contact, accidents can happen, and sometimes, a hit lands.

I grab a large pair and hold them out for Xavier, who takes them and slips his hands into them. "Do you want to go full contact?" he asks, nodding toward the basket of shin and body pads as well as face guards.

I shake my head. "No, it's been a while. If we could just do some light contact, I would appreciate it. I have a morning meeting I can't miss, and I'm assuming you have to be at college sometime today."

He looks at the clock on the wall. "Yeah, I have a self-defense lesson to give this morning, with a class in sports psychology this afternoon."

My eyebrows rise. "I thought you were doing a business degree like Gio," I say, and he avoids looking at me as he pulls his gloves on.

"Yeah, I'm just auditing the class. I thought it might help with my self-defense classes," he mumbles before gesturing to the mat. "Shall we?"

I pull my gloves on while thinking about what he just said. I guess it makes sense to know more about the mind of someone you're training, but what would I know? I haven't even considered college classes, since I knew what my life was going to entail. Not all of us have the luxury of deciding what we are going to be when we grow up.

I pull my phone out of my pocket and connect it to the sound system, and a playlist heavy in eighties' rock music starts playing. I toss my earbuds and the phone onto a weight bench and step out onto the mats, the softer surface giving way beneath my feet. Standing in front of Xavier, I hold out my gloves, and he bumps them before we both put our hands up to guard our faces. I watch him carefully as we circle each other, waiting for the minute movement of a muscle to telegraph his movements. He jabs at my face, fast and straight, and I duck just in time, but I still feel the rush of air on my cheek. I stumble back slightly, my eyebrows rising at the force he put behind it. "Okay then, I guess we aren't going to pull our punches. That would have fucking hurt if it connected."

He smirks, and there's a wicked glint in his eye. "Aren't you the angel of death? I thought that would have been easy to see coming."

I growl and get back into position with my hands up. I guess it's going to be like that. This time, I don't wait for him to move, and I strike hard and fast, a jab cross combination. He manages to duck the first punch, but the second clips his cheekbone, and while he's distracted by that, I follow with a right hammer fist toward his temple, but he ducks and quickly steps under my guard.

He counters with a sharp burst of punches to my body—left, right, left—his elbows driving into my ribs and solar plexus. I can tell by the hits that he's not putting his full strength behind them, but it still stings. I gasp in a quick breath of air before pivoting on my front foot and firing back with a short hook to his jaw. It connects, and he stumbles back slightly, shaking his head.

It's my turn to smirk at him and raise an eyebrow. "That all you've got?"

He doesn't say a word, unleashing another volley of punches to my face and body, the blows drive me back, but I bring up my forearms, blocking high to protect my face. He follows with a low kick to my thigh that has me dropping my guard slightly, and he lunges in with an elbow strike straight to my temple. I twist so instead of knocking me out, it glances off my shoulder. I can't stop the grunt of pain that leaves my mouth. Damn, there was some heat behind that one. If I didn't know better, I would say he was trying to knock me out. That elbow strike certainly would have done that.

Twisting, I grab his wrist, trying to trap and counter, but he slams his forearm down on my arm and breaks free, and we stumble apart to regroup. He looks completely focused, but I'm slightly shaken by the intensity of this fight. A rush of excitement flows through me. I'm impressed with how skilled he is, and I'm getting the surge of adrenaline I'm addicted to. He comes at me fast and hard, trying to grab hold of me to use his weight as leverage against me.

My knee shoots up, aiming for his groin, but he turns his hips and absorbs the impact on his thigh. He fires a short elbow strike into my sternum, and the breath rushes out of my lungs. Still, I try to fight back despite struggling to get air into my lungs. He has me locked against him, and I try a punch to his face, but it glances off. Lifting my head, I aim a headbutt at his cheek, but all it does is make my head spin and my vision turn blurry while he remains unshakeable. I sag in his arms to get my bearings, and he hooks my shoulder, pivots, and sweeps his leg. I go down hard, my back smacking against the floor as his full weight comes down on top of me. I close my eyes and groan, knowing he handed me my ass, and try to regroup.

I feel his breath across my lips, and when I open my eyes, he's right in my face. "Why did you run off last night?" he asks harshly, his breath heaving from his lungs as much as mine is, and I feel a moment of satisfaction that I gave him as much hell as he gave me. There's a slight bruise blooming on his cheek where my head connected with it. "If you didn't want it, you should have just said no, and we would have backed off. Tristan is miserable because he thinks we violated you."

I close my eyes, lean my head back on the mat, and shake my head. "No, it's fine. I did want it," I reply, unable to meet his gaze.

"Then why rush out of there like a bat out of hell? Shit, you didn't even have pants on, and you left your gun."

I blow out a huge breath of air before opening my eyes and looking at him. "You know who I am, right, and what my family does?"

He frowns. "Yeah, we know who you are," he says gruffly.

"Our life is not conducive to relationships. Letting anyone close makes them a target. Hell, what Gio has done with Casey has put her right at the top of the *ways we can make him suffer* list. I don't want that for you or her. She's too nice and not cut out for this life."

He scoffs and releases my arms, then he sits back on his heels, allowing me to raise my body off the mat.

"You're scared," he accuses, and I push a stray sweaty lock of hair off my forehead.

"Damn right I'm scared. Before I got involved with Sage, my sexual experiences were strictly women and no emotions were involved. I got my orgasm, then I got out. No messy emotions, commitment, or danger of my heart getting involved."

"Well, that isn't strictly true, is it? You've been playing with Colt for a few months now," he points out, and I feel my face flush.

"That's another aspect of me that isn't easy to accept. I like blood. I like to make my subs bleed. Is that something you are into?" I ask boldly, and he shrugs.

"I don't mind a little blood play, but let me ask you this. Do you make Sage bleed? Or when you were with Vienna last week, did you want to make her bleed?"

My eyebrows jump in surprise before I can stop them. I guess they have no secrets from each other, not that I needed them to keep it a secret. I think about what he asked and shake my head. "No, I don't need to make them bleed. Sage doesn't like anything remotely like that—old childhood trauma," I explain, and he nods.

"Exactly, so as long as you still have Colt who can

fulfil that need, then I don't see what the problem is, and trust me when I say Colton needs it. He might seem like a geeky computer nerd, but that boy has demons. Letting you bleed him is a release he craves."

"But—" I begin to argue that sex isn't the issue, but he doesn't let me finish. He stands up and offers me his hand. I slap mine into it, and he hauls me to my feet.

"No buts, we are all adults and capable of making our own choices. Trust me when I say we can all look after ourselves. Even Casey, who might seem sweet and innocent, has her own drama. She can handle all of Gio's shit. Also, let the four of us make our own decisions. We know what we want, and right now, that's you and Sage, and if things progress, we can be adults and talk about it."

"In public we're going to have to pretend to just be friends if we ever hang out together," I warn him, and when he goes to argue, I put up my hand. "No, I know you're all adults, but I won't put you at risk. If my enemies find out I feel affection for any of you, they will take advantage of that, and the last thing I want is for anyone else I have feelings for to die. Losing my dad and aunt Carla almost destroyed me, and with Uncle Mickey barely clinging to life, I wouldn't be able to survive another loss, so those are my terms. If you can't handle them, then we need to stop whatever this is right now." I'm firm, and I can tell that Xavier understands I'm serious.

"Fine, but in this house, none of us will hold back. Are you okay with that?" he asks, and I shrug.

"Sure, but know that my business comes first. If I get a call and need to leave for whatever reason, then you have to let me go. You can't come with me or be my white knight, riding in to save the day. That's not how my life works, and you would only end up getting hurt or worse."

"So Sage can protect you, but we can't?" he asks stubbornly, crossing his arms and glaring at me.

I sigh. "Sage is in the life, Xavier. He knew what he was in for when my dad gave him a home."

He drops his arms but doesn't lose the hard expression. "Fine, I'll let it go for now, but I will prove to you that we can take care of ourselves, and maybe then, you'll feel comfortable with us in public."

I give him a wry smile. "I don't want you to think I'm embarrassed or anything. I promise it's not that. I just don't want you to regret any of this."

He steps a little closer, sliding his hand onto my waist and tugging me against him, and my heart rate picks up again. He lifts his other hand and cradles the back of my head, then he gently pulls me toward him, stopping when his lips are just inches from mine.

"I assure you, I'm not going to regret this in the least," he says before pressing his lips to mine, his tongue asking for entrance. I sigh and open for him, sinking into the kiss. There's nothing hurried about it as he slowly maps my mouth with his, my hands wrapping around his waist as I fully submit to his strength. Before I know it, he's pulling away, and I blink owlishly at him, my mind wiped of all worries by one freaking amazing kiss.

"See you later," he tells me. "Maybe we can have a rematch tomorrow. I like having you under me." He pulls away and strides off without a backward glance. I blink and shake my head, clearing it of all the lustful thoughts that replaced any resemblance of clear thought.

"Don't think you will get me on my back quite so quickly next time," I call after him, my voice shaky with desire, and his loud chuckle echoes back to me.

Chapter Fourteen

I take a long shower and wash my hair, enjoying the warm water flowing over my sore muscles. That's the hardest workout I've had in weeks, and I know I'm going to feel it tonight. Once I stand under the spray for way longer than I should, I turn off the faucet and climb out, wrapping a towel around my body and grabbing another to dry my hair. Sage is no longer in bed, but the room still smells like his cologne, and I smile at the rumpled bed sheets he left behind. I bet he's already harassing Suzy for breakfast. We have that meeting with Sam and Dean first thing this morning, and I'm hoping they have a solid lead on the Lorenzo issue.

Before I can enter my walk-in closet and find some clothes for the day, there is a knock on my door. When I open it, I find Colton standing on the other side.

"Hi," I say cautiously.

"I was wondering if we could talk for a moment

before you leave today." He shuffles his feet, looking uncertain, and I feel my heart soften a little more.

"Come in." I open the door wider, and he steps in. "I was just getting ready, but we can talk now if you want."

He looks around my room in interest. As pretty as it is, there isn't a lot that shows my personality in here. I gave up all my interests when I realized I wasn't going to have time for anything else. I also disposed of all of my high school and childhood memorabilia in a fit of rage after the Stacey situation, so the only thing that says anything about me is the box of wool and knitting needles next to the small couch in the little cove next to the window.

"What can I help you with?" I ask, using the spare towel to dry my hair before tossing it on the bed. He frowns, picks it up, and takes it into the bathroom. I can't stop the bemused smile that crosses my lips at his actions. It's cute. Both Sage and I are kind of slobs. We're lucky we have people to clean up after us.

I sit down on the bed and wait for him to return, and when he does, he looks at me intensely.

"Are you planning on going back to the Black Rose anytime soon?" he asks with a desperate sort of breathlessness. I look at him carefully. His shoulders are slightly hunched, and the fingers on one hand constantly clench and release in a nervous tick.

"I wasn't planning on it. I have a lot going on, and after our untimely exit last week, I'm not sure if I was recognized or not," I tell him honestly, and his entire body seems to cave in on itself, so much so that I'm not surprised when he drops to his knees in front of me, reaching for my hands.

"Please, Tori, I need Mistress V. I need to hurt," he begs so prettily, his head bowed as he stares at the ground.

I feel a rush of adrenaline, and my hands clench the sheets on either side of my thighs. "How badly do you need it?" I ask huskily and lift his chin so he's looking at me. I can see the torment and desperation in his eyes, and a shiver of desire flows down my spine.

"So much," he replies, a tear glistening in the corner of one eye.

"Hmm, come with me." I stand up, and my towel loosens, but instead of grabbing it, I let it fall to the ground, exposing my naked body to him. His pupils blow, but he scrambles to his feet and follows me as I leave the room and walk down the hallway toward my hidden room. I hope Gio and Casey are already down at breakfast, because I don't want them seeing me parade naked through our hallways, and I also don't want them knowing about the room. Gio has no sense of decency and would probably use it for his own enjoyment.

I don't need to look back to know Colton is following me. I reach the bookcase at the end of the hall and pull out the book lever. The wall clicks open, and I pull the secret door ajar then step back for Colton to enter. He doesn't even hesitate as he hurries into my secret room. He looks around in awe.

I walk past the bed, trailing my finger over the lush coverings before moving over to my cupboards of toys. I don't have my favorite knife with me, but I do have some in here just in case. I pick one of those up now and test the sharpness against the pad of my thumb. There's a brief bite of pain, and a drop of blood wells on the digit. I lick it off before looking up at Colton. He's staring at me with lustful eyes, and I can see the outline of his cock in his sweatpants. I put the knife down, walk over to the St. Andrew's cross, and trail my finger over it. "I've never had you on one of these. I can't wait to see you spread out and at my mercy. You'd like that, wouldn't you?" I ask him, and he nods, tracking my path toward him like a gazelle watching a lion.

When I reach him, I grab his hair and pull it so he has to bend down to my level. Without my heels on, he's a good head taller than I am.

"Use your words," I growl, tightening my fist in his hair, and he groans before mumbling, "Yes, mistress."

"Good boy," I praise and release some of the tension without letting go completely. Before I can second-guess myself, I kiss him. Whenever we've been in a session, his plump lips always tempted me to bite them, and knowing I have no such restriction now is exciting. He holds still like a good, obedient boy, kissing me back without grabbing for me or trying to take things further.

"Oh." A voice in the doorway has me freezing and turning to see Vienna staring at the two of us. "Sorry, I was looking for Colt to tell him breakfast is ready." She looks around the room in interest, stopping at the stocks, and a memory comes to my mind.

"I saw you, Tristan, and Xavier doing a scene in those one night at the Black Rose, didn't I? I recognize their tattoos now," I ask her, not releasing Colton, and she blushes prettily.

"Yeah, sometimes we play around while Colton is at one of his sessions. None of us knew it was you doing them," she tells me, not hiding her appreciation of my naked body. My nipples pebble even harder at her perusal, and I grow damp between my thighs. I don't want to go to work feeling needy. I have too much to do today to be distracted, so these two are going to give me what I need.

"And you don't mind if Colton and I continue his... therapy here?" I ask, and she shakes her head, looking relieved.

"No, not at all. None of us can cut him and enjoy it, so knowing you can give him what we can't is a relief."

"And what about you? Do you enjoy a little pain with your pleasure?" I ask her, and she shakes her head.

"I don't enjoy being cut, but I don't mind other things."

"Like what?" I prompt, wanting to know it all.

"I like to be spanked, and I like nipple clamps. I also like to be both praised and humiliated," she replies, not meeting my eyes.

I run my gaze over her body. She's already dressed

for the day, and she's wearing a short black skirt with an equally tight white shirt and has Converse on her feet. She looks cute in a college girl kind of way, and I want to see her on her knees, choking on Colton's cock.

"Close the door, Vienna," I say slowly, and she quickly does what I say, pulling the handle on this side to lock us away in private. This room is completely soundproof, and even someone standing on the other side wouldn't know any of this is in here.

I lean in to whisper to Colton, who has stayed nice and still in my grasp. "I'm not going to cut you today. I don't have time. We can discuss that tonight if you wish, but I am going to see that you get a bit of relief from that." I nod down at the bulge in his sweats, and he shudders in desire. "Get over here," I tell Vienna. "I want to see you on your knees and your mouth on Colton's cock. I want to see tears rolling down your face and spit dripping off your chin. I want to hear how much you love sucking his dick, you dirty little slut."

Her eyes widen, and I see a tremor run through her body as she follows my commands. I feel a rush of appreciation and release Colton's hair, allowing him to stand up straight.

"Now be a good boy and fuck Vienna's face so I can watch her swallow all your cum." I run one hand over his cheek and down his front until I get to his sweats. Grabbing the waistband, I peel them down his legs as Vienna kneels obediently at his feet. His cock springs free, and I stroke it with one finger.

"I was always so tempted by this. It wasn't until that last session when I broke my own rules, that I allowed myself the pleasure of knowing what he tastes like. Did you know that Vienna? Did he tell you all about what Mistress V did to him? Did you know I tasted his cum? Oh, I didn't suck his cock, I just had a little taste of the precum, and then I used his release to get myself off after. Did he tell you about it? Did you get jealous at the thought of another woman tasting your man?"

When I look down, her eyes flash with anger and lust, and she nods. "He told me. I wanted to find you and gut you with your own knife for pushing past his limits without permission," she admits, and I laugh wickedly at the admission.

"Oh really? And how do you think that would have gone?" This time, I grab her hair and kneel so I'm face-to-face with her. "Do you think you would have come out the winner, or would you have been at my mercy?" I ask, and she squirms in my grip, so I pinch one of her nipples through her shirt. She squeals, and I smother the noise with my mouth, plunging my tongue into hers and swallowing her moan of pleasure before quickly pulling away.

"Good girls get rewards, and you have not been a good girl." I encourage her to rise up on her knees, then I reach for her skirt and tug it up to her waist, seeing her panties damp with her desire.

I smirk at her. "Dirty bitch is already wet. She's practically begging for your cock, Colt. How about you give it to her, and we'll see just how good she looks with her throat bulging." I release Vienna and stand up as she leans forward, and Colton feeds his cock into her mouth. I almost moan out loud at the sight. Fuck, they are pretty, but I need to see more.

I want them to be a work of art. I move over to my cupboard of toys and pull out a riding whip and a double-sided dildo, pulling it from its packet. It has one end that goes into me and the other into Vienna. I've been dying to fuck her, and now I'm going to do exactly that. Maybe I should start all my mornings like this.

Grabbing one of my knives, I return to the couple and frown, not liking how gentle Colton is being. I place the dildo and knife on top of his sweats then walk around him, running my riding crop over his ass before giving him a sharp tap on one of his round butt cheeks. He flinches forward, and I hear the delightful sound of Vienna choking and smile.

I rub a gentle hand over his red butt cheek and coo into his ear. "That's a good boy. I want to hear her gagging for you."

I walk around and grab my knife before crouching in front of Vienna. She glances at me, pulling back from Colton slightly, so I use the crop to smack the mound of her pussy. She cries out around his length, and tears trickle down her cheeks.

"Look at you. You're so fucking gorgeous." I stroke

a damp cheek with my finger before swapping my crop for my knife, then I cut each side of her panties and take them off her. She shivers when the dull side of the blade presses against her skin.

"Hmm, you don't like to be cut, but the element of danger excites you, doesn't it?" I reach forward and run a light finger through her folds and discover she's soaking wet. "Excites you a lot." I put my finger to my mouth and suck off her glistening arousal as I run the blunt side of the knife over her covered breasts. "As much as I would like to cut you out of these clothes, I also love how you look, so I'm going to leave them on," I tell her before turning and slicing a small cut down Colton's thigh, just enough for a small trickle of blood to run down it.

I hear Colton groan, and when I glance at him, his legs are shaking. "Neither of you are allowed to come until I say so. If you do, you will be punished, and you won't like what I do to you," I warn them, my hand shooting out and gripping Vienna's throat. "Now skull fuck her, Colton. I want to feel your cock in her throat."

I tighten my hand as he listens, thrusting in and out with long, hard strokes. Vienna's hands brace against his thighs, and she chokes and splutters, spit dripping out of her mouth as more tears run down her face. I can feel his cock under my hand, and I tighten my grip ever so slightly, cutting off her airway for a moment before releasing her. I use my other hand to circle her clit, putting the perfect amount of pressure on the slippery, swollen bud as I tighten my grip around her throat once more.

"Fuck, Tori, I can feel you cutting off her air." Colton's voice is guttural, and his breathing is choppy. "I can't hold on much longer. Please let us come, please."

I release Vienna's throat and gesture for him to pull out, and she gasps for breath, sucking in air.

"You two did so well following my instructions, and Colton begs so prettily, doesn't he, Vienna? Should we let him come? Are you going to swallow everything he gives you?" I ask, and she uses one hand to swipe away a stray tear before nodding.

"Yes, I will swallow everything. Please, just let us come," she begs, sounding just as pretty as her partner.

"You two are lucky I have an appointment this morning, otherwise I would keep you on edge for hours and wreck you, but business comes first." I grab the dildo and knife and slice another couple of small cuts in Colton's thighs. Vienna's eyes widen in shock as I roll the dildo around in the trail of blood.

"I know Colton is disease free, as it is a requirement to be tested regularly before each blood play session, and using it for lube turns me on," I explain as I spread my legs and slide one end of the dildo into my throbbing wet pussy. "Now Colton and I are going to spit roast you, and when he comes, if you don't swallow everything he gives you, I'm going to use the handle of my crop to fuck your ass as well," I threaten, and she shudders before nodding.

"Good girl." I give her a kiss, and she almost melts into me, but I push her back and move behind her. "Bend forward slightly," I instruct, and as she does, she exposes the gap between her thighs, wet with arousal as her pussy drips with need. I lean down and run my tongue over her folds, and she moans loudly. She really is fucking delicious, and I can't wait to make her come. I shuffle into position and guide the other end of the dildo into her pussy, flicking the button to make it vibrate on both ends. She moans and drops her head forward as I thrust deep and shudder at the heady feeling of fucking this gorgeous woman. The end inside of me throbs, and my pussy tightens around it. This is going to be fast and furious, because I don't think I'm going to be able to stop the orgasm that is quickly barreling forward. I grab hold of her hair and yank her back against my body, using it to hold her in place while I slide my other hand around to circle her clit.

"Okay, Colt, fuck her, and don't stop until you're spilling down her throat."

He steps forward and grabs her head with both hands. Now that he's holding her in place, I slide the hand from her hair back to her throat, and we start to thrust in tandem.

She's pinned between us, and neither of us are gentle. My hips thrust back and forth, the end inside me jamming against my G-spot with every movement. My other hand circles her clit, and she moans and groans around Colton's cock, struggling as her orgasm barrels toward her. Her cunt muscles tighten, and it makes fucking her a little harder, but I just push through it.

"Come, my pretties," I shout harshly as my own orgasm rips through me. I struggle to keep going, but I want to milk Vienna's pussy for all it's worth. Colton groans and pauses, his cock lodged deep in her throat. I reach up and put my hand around it, and I feel her swallow his release. "Good girl," I coo and stroke my other hand over her hair. "That's it, swallow it all."

Although I threatened to fuck her ass with the riding crop handle, I don't think I would have. I've never tried that before with any of my other lovers, and I don't really want to hurt her like that.

She's a sweaty, sticky mess when Colton pulls free and sags to his knees, wrapping his arms around her. I pull out and remove the toy, tossing it off to the side to be washed. I watch as Colton murmurs to Vienna, checking to make sure she's okay, and I feel a little awkward. Do I join them, or do I get up and leave? Then I catch sight of Colt's cuts, and I know I need to look after them. I get up and move into the attached bathroom and grab two cloths, wetting them, and find some antiseptic cream. When I return, they are where I left them.

Colton looks up when I cross to them, and I pass him one of the cloths. He uses it to clean Vienna while I tend to the cuts on his thighs, cleaning the trail of crusted blood before applying some of the cream. When I'm done, I get up to leave, but before I can,

Colton grabs me and tugs me into his arms, and Vienna wraps her own arms around me too.

All of us are breathing unevenly, and nobody speaks for a minute. I decide it's time to leave, but before I can, Colton lifts my chin, and he kisses me. He's unhurried with his exploration of my mouth, and I relax into him as I feel Vienna stroke her hand over my naked back.

"That was fun," she murmurs as her hand cups one butt cheek and gives it a squeeze. "You are one sexy domme. I don't think I've ever come so hard." Vienna giggles. "I better not tell Xavi, or he will turn it into a competition."

Colton pulls away and stares at me intently with those beautiful blue eyes. "Thank you, that helped."

I smile. "We can have another session soon, but now I'm really going to be late for my meeting. I have to go." I press a kiss to his lips before turning and doing the same with Vienna. "Don't shower today. I want you to go to school smelling like us." I instruct them before standing. "But I need to be quick if I'm going to have another one. I don't want to go into my meetings and having everyone smell what we've been doing. They'll lose all respect for me. I'll clean up the room later. The longer we're missing, the more suspicious the others will get. Please don't mention this room to anyone else. Gio doesn't know it's here, only Sage. Suzy and Ben know, since they were here when I was having it installed, but they are discrete."

I hold out a hand and help Vienna up, pulling her

skirt down over her ass. "No panties today," I tell her, patting her butt. "If the other two ask why, I want you to tell them in great detail what we did." I wink at her, and she giggles again.

"You're asking for trouble, aren't you?"

I bend down and pick up Colton's sweats, passing them to him as he stands, then I grab the knife and dildo and place them on the bed—I'll deal with them when I get home. Once Colton is dressed, I use the peephole in the wall to make sure no one is in the hallway, and the three of us leave.

"I'll see you at breakfast. I won't be long." I shoo them away, and they continue down the hallway, with Colton's arm around Vienna to keep her steady. I usually like a little more aftercare, but for today, this is just going to have to do.

Chapter Fifteen

When I get down to breakfast, everyone is at the table. I guess having meals in the dining room is going to be a new thing with too many people to hang out in the kitchen. I need to check in with Suzy and Ben to see if I need to hire a chef now that we're feeding five extra mouths with three of them being boys. There's a huge spread of fruit, pastries, and pancakes set out, but I hear Sage whining.

"Where's the meat, Suzy? You know I like my meat."

Suzy scoffs indelicately. "That's what she said."

Tristan chuckles and holds out his hand for a fist bump, which she indulges as she places a platter of bacon and sausage links on the table. "There, are you happy now? Make sure you eat some fruit to go along with all that meat. You need a better diet."

"Oh, I'm starving. I'll have some meat too," Vienna, who is sitting next to him, says, holding out her plate to Sage who places a couple of pieces of bacon on it and a sausage.

"Who the fuck are you and what did you do with Sage?" Gio gapes at him in surprise. "You usually get stabby with your fork whenever I ask for some."

"That's because you don't deserve any. You are an asshole, but Vienna needs it for brain power for school, although I am almost certain Vienna has already had her protein this morning." He wiggles his eyebrows suggestively at her, and she blushes prettily. Casey chokes on her juice, carefully placing her glass on the table. Sage leans in and inhales deeply near Vienna's neck, making her giggle. "Yup, someone had a workout this morning and needs to replenish her energy."

The table falls into an awkward silence before Gio grabs a pastry and throws it at Sage. "Shut it, I'm fucking eating. I don't need any details of whatever kinky shit you have gotten up to."

Colton and Tristan are ignoring the commotion and talking quietly between them, so only Xavier has noticed me paused in the doorway. I wink at him before grabbing a mug and filling it with coffee off the side table. I sit down next to him. His hand finds my thigh, and he gives it a squeeze.

"Good morning," I say cheerfully to everyone else before grabbing a Danish to go with my coffee. I love Suzy's strawberry Danishes. They are my biggest weakness. I take a big bite and groan. "This is so freaking good." They are still warm and the perfect balance of flaky pastry and sugary filling.

Tristan smirks, and Xavier's hand tightens on my thigh. Colton and Vienna stare at me with undisguised desire. I guess they are still riding the high from our little session.

Sage leans back in his chair and looks at me, his eyes sparkling. "Well, someone seems to be in a good mood this morning. I wonder why that is?"

"You've finally joined us. I want to discuss what you've been up to this week," Gio says, and I can tell by his tone he's grumpy. Is he really looking to pick a fight this morning? What is his fucking problem?

"You know we don't talk business at the table," Suzy says, slapping him on the back of the head before retrieving an empty platter and returning to the kitchen. He glares at me, and I shrug.

"I don't want to piss off the person who makes our meals. You can come see me at the office after school if you want and we can talk there," I tell him, and I practically see steam pouring out of his ears. I know he can't because he and Casey have a prior engagement. All I'm doing is pissing him off, but it's time he's gotten a taste of his own medicine. Oh well, he will get over it. It isn't like he has shown any interest lately anyway.

"Here, you left this at the range yesterday." Tristan reaches behind him, pulls my gun out of the waistband of his pants, and passes it to me over the table.

"Oh good, thank you. That saves me from having to retrieve it." I tuck it into the holster in my corset and take a sip of my coffee.

"What the fuck? Who are you, and what have you done to my sister?" Gio asks the same stupid question he asked of Sage. "You never go anywhere without that gun."

I flip him off and ignore his question. He doesn't deserve to know anything.

"I guess she was completely mesmerized by my and Xavier's marksmanship. We totally kicked her ass," Tristan crows, and I didn't think Gio's eyes could get any wider, but he continues to surprise me.

"You beat Tori at shooting?"

"They cheated," I grumble, remembering the taunting words Tristan and Xavier whispered to one another.

"Don't be a sore loser. You still won in the end," Xavier says quietly in my ear, "and I kicked her ass on the mats this morning," Xavier adds louder for everyone to hear.

I feel my cheeks heat as everyone turns their attention to me. "What? I'm freaking tired, okay? I'm working my ass off, unlike some other people," I say, pointedly looking at my brother. "It's been a few weeks since I've worked out with Lorn and Castiel."

"We should have a spa day and get some massages and a facial. That will make you feel better and more refreshed." Vienna bounces in her chair with enthusiasm.

My cheeks heat even more. "I've never had a spa day before," I tell her. I've had manicures and pedicures, but none of the other fancy things.

She claps her hands together. "It's a date. I'll organize it. Are you free tomorrow? I don't have any classes."

I think about my schedule. It's hard to know, because I don't know what the meeting with the guys will yield today.

"Yes, she can clear her schedule," Sage states firmly, and I frown at him.

"I don't know if I can."

He waves a hand at me. "If something comes up, I can handle it. Go get pampered. You have been working overtime and deserve it."

I sigh. "Fine, why don't you make an appointment at the Lucky Diamond? We won't have to pay for it, and apparently, the spa there is excellent," I suggest to Vienna.

"Oh, I've heard really good things about it. I'll call them today." She's practically vibrating with excitement.

I hear Gio grumble under his breath, and Sage glares at him. What the fuck is his problem? I decide to take one day off in I don't know how long, and he gets pissy.

Casey puts her hand over his and whispers something to him, and he shuts up. Huh, she must have some magical powers to be able to get my brother to stop whining. Maybe just a magical pussy.

"Okay, well, on that note, I have to go. Sage, are you ready?" I ask him, and he stands up and stretches. His shirt rises, leaving a patch of bare skin between the hem and the waistband of his dress pants. He grabs a suit jacket off the back of his chair and pulls it on.

"Yup, I ordered the limo for this morning since I knew you were tired. You can nap between meetings if you need to, and no driving."

Wow, that was thoughtful of him. I thought I was hiding how exhausted I was, but I guess I'm not fooling anyone.

Gio stands as well. "Good, you can drop us off at school on the way. Saves us all from driving."

"I'm not sure how long my meetings are going to be," I warn him.

"But how will we get to our appointment and then home?" Casey asks, biting her lip with worry.

"I'll have another driver pick us up. Tori isn't the only one with access to family perks." Gio glares at me again, and I narrow my eyes and glare back. Neither of us want to break the stare down.

"Well, that's all settled. Shall we get moving then?" Sage says loudly, interrupting our stare down. The others hurry to finish their breakfast. Suzy offers to prepare to-go cups of coffee for those who want them while everyone grabs whatever they need for the day. I head into the kitchen to talk to Suzy and Ben.

"Have we heard from Mickey about that back-ground check yet?" I ask Ben quietly, and he shakes his head.

"No, we haven't heard from him since we gave him the information."

"I'll give him a call today. I might even go out and

see him. It's been a while, and I miss him." I turn my attention to Suzy. "Should we hire a chef to give you a break?" I ask her, but she shakes her head.

"Absolutely not. Finding one that passes the background checks will be a pain in the ass, and I like having this many people to cook for. It gives me something to do. Our lives were so lonely for so many years, it's nice to have people to take care of." I see the sadness in her eyes.

Ben and Suzy tried to have kids of their own for many years, but it just wasn't in the cards for them, and because of Dad's choices, they missed out on seeing me and Gio grow up. I think they are making up for all that lost time and trying to fill the void Dad left behind.

"Okay, but if it gets to be too much, let me know," I tell her, placing a kiss on her cheek before doing the same to Ben. "I'm going to see what Sam and Dean learned about Lorenzo. I'll fill you in later."

"Gio is getting annoyed at being shut out," Suzy points out, and I shrug.

"He knows the deal. We don't discuss family business around nonfamily members. He shouldn't have asked about it this morning or last night. If he wants to know what's going on, he can come into the office or approach me privately. We can always use the secret meeting room, but he keeps bringing it up around the others."

Ben sighs. "That boy needs to get his head on straight and decide what he really wants. If he wants to have a white picket fence kind of life with a wife, two point five kids, and a dog, then he should really step down as the head of the family. I mean, he's basically just a figurehead now."

"I don't remember the last time he came into the office for work. I know he has college, but it's like he's completely forgotten he has other responsibilities. He was good right after Dad died, but for months now, he's been shady as shit. I guess that was when Casey came back into his life."

"I don't think she ever left his life. He's just gotten careless. From how she tells it, they've been together since they first met." Suzy breaks the news to me, and my hands curl into fists.

"Are you freaking serious?" I ask, grinding my teeth together. "Even when Dad was alive?"

"Yeah. He suspected. It was one of the things he wanted to talk about on the day of the explosion. He made some kind of deal in the hopes it would keep the two of you safe, but he never gave us the details." Ben frowns. "Maybe Penelope knows."

I scoff. "Why would she know? She was pretty arm candy and not much else."

They exchange a glance. "Although he never loved her like he loved your mother, she was a comfort to him, and she loved him. I think he told her things he never told anyone else, which we thought was stupid, but he wouldn't be swayed," Ben explains.

"I think he felt sorry for her. She came from a family who believed the only thing women were good for was spreading their legs for the right person. Her family practically shoved her at Stefano. I think that was probably why she was so resentful of you, Tori. He gave you choices she was never allowed," Suzy adds.

I bite my lip, thinking about everything they just shared. "I had a weird conversation with her yesterday. She all but apologized for her behavior when I was growing up, and she actually showed some emotion, like she isn't really the cold, callous bitch I thought she was. It was so confusing," I admit, not mentioning the small child she had with her.

I don't want to tell anyone that Mario has a grandchild, but Suzy and Ben wouldn't tell anyone anyway. I don't want someone to suggest that she would be a good way to get to him. I had the thought briefly but dismissed it once I got to know her a little better. No child deserves to be used like that, and I refuse to stoop so low. I didn't even press her for information on her parents. It seemed to make her sad when I asked her where her mom and dad was. All she would say was they were gone. I don't know if she means they are dead or something else. Penny seemed to imply something else.

"She had Mario's grandchild with her, and she actually seemed fond of her. I've never seen anything maternal from her."

"I know one thing, she did love your father, but she was also good at looking out for number one. You said she was seeing Mario Maricuso, so I can guarantee she has an agenda. Whether it's to benefit us or not is the question, but I can assure you it will definitely benefit her, and if the child somehow gets her what she wants, then I don't doubt she would use her." Suzy doesn't hide her disdain.

"Hmm, I don't know about that. You didn't see her yesterday. She looked rough, or rough for her at least." I think about the bruises on the little girl. "She implied that Mario is neglectful of the child, and she seemed angry about it."

"Penny always wanted kids, but your dad got a vasectomy after you were born and your mother passed." Ben's eyes are sad. "I think Penny resented the fact that he took that choice away from her. It's part of the reason she wasn't particularly kind to you. You were a constant reminder of what she couldn't have."

"I was just a fucking kid. I didn't deserve her resentment," I argue angrily.

"No one deserved any of what they got. Stefano didn't deserve to lose the love of his life, you and Gio didn't deserve to grow up without a mother, and Penny didn't deserve to be bartered away to a man who was never truly going to love her," Ben points out, and I sigh.

"You may be right, but I don't trust her."

"So don't trust her. You shouldn't, but maybe think about what her angle is. It may work in your favor," Suzy suggests as the door to the kitchen bangs open and Gio stomps in.

"Are you coming? We're going to be late," he snarls.

"Hey, asshole. You could have taken your own car. Don't treat me like this," I snap at him as I follow him through the house and out the front door. The limo is waiting for us on the driveway, and the others are already in the car.

Gio stops and grabs my arm tightly. "Watch yourself, Tori. I am still head of this family."

I look down at his hand on my arm and channel my angel of death stare. "Remove your hand from my body before I remove your hand from yours," I snarl, and he tightens his hold for a moment before releasing it.

"You overstep," he hisses.

I take a step closer so our chests press together, my heels almost making me as tall as him. I glare at him. "Do I? Or are you just now realizing how out of touch you have become? Careful, Gio, your ignorance is showing. I am the one who has kept this family going while you have been busy trying to have a normal life. Maybe all of that is now biting you in the ass. You need to make a decision. Are you going to man up and be the leader this family needs, or are you going to let a delicate piece of ass be your ruin?"

I say this quietly so no one can hear, but it's like Casey has a sixth sense. She sticks her head out of the limo. "Are you guys coming? We're going to be late to class."

Gio glances toward her before muttering, "This isn't over."

Before I can reply, he hurries toward the car.

"And you just proved my point," I mutter deject-edly before following him. I'm going to have to deal with Gio sooner rather than later, but should I kill him or his girlfriend? One is going to destroy me, and the other will destroy him, and it's a decision I'm not willing to make just yet.

Chapter Sixteen

We drop the others off at school but don't stick around longer than necessary. The ride was awkward. The others, obviously picking up on the tension between Gio and me, talked about mundane things that I didn't pay any attention to. None of them lingered when we arrived, saying hasty goodbyes and getting out as quickly as possible. I wasn't sad to see them go. Finally, it's just me and Sage and blissful silence as we wind our way through the city to the Kitty Kat club where I said we would meet Sam and Dean. They want to show me what they found.

"Are you okay?" Sage asks quietly as the limo pulls up in front of the strip club.

I shake my head. "No, but I don't have time to worry about Gio at the moment. Let's go find out what Sam and Dean know."

He looks like he's going to say something, but I don't give him the chance. I grab the handle of the door and push it open. After I climb out, I straighten my suit jacket before brushing my pants to make sure there are no wrinkles. As I feel Sage climb out behind me, I head toward the door of the club. It's too early to be open, so I press my security code into the pad next to the closed doors and let myself in. I walk past the outer reception desk and through the next set of double doors, into the club proper. The stale scents of cigarettes and beer hit my nose, and I can't stop myself from wrinkling it in disgust.

"Ugh, is it time for this club to be renovated? It stinks," I mutter out loud, and I hear Sage chuckle.

"How long do you think the smell of new carpet and fresh paint would last?"

"Maybe you're right," I agree, "but let's schedule someone to come in and at least clean the carpets. They are sticky." I lift my shoe and look to see if anything is stuck to it, but like I suspected, there is nothing there. "Gross."

There are a few lights on in the fridges behind the bar, and we use them to guide us through the mess of tables and booths. The opening staff won't be in to set up for a while. We open at one today, so we will have the place to ourselves for a few hours.

Pushing through the door that leads up to my office, we climb the stairs. I have fond memories of seeing that asshole tumble ass over tit down them, and it brings a smile to my lips. Ah, fun times. That was my first time shooting someone, and it lives rent free in my head.

The office door is open, and I can hear quiet voices murmuring inside, but I can't make out what is being said.

When we enter, Lacey is sitting behind the desk, and Sam and Dean are both on the couch. I look around. There is no evidence of Melissa's death anywhere, and the sex swing is no longer hanging from the hook in the ceiling. Our cleanup crew did a great job. I must send them a bonus.

"Hey, guys." I wave a hand and take a seat on the chair opposite Lacey. Sage goes over to the others and does some manly handshake shit before joining them on the couches.

"How's it going?" I ask the pretty stripper, and she sits up straight in her chair. I smile when I notice she's wearing a suit very much like mine.

"It's good. I'm just going over the roster for this week," she tells me, glancing at the boys and biting her lip with worry, but then I see her metaphorically pull up her big girl panties. Her back straightens, and her eyes narrow.

"I want to be inducted into the Russo family," she states firmly, and I smother the smile that wants to cross my lips. I guessed this was coming, but I thought it would take her longer to get the guts. "I'm loyal, and I want to be able to repay you for everything you've done for me."

"Hmm..." I turn my chair so I can see her, Sam, and Dean. "How do you feel about this?" I ask them, and Sam shakes his head.

"This is her decision to make, and if this is what she wants, then we will support her."

"Yeah, and you can't deny her because she's a woman. That would be hypocritical," Dean points out, and I scoff.

"Please, I wasn't going to deny her for that reason." I turn back to look at Lacey. "You know it will come with much more danger than just running this club, right? You will be asked to do things you aren't comfortable with."

I'm not trying to change her mind, she's entitled to her wants, but I want to make sure she really knows what she's getting into. I kind of also want to appoint her to oversee all the Kitty Kat clubs. It would be one less thing on my never-ending list of things to do. She's proven herself capable, and if I assign Sam and Dean to be her permanent protection, then I don't see it being a problem.

"I have been working with Sam and Dean. I know how to use a gun, and I'm getting really good at it. I have also been working on self-defense, and look."

She picks up what I thought was a letter opener, but I can now see it's a small throwing knife. She lifts her hand, and with a flick of her wrist, it flies across the room and hits a target on the wall dead center.

Sage blows out a whistle of appreciation. "Damn, Lace, you have some mad knife skills. Watch out, Tori, she may take your title of knife queen." I know he's joking around, but he's not wrong, that was a nice throw.

I nod my head. "Fine, but once you're in, there's only one way out," I caution, carefully watching her to make sure she understands exactly what I mean.

"Death is the only way out." Her jaw is set stubbornly, and I can tell she's serious.

"Fine, take her to the tattooist and get her the mark. Make sure she has the skills she needs to survive," I instruct the boys who nod. Sam looks resigned, like he didn't really want this but knows there is no point in arguing, and I can understand why he feels that way. Dean, however, looks excited, and I know he will make sure she can protect herself if she needs to.

"But know this, Lacey. Fuck me over like Candy did, and I won't hesitate to take care of you like I did Melissa," I threaten. I like the girl, but not enough to save her precious sensibilities. She needs to know that there is no backing out once she's committed.

"I'd sooner cut off my own hand than betray you, Tori." I'm surprised but pleased by how serious she is.

"Okay, well now that's out of the way, shall we talk about what the two of you have been up to?" I turn my attention to my henchmen. Lacey stands up and starts gathering her papers and her laptop. "I'll just take my work downstairs and get out of your way," she says, but I wave a hand, gesturing for her to sit.

"No. If you want in, then it's time to see if you can kick it with the big kids." She settles into the seat, a slight gleam of excitement in her eyes. "So what has my dear uncle been up to?"

"We've had a tail on him twenty-four hours a day since you discovered the tunnels, but he hasn't gone anywhere that could hold the people scheduled for auction on Saturday. There has been a lot of socializing with the usual characters. He had lunch with Penelope and Mario Maricuso at the Lucky Diamond two days ago, and he's been hanging out in some dive bar down near the docks," Sam replies.

"He also visited an apartment in that newly gentrified area of Suncity. You know, the one on the river, but it was gated, and we couldn't find who the registered owner is. A woman answered the door and was happy to see him, so we're assuming he was there for personal reasons."

"And he hasn't been back here?" I ask Lacey who frowns.

"He was here two nights ago with another man I didn't recognize, but all they did was sit and watch the strippers, have a few drinks, and leave."

"Pull up footage of who he was here with please." I nod at the laptop, and she runs her fingers across the keyboard, accessing the footage I want to see.

"What about the tunnels? What did you discover?" I ask the boys while she does that.

"We had men explore them in either direction. One leads directly to a warehouse at the docks, but it was empty with a few signs of occasional vagrant inhabitants and nothing else suspicious. Even the office was wiped clean." Sam frowns. "Which in itself is suspicious. Unused warehouses are usually filthy with dust and debris, but this one was kind of immaculate, like they don't want fingerprints left behind."

"Hmm," I hum. "What about in the other direction?"

"That was more interesting, but no less of a dead end. That tunnel branches out farther down and leads to four separate locations. One is caved in and useless, but the other three were more interesting. One leads to a private airfield on the outskirts of Suncity. We did some surveillance, but didn't notice anyone who would trip alarms. There's a full-time mechanic and grounds person as well as a manager. I've had someone sitting on it, logging all the tail numbers of planes that arrive and depart, and watching for any suspicious activity, but so far, it's been a dead end. Nothing to note." Dean sounds resigned.

"What about the other two?" I ask.

"One leads to the rail yards. We tried to have someone watch them too, but there are too many security guards, and they kept chasing our guys off. There is a surveillance system, but our tech guys have been having trouble hacking into it, and there is nowhere to hide in the tunnels, so we haven't been able to have anyone watching them," Sam explains. "I think this is probably the route where they are bringing in the merchandise. It would be easy to smuggle people in railcars and pay authorities to look the other way."

"Did we get cameras installed in the tunnels like I asked? Ones that are motion activated and will send an alert if anything happens? Is there anywhere in the tunnels to stash the merchandise? Do you think they know we know the tunnels are there now?" I fire question after question, my brain trying to compute everything they shared.

"Yes, but they haven't been activated yet," Sam confirms.

Lacey frowns. "Lorenzo asked me where Candy and Melissa were the other night. I told him they disappeared after stealing money from the safe and clearing out the stash of drugs from the office. I acted like they better run as fast as they could, because you were pissed and calling for their heads."

"That was quick thinking and a good idea," I say appreciatively, pleased with her initiative. "How did he react?"

"He lost his shit. He picked up his glass and launched it at the wall, but the gentleman with him quickly got him to calm down. I couldn't hear what he said, but Lorenzo calmed, and I didn't speak to them again. One of the other waitresses dealt with them. I asked her if he questioned her, but she said he didn't. Nobody else knows what happened except for Joe and Bill, and they are loyal. I would say it's probably safe to assume they don't know that you know about the tunnels."

Some of the tension in my body eases. "Okay, what about the last tunnel? Where does that go?"

The two guys exchange a look, and I feel the tension in my body return. "What?" I demand.

"It comes up in the warehouse under your place," Sam says, and I feel my eyes widen with shock.

"Seriously?" I ask him, and he nods. I look over at Sage to see his reaction, but he looks as surprised as I am. It's obviously news to him too, and I'm relieved it wasn't a secret he kept from me.

"Yeah. I'm guessing they used them to transport goods in your grandfather's time, or maybe even before that. Did you know it was there?"

I shake my head. "No, and Dad never mentioned it to me. I wonder if Gio knows it's there." Damn it. I have been avoiding him, but now I'm going to have to sit down and ask him about it, which will lead to more questions from him—questions he should already know the answer to, but it's his own fault he doesn't know. I sigh. "I'll ask Gio when I see him tonight. He may have more information, but at least we know the merchandise isn't coming from that tunnel. You will have to show me where it is so I can make sure it's secure. I don't like that there is another way into our place I had no idea about, but I bet Lorenzo does, and whoever he has told makes it a serious security breach."

"We need to get someone to close it. Do we have anyone on the books who is a contractor?" I ask them. They would have a better idea about who has the skills we need.

"Do we want to block it up? It would be another escape option if we needed it," Sage suggests.

"I don't like the idea that people can access it from the other side, especially because our enemies know about the tunnels. I'm surprised we haven't been breached yet, to be honest, not that they could get up to the house without the code, but they could have hijacked any of our shipments."

"Or destroyed my grow house." Sage shudders. "We need to get it fixed today." He sounds panicked, more worried about his plants than our lives, and it makes me smile. Leave it to Sage to prioritize like that.

"Oh, speaking of drugs... Someone tried to breach the new warehouse, but the chemist hit the lockdown button and sealed it up until our security could chase off the intruders. Head of security believes it was a group of teenagers looking for a little bit of fun, not knowing what the warehouse is or who owns it."

The new warehouse is back in Banebridge because Sage didn't want it to be too far away in case he ever had to spend some time there. It looks like an unassuming building from the outside with excellent defense on the inside. Much like our house, it can go into lockdown if a breach is ever attempted.

Sage sits up straighter, his body tight with tension. "Is Anthony okay?"

I don't particularly like our new chemist. He's a fucking weasel who's always sucking up to me, and it feels disingenuous, like he's giving me lip service, but Sage seems to like him, or at least he admires his skills.

"He was shaken but fine. I think it would be a good idea just to show your face, though, and remind everyone who is in charge." Sam sounds concerned, and I latch onto it.

"What's wrong? What has you worried?"

"I may be wrong, but when we were there earlier this week, I thought I saw a batch of ecstasy with a different stamp on it, not the butterfly that Sage uses."

I frown, looking at my boyfriend for input. "Do you know anything about this?" I ask him, and he waves his hand, unconcerned.

"Anthony didn't like the butterfly. I guess he decided to use something else."

"Well, I didn't fucking approve that," I growl. "What was the symbol?" I ask Sam.

He winces. "It looked like an eggplant emoji," he admits, and Sage stutters out a choked laugh, but I'm fucking fuming.

"That's classy," Lacey says dryly, and I can't say I disagree, "but it's also weird. I got a delivery of product last night, and they still had the same standard butterfly on them." She pulls one of the drawers open and throws a bag onto the table in front of us. Sure enough, they are the same as the ones Sage used to make.

"So where did the eggplant emojis go?" Sage asks, scratching his head.

"Right, I guess we are taking a trip to Banebridge once we are done here. I need to have a little chat with our new friend."

Sage winces, and I drum my fingers on the table impatiently. Lacey finally turns the laptop around for me to view the security footage. As clear as day, sitting in a booth with Lorenzo is Mario Maricuso.

"Ballsy of him to walk into our establishment. It's like he's flipping you the finger," Dean comments when he sees the man.

"But it helps solidify the idea that the two of them are working together. To what end though? Lorenzo wants to be the head of this family. Does Mario want an alliance, or does he want to make Lorenzo the head then kill him and absorb our organization? That is the million dollar question. And what is Penelope's role in all this?" I have so many questions and not enough answers. "We have a week before Lorenzo and his goons send out his next shipment of people. We need to find a way for the FBI agent to catch him red-handed. That will take him off the board completely. We need to find out where they are keeping the victims."

"And for the moment, we don't have any idea, not even a hint of where they might be." Sage sounds dejected. I know he's as anxious as I am to help the missing people.

"Oh, speaking of clues." I dig into the pocket of my pants and take out the crumpled note that was left under my wiper yesterday. "Someone left this on my car when I was at the Lucky Diamond. Lacey, can you google the address? I'm worried it might be a setup, but I'm also curious."

I pass it over to her, and she takes it, running her fingers across the keyboard.

"Did you check the hotel footage to see who left it?" Dean asks, and I shake my head.

"My spot is in a dead zone in case I ever need to defend myself with extreme measures. No cameras."

"Huh." Lacey sounds surprised. "It's an address in Banebridge." She spins the laptop around so we can all see.

"Hey, that isn't far from the warehouse Anthony works in." Sage points at a building on the map. "Let's see if there is a street view." He leans in and does something, and sure enough, pictures of the warehouse come up, and Sam whistles quietly.

"That is a mighty high security fence around it."

"Look, they have dogs and security cameras." Dean points at two different images.

"What could they be guarding that needs such high security?" I murmur, starting to feel excited. "What do you say to a little breaking and entering tonight?" I ask Sage who winces.

"Are we going to be able to get past all that?" He waves at the dogs, cameras, and fence.

"Ah, my little green thumbed chemist. While you were playing with plants and chemicals back when he was alive, Dad had me doing extensive training, and one of them just happened to be with a world-class thief. I have some pretty nifty tricks up my sleeves."

"So I'll be like the magician's eye candy?" he asks, and I chuckle.

"You sure are pretty enough for it." I give him a wink, and he grins before shrugging.

"I guess we're committing a felony tonight."

"What if the tunnels and all of that was just a

smoke screen?" Sam has his fingers steepled in front of him. "What if they were deliberately seen going into the basement so we would follow them and find the tunnels? I'm sure Lorenzo would guess that someone would tell you eventually. It would be a good way to distract us, so we actually weren't looking in the right direction. With us distracted, it gave them an opportunity to get the merchandise into town without being seen."

"And they'll probably just ship them to the docks by truck. No one would question a container coming and going from a warehouse like that. Hell, anyone would see it on the street and not suspect anything," Dean remarks, following his partner's train of thought.

"We need to find out who owns the building. Is it one of ours?" I ask Sage, and he shakes his head.

"No, I don't think so, but I don't have the list of our assets memorized. If it was, I probably would have picked it for Anthony. It has wicked good security."

Lacey turns the laptop toward her. "I'm sorry I don't have those kinds of computer skills."

"Don't worry about it. We have others who do that kind of thing for us. I'll have one of them look into it." I turn to my henchmen. "You know, I think you may be on to something. If that warehouse is a holding zone for the victims prior to transport, then we need to find a way to get Lorenzo to go there so he will be implicated. If the FBI raid it and he isn't there, then there will be no proof."

Sage stands and stretches. "We will figure something out. Let's worry about getting into it tonight. For all we know, it could be storing drugs or guns like we do."

"That would still be enough to put Lorenzo away," Sam points out, but I shake my head.

"Yes, but then we still have a whole heap of missing people, including the FBI agent's sister. We need to find her, even if it's to save our own asses."

"Yeah, I'm not sure that letting him go was your smartest move to date." Sage runs a hand through his unruly mop of curls. "Gio will be pissed."

"Fuck Gio," I snarl, standing up. "Alright, we're heading to Banebridge. You guys stay here and get Lacey sorted. Welcome to the family, Lacey. We will have a more formal celebration when things settle down a little," I promise her.

"We needed a bit more feminine energy. It's a real sausage fest," Sage says brightly. "I'm sure you are going to be great."

"I won't let you down," she promises, standing up and giving me a nod of respect.

"Get the girl a firearm, and Lacey, make sure you always have it on you. Take her to the same place I get my corsets from." I lift the back of my jacket so she can see. "It's way more comfortable than a holster and safer than shoving it into the back of your pants like the movies." I roll my eyes, and she grins.

"Will do, and be careful tonight."

Sam and Dean murmur their own warnings and goodbyes, and Sage and I leave the club.

Chapter Seventeen

I try to take a small nap in the limo on the half an hour drive to Banebridge from Suncity. Sage's lap is warm and a comfortable place for my head, and he hums along quietly to the music, but I can't shut my brain off. Thoughts of everything we just discussed interspaced with what I did with Colton and Vienna this morning play on a never-ending loop inside my mind, and I toss and turn until I finally give up and sit upright.

"You know if you wriggled around much more, I probably would have came in my pants." Sage chuckles. "You're restless. What's going on?"

"Got a lot on my mind," I reply distractedly as I stare out the window.

"Does it have to do with what Colton and Vienna got up to this morning?" he asks slyly, and I turn my head to look at him.

"How did you know about that? You hinted at breakfast."

"Vienna gave me a kiss good morning, and I could smell sex on her, and Colton looked a little less tormented than normal. I figured maybe you helped him with that."

"You're a little too observant," I grumble, and he grins and bounces in his seat like a kid going to the carnival.

"Did you use the sex dungeon? I came looking for you when I saw your door was open, but when you weren't there, I thought you must have already gone down to breakfast. When I got down there, you and the other two weren't there. Tristan mentioned Vienna had gone to search for you and Colton."

"Hmph," I grunt and nod. "It's not a sex dungeon."

"It so is," he teases. "Ugh, I'm jealous now. I would have loved to have been a fly on the wall and watched what you did."

I smile slowly and raise an eyebrow. "Is that so?" I ask him, and he adjusts the growing bulge in his pants.

"Ugh, a hard-on in dress pants sucks. Of course I want to know or watch or join in."

I pull my phone out and open the secure app I have on it—the one that receives video footage of the camera I have in the room. I am the only one who knows it's there or how it can be accessed. I pull up the footage from this morning and press play before handing it to Sage.

"Don't say I never give you anything," I tell him as he grabs it eagerly, his eyes widening when he sees what's playing.

"Oh, you dirty little bird, recording your home porn sessions for posterity... or to use at a later date. I approve."

He groans loudly, and I watch as he bites his lip, his eyes locked on the screen. "Holy fuck, that's hot. Look at you with that riding crop. Fuck, Colton is packing. I haven't had the pleasure of feeling or seeing all of that yet, and look at Vienna on her knees. Now that is a pretty sight."

Sage falls silent as the video continues to play, the soundtrack loud. My voice can be heard as well as the moans and grunts of pleasure from the other two. Sage drops one of his hands to his pants again and palms his cock, pressing to ease some of the pain.

The sounds remind me of everything that happened this morning, and watching Sage watch us turns me on, so I push his hand away and unzip his fly, going to my knees. Sage spreads his legs so I can slide between them, and I manhandle his erection out of his underwear then flatten my tongue to run it under the backside of the tip. I've never done this before, so hopefully I don't suck at it—no pun intended.

Sage groans, this time a little louder, and his free hand comes to the back of my head. He pulls out the clip that was holding all my hair up and slides his fingers into the curls, encouraging me to take his dick into his mouth. I tease him for a little longer, running my tongue from base to tip, savoring the salty taste of his skin, but I want to feel him slide deep and hear his reaction to what I'm doing to him.

I relax my jaw and brace my hands on his thighs as I slide my mouth down his length before retreating and sucking firmly on the head, swirling my tongue over the sensitive ridge. Inch by inch, I bob with rhythmic pulls, getting lower and lower, until his tip nudges the back of my throat. I struggle to control my gag reflex, breathing through my nose as my lips stretch around his girth. Sage bucks his hips slightly, fucking my mouth with shallow thrusts. I hum, and Sage's whole body jolts in reaction to the sensation as his hand tightens in my hair. I gag slightly as his cock slips deeper, the sounds louder than the soundtrack of the video.

"Feels so fucking good," Sage mutters, and when I glance up, he's lost interest in the video and is watching me. "Looks fucking good too."

I reach up and cup his heavy sack through the fabric of his pants, hollowing my cheeks even more and sucking harder. His breathing becomes ragged, and I feel his thigh tense under the hand I still have braced against it. His head drops back, and he moans loudly, cursing as he floods my mouth with his release. I swallow greedily, my throat working around him, prolonging his pleasure as he sags into the seat, spent and satisfied.

"Wow, that was awesome," he mumbles, patting me on the head like I'm a dog. I push his hand away and sit up, wiping at my mouth with the back of my hand.

"Well, I can't have all the fun, can I?" I ask him as he lifts my phone and continues to watch our session this morning.

"Next time, I want an invite. There were two perfectly free holes for me to make use of." He points to me and Colton as I sit back next to him and grab a bottle of water out of the little fridge.

I roll my eyes. "Fine. Next time I'll make sure you are invited. We're almost there, so zip it up." I nod at his fly and spent cock, retrieving my phone from his hand and closing the app. "Colton's bi, right?" I ask. I think I remember him kissing one of the others, but I'm not a hundred percent sure.

"I sure hope so," Sage replies, excitement in his eyes. "I'd like to be the meat in a Vienna and Colton sandwich."

I chuckle. "Me too, or maybe make Colton the meat in a Vienna and Tori sandwich."

Sage looks at me, a grin spreading across his face. "Look at you, admitting what you want unashamedly. I'm so freaking proud of you, Victoria Russo, you're growing up." He presses his hand against his chest and wipes at a fake tear as the car comes to a stop, pulling into a small parking lot a few hundred feet from the warehouse. I flip him off and climb out, not waiting for our driver. I instructed him to park out of sight of the warehouse so Sage and I could get the lay of the land without giving ourselves away.

I glance around, and I don't see anyone suspicious hanging about. There doesn't appear to be any surveillance, so maybe it really was kids goofing off, thinking they could break into a warehouse.

Neither of us are dressed particularly inconspicuously, but we hold each other's hand and try to look like a couple out for a walk on our lunch break. The warehouses that surround this area are filled with a large variety of inventory, and suits are occasionally seen as well as tradesmen. Thankfully the council planted plenty of trees along the sidewalks in hopes of neutralizing how industrial this area looks. It hasn't worked, but it gives us cover if we need it.

My phone rings, and I stop to answer the call. "Hey, Sam, what's up?" I ask, wondering why he's calling after we just parted ways.

"Hey, boss. I was thinking about that newly branded X I saw in the warehouse, so I did a little digging. I spoke to one of our contacts in the Suncity Police Department, and they said there have been five overdoses attributed to the eggplant emoji X in the last month. The cops are trying to figure out where it's coming from. They know it's not a Russo product because we don't supply dirty drugs. That's at least one thing we have going for us."

"Five? Any deaths?" I ask him, and he sighs.

"Yeah, apparently one didn't make it. He overheated before anyone found him. The cops questioned the others, and two of them had been partying at Essence nightclub, but two of them said they got the drugs at Club Hell." He sounds reluctant to relay this information, and I feel my blood boil.

"Somebody is peddling dirty drugs in my fucking club?" My hand clenches around my phone, and it's all I can do to stop myself from throwing it across the street. "Fuck. I'm going to kill him. He must be adding something to it to cause that." I look at Sage for confirmation, and he appears as livid as I do, having heard my side of the conversation.

"He could be adding anything—cocaine, meth, or fentanyl just to name a few. I don't use any of those in my recipe because mixing drugs like that increases the risk to the user. We don't deal in meth or fentanyl. Your dad drew a line in the sand. He wanted happy return users and didn't want our drugs to become synonymous with death. It was smart of him, and we try to keep all of those highly addictive drugs out of our cities," Sage says.

We've had to destroy a number of gangs who tried to peddle those other filthy drugs in our cities. They keep popping up, and we keep sending bodies back to the people trying to infiltrate our territory.

"Thanks for letting me know. I'll deal with this," I assure Sam, and we hang up.

"God, Tori, I'm sorry."

I shake my head. "It's not your fault. The only person I blame is that little fucking weasel. I'm going to gut him like a pig." I search my cleavage for my favorite knife and smile. "Today is a good day. I get to make someone else bleed."

Sage winces but doesn't look too worried for the man he considered a friend.

"I'm sorry he betrayed you." My EQ levels aren't great at the best of times, but for Sage, I want to try. "Would you like the honor of gutting the betrayer?" I ask, but from the way he turns a little green, I guess maybe I was off the mark.

He shakes his head. "No, absolutely not." I feel my smile drop, and he hurries on. "But it was nice of you to offer," he says, giving me a gentle smile. "It was very thoughtful of you."

I perk up again and give myself a mental pat on the back. See? I can be a good girlfriend.

"Come on, let's go take out the trash."

We're approaching our warehouse when a car pulls up to the front of the building and someone I don't recognize gets out. He looks around, checking for anyone watching. We duck behind one of the large trees. I see him press the buzzer at the side door, and after a brief pause, he is let in.

"Who was that?" I ask Sage, who would know better than me who should be visiting the warehouse. As far as I know, the only person who should be here regularly is Anthony. The only other people who know about this place are Sage and my henchmen, who collect the products for delivery. We kept everyone else out of the loop because we didn't want anyone else knowing where it was. I don't even think Gio knows where this place is.

Sage is frowning. "I don't know, but I'm going to

go out on a limb and suggest he might be the recipient of the bad drugs," he says darkly.

"They are bold enough to come to my warehouse in the middle of the day? I don't like this at all, Sage. I bet Lorenzo has something to do with this," I growl and stop walking, grabbing my phone and pulling up the surveillance feed.

There's nothing but snow, and I know there is a problem. I show Sage, and he swears colorfully.

"Fucking Anthony. I knew he was a snake. He always gave off a slimy vibe," I tell him before pulling up the camera nobody knows about but me. Much like the one in my office, this one is placed in an inconspicuous item. In this case, it looks like a chemistry book, one of many on the shelves close to the chemist's workspace.

"I'm sorry, Tori, I thought he was trustworthy. I worked with him before your dad found me. Two kids just trying to get by. I thought he would be loyal for a steady, generous, and reliable paycheck." I hear the regret in Sage's voice because he knows what is about to befall Anthony.

Unfortunately, this camera only points in one direction, toward his workspace, but it does pick up all sound, and we can both hear Anthony betray us loud and clear.

"What the fuck are you doing here?" he hisses to his visitor.

"We need a new batch. We are out of the one you supplied us. We need way more product than you've been providing." The man's voice is deep, and he sounds annoyed.

"I can't produce more at once, I told you that. The Russos would question why I need more ingredients so quickly, especially Sage. He knows exactly what it takes to make their supply. If you want more, then you're going to have to supply the ingredients." Anthony's nasally voice grates on my nerves.

"Mr. Russo assured Mr. Maricuso that you would be able to provide us with another batch. Now I suggest you quit whining and get on with it. We want it within twenty-four hours."

"What? I can't rush the process. It's dangerous," Anthony argues, and I hear the panic in his voice.

And just like that, I have the proof I need. Lorenzo is working with the Maricuso family. I just need to find the warehouse holding the trafficking victims, and I can be done with the sorry excuse of an uncle for good.

"Maricuso. I knew he was going to be a thorn in our side. Fucking Penelope probably set this whole thing up. She wasn't happy with what she received from Dad's will, neither was Lorenzo. Those backstabbing family betraying snakes," I hiss, closing the camera app and shoving my phone into my pocket. "Let's go break up this little tête-à-tête," I tell Sage, reaching for my gun.

Sage pulls his own from his back holster, and we march toward the front door. The good thing about the security cameras being off is that they won't even see us coming.

"I'm even more determined to check out the warehouse tonight. I want to be done with Lorenzo, then we can focus on the Maricusos. It's time they learned that the Russos are not going to give up. Our territory has been ours for generations. We aren't letting it go without a fight."

"Okay, take a deep breath," Sage tells me as I reach for the handle. "Where is the cool, calm, deadly angel of death? You're going to get hurt if you go in there with a head full of steam."

I do as he says, letting all my anger and emotions drift away until I feel nothing but the cold, blazing chill of violence. "Let's do this."

Chapter Eighteen

Sage and I stealthily enter the warehouse. There is a small outer office before the rest of the warehouse opens up. It isn't large, just big enough to store all the ingredients the chemist needs and a workstation. It's also kept dry by an impressive exhaust system, since humidity can fuck with the product, or so Sage tells me. There are no windows, but the warehouse is well lit.

"I'm pretty sure if we go barging in there, that guy is going to start shooting willy-nilly, and that would not be good around all those chemicals," Sage cautions me, putting a hand on my arm to stop me from doing exactly that.

"So what do you suggest?" I ask, praying for patience. I really was going to go in guns blazing, so I'm glad he stopped me.

"How about we flick the breaker on the lights? The box is just there." He points out the circuit breakers on the wall. "Anthony will come out to check it, and I can capture him while you sneak in under the cover of darkness and get the other guy."

"They won't be suspicious?" I ask, and he shakes his head.

"No, he called me the other day, telling me the grid has been unstable, and I promised to get him some generators, which should be arriving tomorrow. He needs stable electricity so the cooking process doesn't get interrupted."

"Do it," I agree. "Just knock Anthony out. I want to question him before we kill him."

Sage moves quietly over to the box, opens it, and flicks the breaker. We are plunged into darkness. I hear him move toward the door, preparing to ambush Anthony when he leaves. I do the same thing so I can slip out behind him and take care of the other guy. Do I want to question him too? I think I have all the information I need from him from the video feed. Excitement starts to rush through my veins as I pull my knife out and open it. The door leading into the warehouse opens, and Anthony comes out, cursing up a storm. I trust Sage to take care of him, so I creep into the warehouse.

I move around the perimeter of the building, hugging the walls and weaving in and out of barrels of chemicals and shelves.

"Hurry up, I don't have all day," Maricuso's man calls to our slimy chemist.

Luckily for me, he is looking at his phone, and the

light from it shows me exactly where he is standing. I creep forward, thankful for the rubber soles on my heels, until I'm directly behind the guy.

He must feel my movement, because at the last moment, he starts to spin around, but it's too late. I whip out my hand and draw my knife across his throat, pushing down hard. His shout turns into a gurgle, and he drops his phone, clasping his neck just as the lights turn back on. I watch with satisfaction as blood coats his hands as he tries to stem the flow. It's no use, I made sure to cut deeply and get all the necessary vessels to make his death quick and painful.

He sinks to his knees, his eyes wide with panic as he gasps for help, but I just watch with immense satisfaction before pulling out my phone and sending a message to Dean, asking him to send the cleanup crew to the warehouse in an hour. That will give me plenty of time to deal with Anthony.

Sage comes in carrying an unconscious Anthony over his shoulder. He slams his dead weight into a chair and ties his hands behind him with a couple of zip ties before doing the same to his legs, making escape difficult.

Sage looks down at the enemy, whose gasps for breath get shorter as his blood spills all over the pristine white floor.

"Cleaning that up is going to suck," he comments as the two of us wait for the final bit of life to leave the man. "I'm glad we have someone to do it for us." He leans against the metal counter that holds some scientific equipment.

"Ugh, I should probably give the team a bonus. They've had to deal with two of my messes in the last week or so."

Sage puts his arm around me and pulls me against his chest, giving me a hug and pressing a kiss to the top of my head. "Don't be silly. That's why you employ them, and you pay them enough for discretion as it is."

"I'll comp the team a weekend stay at the Lucky Diamond. Happy employees equal loyal ones, or so Dad used to tell me. That doesn't explain this asshole." I kick Anthony's leg and pull away from Sage as he starts to come around. He was being paid very well for his services, and he still betrayed us.

Sage crosses his arms and glares at his former friend while I step behind him so he can't see me when he comes around. I love the element of surprise and seeing them just about shit their pants when they realize that I'm personally seeing to their torture.

"Sage?" Anthony sounds groggy, and he struggles with his bonds, but my man has him locked down tight. He might not enjoy torture like I do, but he can lock a body down like a champ.

I look over my surroundings, cataloguing the tools I have to work with, which is limited compared to my usual workspace, but I'm nothing if not practical.

"What the fuck, man?" Anthony sounds annoyed. "Fucking untie me," he demands, and Sage makes a tutting sound.

"Anthony, man, you fucked up. So what did the Maricusos offer you to betray us? What was your life worth?" Sage sounds bored.

I guess Anthony must finally get his wits about him and catch sight of the dead body, because he starts babbling.

"Oh my god, you killed him. I can't believe you killed him. I'm a dead man now."

"Yes, you are, but I'm not going to be the one who kills you," Sage says genially before nodding in my direction. "She is."

I step into Anthony's view, and his face turns an ashen shade as I tap the pair of forceps that I found against my palm. I'm not sure why they are in the lab, but they have a nice pointy end that has potential.

"I swear, Ms. Russo, I had no choice. They have my sister," he pleads, tears welling in his eyes. "They threatened to kill her if I didn't do what they told me."

Sage scoffs. "What a load of shit. You're an only fucking child—a spoiled rotten only child rebelling against two wonderful parents who would have gladly given you the world."

The tears instantly dry up, replaced with a vicious scowl in Sage's direction. "Shut your fucking mouth, you freak," he snarls. I step forward and drive the forceps into the meaty part of Anthony's thigh. His thin, cotton scrub-like pants do nothing to protect him from being impaled, and his scream reverberates around the warehouse.

"I don't like it when people call Sage names," I remark conversationally.

"Aww, what do I keep saying? You are such a softy, Victoria Russo." Sage blows me a kiss, and between his gasps for breath, Anthony starts spewing vitriol.

"She's a fucking psychotic bitch who should have been put down years ago. Only thing she is good for is sucking or taking a cock. Thinks she's something special now that her brother has turned into a fucking pussy and can't run this family, but all she's doing is making it ripe for takeover."

"Ah, and that is the root of this very situation. Why were you making product for the enemy?" I ask, and he clamps his lips shut, a stubborn set to his jaw as his nostrils flare as he tries to breathe through the pain.

I grin at him gleefully. "Dude, you can be as stubborn as you like. It's been a while since I have been allowed to torture someone, and you are giving me all the motivation I need."

I lean forward and grab each side of the forceps before yanking them open. Inside the wound, the two ends dig through more flesh. He howls again. It's music to my ears, and I feel my nipples pebble with excitement.

"Stop," he rasps. "Please stop. Fuck, first I told him I wanted you." He opens his eyes and looks at me with a mixture of hatred and lust. "Wanted to parade you in front of Sage, knowing I had you and he didn't. Wanted to fuck that pretty mouth and ass and make him watch while you screamed my name."

I raise my eyebrows at Sage. "I thought this guy was your friend. That doesn't sound very friendly."

Sage leans back against one of the benches and crosses his arms. "I did too. I guess I was wrong."

"Why would I be friends with a gutter rat like you? You were useful in helping me with my chemistry career, but I am so far out of your league, it's ridiculous." Anthony is nasty as fuck. Sage is a way better man than he will ever be, no matter where he came from. Being well off doesn't automatically make you a good person.

"So Lorenzo promised you me?" I ask him, and he shakes his head.

"No, unfortunately, you've been promised to someone else. Then I asked him to make me a Russo like Sage." I can see a theme behind his requests. "But Lorenzo said the Russo name should never have been given to someone not of Russo blood. You were not going to survive the takeover." He grins at Sage with glee, so I pull back my fist and punch him in the face. He starts to laugh, blood flowing from his nose.

"But the funniest thing is, both Lorenzo and Mario are plotting against one another. People forget the insignificant chemist is in the room and tend to talk about things they shouldn't. Both of them have plans to take one another out. I can't wait to see who will win."

I tut sympathetically at him. "If you think you're going to be around to see that, then you are delusional."

I grab my blood encrusted knife from where I placed it on the countertop and walk a circle around the chemist, running the blade from the corner of his eye to the corner of his mouth. I don't cut him, but he gets the idea. "What should I take first? The tongue that spews such awful words, or the eyes that covet everything they shouldn't?" I ask Sage conversationally, and Anthony starts thrashing his head, almost impaling his own eye with his desperation.

"No, stop! I'm useful. I know things."

I pull the knife away and gesture for him to go on.

"Uh, um, they are bringing in meth and fentanyl in the hopes they can distribute here. They have a deal with the Mexican cartel. The cartel provided the drugs in exchange for warm bodies they can sell."

I assume an exaggerated pout. "Boo, we already knew all of that. You will have to do better," I tell him.

His eyes roll around in their sockets in his panic to give me some kind of useful information.

Sage yawns and stretches. "I know you've been dying to do some cutting, but do you think we can get a move on? I'm getting hungry."

I gape at him in wonder. "But you had a huge breakfast."

He pats his flat stomach. "But I'm a growing boy, and I need my energy for fun times." He winks at me, and I shake my head at him.

"Whore." I guess Anthony gave up on trying to recall some useful information for me. I suppose he wasn't as important as he thought he was.

"Sticks and stones, Anthony. Sticks and stones. Shaming someone for their sexual proclivities is low class. It smacks of jealousy. I bet if I was bending over for you, you wouldn't be calling me a whore."

"I wouldn't bet on it," Sage mutters.

"Okay, well, I guess you're in luck, Anthony. I'm feeling pretty fucking generous today. I've had a pretty outstanding start to my morning, so I'm going to take it easy on you." I see him sag a little in his chair as some of the tension bleeds out of him and frown. "Oh no, that was not a cue for you to relax." I reach forward and yank the forceps out of his leg.

His screams fill the warehouse like a symphony caressing my ears. I straddle his legs and lean over to whisper in his ear.

"Wait, wait, please. I know where they are keeping the people for the shipment. I can show you," he pleads, snot and tears streaming down his face. I pause and tilt my head to the side.

"How do you know?" I ask curiously.

"I dropped the last shipment of drugs off there. It's not far from here." He rattles off the same address that was on the note left on my car, and another rush of adrenaline runs through my body. We are finally getting somewhere. I'll still check it out tonight, but hopefully I can call Agent Garcia tomorrow and put all of that drama behind us, but first, I need to deal with this disgusting worm.

"You played fast and hard and lost, Anthony. You betrayed someone I care about very much, and that makes me mad. For that, you will lose your tongue." He clamps his mouth shut, but I stick my knife between his lips, and he has no choice but to open them wide. I slide the bloody forceps into his mouth and clasp them around his tongue, yanking it out. He gags and flails his body, but I just pin him down with my weight and use the knife to sever the flesh. I wrinkle my nose at the bloody chunk of meat when it's been detached and toss the forceps onto the ground as blood pools in Anthony's mouth. He starts to choke on his own blood, and the grunts and groans coming from him sound wet and kind of gross.

I climb off his lap and look down at myself. Unfortunately, severing someone's tongue is a little messy, and blood is splattered all over me. Thankfully I'm wearing all black, so I won't be walking around like a Jackson Pollock painting.

"Okay, he'll be dead by the time the cleanup crew arrives," I tell Sage, wiping my knife on Anthony's shirt in a spot where there is no blood. I depress the hinge and fold the blade over. I'll clean it later tonight.

"Huh, I've never seen you do that before." Sage looks a little pale as he watches Anthony's eyes flutter, and he starts to lose consciousness. He'll either bleed out or choke on his own blood, so my work here is done.

"To be honest, I don't do it very often, because as you can see, they die pretty quickly after their tongue is severed. Usually, I like to drag it out, but we have things to do today. I want to drive past that address and get an idea of what we are walking into tonight, and we probably shouldn't do it from the limo. We need something inconspicuous."

"Hang on, I have an idea." Sage wrinkles his nose but shoves his hand into Anthony's pocket and pulls out a set of keys.

"He has a POS he drives here so no one sees his flashy car and gets tempted to boost it. No one will recognize us, and it won't matter that you're covered in blood splatter. Afterwards, we can go to the hotel, and you can change in our apartment there." He swings the keys around his finger.

"Good thinking." I give him a kiss on the cheek before washing my hands and the outside of my knife. Pulling some paper towels off the roll, I dry both before tucking the knife back into my cleavage. I pat the blood splatter with more damp towel, but it doesn't do anything.

"Ugh, it's going to have to do. I don't think I'll get any on the car."

"If you do, we'll ask the cleanup crew to make it look like he was in a car accident. They can make it appear like he severed his tongue in the crash. Maybe push it down a ravine somewhere."

"Good thinking. Let's get out of here."

"Hang on, let me just make sure he isn't in the middle of a batch. I don't want this warehouse to go up in a ball of flames, and I want to inventory how much product we have. I might need to speak to our suppliers to get more if he's been skimming them for the Maricusos."

Sage has a little crease of worry between his brows as he looks at the storage area. I know he's feeling guilty about Anthony, since he was the one who recommended him, but he isn't to blame. He had well and truly been played.

"Don't worry, we'll figure this out. I'm sure we can find ourselves another chemist." I try to reassure him, but I don't think it helps.

"Maybe I should just go back to it full time," he suggests, and I start to vibrate with anger again. Fucking Gio. If he was pulling his weight, Sage wouldn't be split in two, helping manage all the slack.

"Don't stress about it. You stay here and set things right, and I'll come back once I've done my reconnaissance. We don't need two of us for surveillance," I tell him before grabbing the keys out of his hands. "I'll see you soon." I wave goodbye and hurry out before he can argue.

There are only two cars in the parking lot, and one of them is the one we saw arrive, so I logically assume the other is Anthony's. It's such an old clunker, I need to use the key to actually open the door, but before long, I'm using google maps to direct me where to go, excited at being that much closer to dealing with Lorenzo. If the victims are at the warehouse, I just have to figure out how to get him there when it's raided, but that's a problem for future Tori.

Chapter Nineteen

The drive past the warehouse is uneventful. Unlike ours, it has a fence around it, and I saw guards and dogs patrolling the perimeter, which is going to make it tricky to break into tonight but not impossible. I make some calls and arrange to have everything I need delivered to the house in Banebridge, since that's where we will be leaving from. Sedatives for the guards and dogs are the easiest way to get past them both, and some det cord for any locked doors we come across, although I don't really want to make it noticeable that the place has been breached. I couldn't tell what kind of locks the door had, so that's just in case, but I'll take my lock picks.

I'm not computer savvy enough to hack an electronic lock, hence the det cord. A window is an option, but the only ones I could see were up high. Scaling the building will take more time than I want it to, and the fire escape wasn't close to any of them, unless there is an entrance on the roof. I plan on checking that out by using the fire escape first. Lots of people get lazy and forget to guard the roof entrance because it's harder to get up there. That's going to be my first option. I'll rework the plan if it turns out to be a dead end.

On my drive back to pick up Sage, I get a message from Vienna.

Vienna: Can you come pick us up? Gio and Casey left for their appointment, and we don't have any way of getting home.

I look at the time on my phone and realize it's already a lot later than I thought it was. I guess I won't be able to change before we pick them up, but the black hides everything if they don't look too closely. We've both completely missed lunch, and I bet Sage is starting to get hangry. We're going to have a late night, so it wouldn't hurt to go home early and maybe nap after we have some food.

Tori: Sure. Give us half an hour, and we will be there.

My phone pings again, and when I look down, the screen is covered in hearts.

I feel warmth flow over me and wriggle uncomfortably. This POS of Anthony's certainly has uncomfortable seats.

Sage is waiting for me when I return. The other car has been removed from the parking lot, and he holds out his hands for the keys then puts them in a flowerpot next to the door.

"The cleanup crew will be back to dump this car later. They are going to stage it like we suggested, and they are going to put the other guy's body in the trunk to make it look like Anthony betrayed them and died when he was on his way to dump the body," he tells me as we make our way back to our limo. Our driver remained parked out of the way, but he starts the vehicle when he sees us coming.

"Hopefully they don't notice he hasn't returned for a few days," I murmur, but I have a feeling he was important if he was being sent to lean on Anthony. They wouldn't trust a low-level man for an important job like that.

Sage's stomach rumbles loudly, and I chuckle before giving the driver instructions to head to the college to pick up the others.

"But I'm hungry," Sage whines dramatically.

I pull open one of the little storage areas, and along with a couple of spare guns and ammo, I have a few candy bars for this exact reason. I hand one over to my boyfriend, who snatches it before tearing it open and stuffing it into his mouth. His eyes roll in his head as he moans his enjoyment.

"So fucking good," he says around a mouthful of chocolate.

"Hmm, sexy," I deadpan.

He happily munches for a while before asking, "So why are we going to the college?" He raises an eyebrow knowingly.

"Because Vienna messaged me, and Gio left them

in the lurch. I guess he only arranged for a car for him and Casey and forgot about the others."

Sage tuts. "Typical. So gallant Tori is riding to the rescue of the damsels in distress? You could have just sent a car for them as well."

I shrug. "I figured we could use an early knock off if we're going to be partaking in nighttime activities, and since we're heading home, we might as well give them a ride," I tell him, and he waggles his eyebrows.

"Tell me more about these nighttime activities."

I roll my eyes. "A little B and E, you perv."

He huffs good-naturedly. "I know that, but a nap sounds good."

"I'll message Suzy and ask her to organize an early dinner," I say, but before I can pull out my phone, his eyes light up, and he sits up straight.

"I'll do it," he shouts. I stare at him with surprise, and he looks sheepish. "Sorry, I have a craving, and I'm hoping I can sweet talk her into making my favorite."

"Okay, I'll leave it in your hands. Maybe message Gio and see if he and Casey will be back by then. I doubt he remembered to let her know."

Sage is quiet while he sends his messages, and I watch the city glide by through the window.

I guessed Lorenzo was working with someone, but I thought it was just the Mexican cartel trying to undermine us. Knowing he's actively working with a rival cuts deeper. We expected it, but to have it confirmed is like a slap in the face. I want to kill him, not have him arrested by the FBI, but unfortunately,

I'm between a rock and a hard place, and if I don't give Agent Garcia someone, he will come after the rest of my organization. This will at least get them off our backs for a few years, or that was the agreement. Sometimes you have to make a deal with a demon to take out the devil.

When the limo glides to a stop at the agreed spot at Suncity U, the others are waiting under a big maple tree. Vienna is leaning against Xavier, and his arms are around her while they talk quietly. Colton and Tristan are throwing a football back and forth between them.

They gather their bags and throw them in the trunk, and then one by one, they climb into the limo. Vienna gives Sage a kiss on the lips on her way past before doing the same to me. A warm, fluttery feeling happens in the pit of my stomach, and I blink away my surprise, but when Colton does the same thing, giving Sage a kiss and then me, neither of us can hide our shock. I'm pretty sure our faces match with our mouths dropped open and our eyes wide with surprise. Vienna giggles and points between us.

"You should see yourselves. You both look like stunned catfish."

"Hell, I want in on some of this action," Tristan says, and he grabs Sage by the hand and hauls him from the seat across from him and into his lap. "Hello, handsome," he drawls before kissing Sage soundly. When they break apart, he pushes Sage gently back into the seat he was in before turning his attention to me. Xavier sits down on my other side, and it's him that Tristan speaks to.

"Give Tori a kiss for the both of us, will you?" he instructs, and Xavier doesn't hesitate. He slides his hand behind my head and drags me toward him, pressing his lush lips to mine then firmly stroking my tongue with his. I moan and sink into him, enjoying it immensely as the limo starts the journey back to our house in Banebridge.

When he pulls away, his eyes sparkle, and there is a small smile on his lips. "Hi."

I'm flustered but manage to get myself together and reply, "Hi, that was nice"

He frowns. "Nice? Well, I guess I need to do better next time."

I expect the atmosphere in the limo to be awkward after all that affection, but it's not. The four of them tell us about their day. Xavier talks about his self-defense class, which is just as popular as ever, and Vienna gushes about the party they've been invited to on Saturday night. Apparently, anyone who is anyone is going to be there. I feel my eyes glaze over, unable to contribute to the conversation.

"We'd love to go, wouldn't we, Tori?" Sage startles me with his question, and I tune back in, unsure what he just agreed to.

"Huh?" I ask, feeling my cheeks heat with embarrassment.

"Vienna was just inviting us to go to the party on Saturday night," he tells me before turning to the others. "Tori's never been to a party with kids her own age before."

"Actually, that's not true," I argue. "Before Dad's death, Gio used to throw parties at home all the time." I wrinkle my nose. "Not that they were much fun. I would blow them off and smoke weed in my room with..." I trail off, not wanting to mention who I would do that with, but I can tell they all have an idea.

There's a slightly uncomfortable silence before Vienna claps her hands, breaking it. "Perfect. I can't wait. There will be drinking and dancing, and we will all be able to blow off some steam. You will have a great time," she tells me, and I wince internally.

I'm not sure I will, but I want to make an effort to be more like a normal young adult. I want what Gio has, and I guess some of my anger toward him stems from that, so what will it hurt to take a night off from being a mafia queen?

"And I booked our spa day tomorrow, so you will be all fresh and relaxed for the party on the weekend."

Ha, I'm pretty sure I will be in a situation that will cause me to be tense well before then, but I don't tell her that. "That's sounds great, I can't wait." I'm not lying, really.

I look out the window at the trees flashing by. We're well and truly out of Suncity now and passing through the forest that sits between it and Banebridge. The large tree canopy blocks out a lot of light, so the inside of the limo is a little less bright. The faint hum of the engine is soothing, and the subtle sway of the vehicle gently rocks me, making me fall into a slight daze. It's already been a long ass day. I'm looking forward to my nap later.

A hand caresses my leg, and I look down in surprise, not expecting it. Tristan's hand is pale against my black pants.

"Um, Tori, care to explain why you smell a little coppery and your pants are sticky?" He lifts his hand from the material, and I see a smear of red on it. I guess the blood hasn't completely dried yet. Crap!

"Um, occupational hazard?"

Before anyone else can ask questions, the limo explodes into violence, the screech of metal deafening as the entire interior shudders from impact. One side caves in as the vehicle is sent into a spin. I get thrown onto the floor, my head hitting something hard as stars burst behind my eyelids and pain shoots through my body. Before I can get my bearings, there's another thunderous crash, and the other side of the limo is hit, the vehicle jolting with the impact, sending me rolling around in a tangle of limbs with everyone else who is also in the footwell with me. Finally, the vehicle stops moving, and there's a small pause of complete silence as I open my eyes and see us covered in shimmering shards of glass before noise comes rushing back in. I hear the guys all shouting in their panic and Vienna sobbing as she calls to Colton to wake up.

"Shit, Tori! Tori, are you okay?" I blink to clear the fuzz in my mind. My temple throbs, and my body aches all over, but when I manage to focus, I find Sage staring down at me with a cut on his forehead. His nose is also a little bloody from where it must have impacted something hard.

"What happened?" I ask as he helps me up. The inside of the limo is a mess, but thankfully, it's still intact. I look around and find Colton slumped to one side with a big cut over his right eyebrow. Vienna shakes him, trying to wake him.

Tristan and Xavier both look okay, but Tristan is rubbing his knee and is covered in glass, and Xavier is gently brushing it out of Tristan's hair. He has a rather large, bloody gash on one arm that looks like it could use stitches.

"God, Tori, I knew you were hardheaded, but I didn't know it was that hard," Tristan jokes weakly as I look out the window. My heart starts to race even harder when I see a vehicle scream up behind the two that wrecked our limo and armed, masked gunmen pour out.

"Fuck, we're in trouble. Sage, stay here and protect these guys, and I'll deal with them." I shake his hand off my arm and reach for the gun in the small of my back.

"We can help," Xavier says, narrowing his eyes as the men approach us. "You're outnumbered on your own."

Colton groans, and his eyes flutter open. "Oh, thank God." Vienna sobs. "You protected me, you idiot, and got hurt."

He smiles gently at her. "I'll always protect you, my

love." My heart aches at his declaration, but I'm focused on the incoming enemy. I push the hidden door on the gun cabinet and pull out two more guns and some ammo, then I pass them to Tristan and Xavier. They quickly load the weapons as Sage uses his feet to kick the crumpled door open.

"Stay in here. The limo is bulletproof and should protect you from any stray bullets. Just stay away from the broken windows," I tell Colton and Vienna. "Do you know how to use this?" I ask Colton who nods but groans in pain.

"I'm not sure I could hit the broad side of a barn at the moment, but I can try."

I hear the men shouting to one another. "The driver's dead. Kill the bitch and grab the chemist." I frown in response. I guess they don't know that there are four others in the car with us. That seems like poor planning.

I open another hidden storage area and pull out the other gun we have stored for emergencies.

"Holy shit, is that an AK?" Tristan whistles as I slip a magazine into the slot and slide the bolt back, chambering a round.

"I'm going to lay down some cover so you can move toward the trees and take the shooting away from the vehicle. Colton, don't hesitate. Point at center mass and pull the trigger," I snap, and all seem to listen.

"I can help," Vienna says, her voice shaky.

"It's fine, you look after Colton's head wound.

There's a first aid kit in there." I point to where I pulled out the semi-automatic. "And you can pass me new magazines when I need them."

Without waiting for a response, I struggle to my knees and take a steadying breath. The men are getting closer, moving around the wreckage of the vehicle. If I don't go now, then we're going to be surrounded.

Securing the gun against my chest next to my armpit, I pop out of the skylight and bend my knees slightly, leaning my body against the car frame to absorb some of the recoil. I flip the safety switch to full automatic. These guns aren't legal in the US except for the military, but hey, we're a mafia family, and legality has never been an issue for us. Thankfully, they haven't noticed me up here yet, so I place my finger on the trigger and, with a thunderous burst of sound, spew a full round of bullets out at their feet, spraying chips of asphalt all over the place.

They shout and race for the trees on either side of the road. "Go," I yell, and Sage finally slams the open door with his feet, and he, Tristan, and Xavier exit the vehicle, ducking and running for the opposite tree line on our side of the limo.

I breathe a sigh of relief that they are out of the way. I can now pick off our enemies one by one without having to worry about them.

I press the lever on the gun and eject the magazine. It drops to the floor, and I hold out my hand for Vienna to pass me another. I don't look away from the enemies in the tree line, but I feel her slam one against my palm. I quickly slide it into the gun, making sure it's in properly before slamming the bolt back and chambering the first round. I flick the safety to semi-auto, wanting to have better control over the bullets this time. Automatic is fine for cover, but its accuracy is limited, and I want to have better consistency than a damn storm trooper. Our lives depend on it.

"Fuck, there are other people in there," I hear one of our enemies shout in the silence that seems deafening after the loud burst of gunfire. "We were told there were only two of them."

"Who fucking cares? Kill them all, but not the chemist."

"Which one is the fucking chemist? We were only told there would be one male and one female. It was easy then."

I don't think these guys realize their voices are carrying, but it gives me time to work out where they are standing in the trees, so when one pokes their head out to look, I'm ready. Before I can fire, there's a sharp sound of a gunshot, and a body falls from behind one of the trees face down.

"One down, five to go," I mutter, not looking away. I don't know which of the guys took that shot, but they were effective. I didn't see where they went when they ran for the trees, and I can't let myself get distracted by looking for them.

I scan the dense forest. We need to get this done before anyone else drives this stretch. I'm actually surprised no one has come along yet. I wonder if they have buddies putting up roadblocks to ensure we aren't interrupted.

"Vienna, reach into my pocket and pull out my phone," I whisper quietly, and it doesn't take her but a moment to do as I instruct. "The code is 090524. Scroll through my contacts and find the listing for 'the crew,'" I tell her. "Call them, give them the code word 'salamander,' and tell them we need a cleanup and for them to GPS my location. Tell them there might be hostiles in either direction on the road leading to us."

I know the crew was disposing of our previous bodies, but hopefully they are almost done and can be here to clean up quickly after we get done with these, because I can't accept any other outcome but us being victorious.

I hear her doing as I instructed, her voice, although she's trying to keep her shit together, sounds panicked in the sudden stillness.

Movement off to my right draws my attention, and I know the others went left, so I shift, aiming my gun toward it. Before I can fire, there's another loud shot, and a bullet pings off the roof of the limo. I duck slightly, not taking my eye off the target, and squeeze off a round once it's lined up. It's not the most accurate, but at this point, I just want them immobilized and unable to fire at us. The man screams as the bullet tears through his knee, a spray of blood and bone fragments misting out around it. He falls to the ground, his shouts of pain loud and distracting. I go to aim again, but before I can, another few shots bounce off the limo's surface, and I duck out of the line of fire.

I'm breathing heavily, and my chest hurts. I must have bruised my rib cage when we were hit. I check on Colton to make sure he's still conscious and find him looking at me with a slightly dazed grin.

"You're super sexy handling that weapon," he slurs, and Vienna tuts, dabbing at the cut above his eyebrow.

"I think he has a concussion. He's loopy," Vienna murmurs, and I can hear her concern.

"Call Suzy from my phone and explain what's happening. Tell her I have it handled, but we are going to need the doctor when we get home. She will organize for him to check on Colton and the others. I think Xavier is going to need stitches."

While we are talking, there are more shots exchanged between the guys and the enemy. Through the open door, I see the three of them exchange words and hand signals like they are a freaking military unit. I narrow my eyes in contemplation. Tristan and Xavier don't just have gun range experience. Before I can ask Colton or Vienna about it, though, the other door is yanked open, and Vienna screams, yanking Colton away from it. I turn the gun and fire, my ears ringing from the sound inside the enclosed space. The bullet hits the man with such force, his body is thrown backward, away from the door, which gives me a clean line of sight. I count two more bodies and know only one remains. I'm not wearing my bulletproof vest, which

I'm now regretting. It looks like Sage and I may have to take to wearing them on a daily basis for a while.

I scan the dense forest for the last remaining enemy. Out of the corner of my eye, I see a shadow pass, and I swivel my head to look, but it's just Tristan crouching behind the car and facing in the same direction as I am. I release the sudden breath I took and turn my attention toward the tree line. The silence is almost deafening. There are no sounds other than my heavy breathing and Vienna's quiet murmuring to Colton, not even a rustle of leaves from the breeze.

Suddenly, there's a sharp crack of a tree branch, and I turn to where it came from and fire. I'm not the only one, because a volley of bullets rings out from our side of the road.

Finally, I hear Sage yell, "Clear. They are all down."

I relax, turning the safety on my weapon and sagging to my knees in the ruined vehicle, placing the rifle on the floor.

"Fucking hell," I mutter, pushing a hand through my hair. It's a tangled mess, and I feel little pieces of glass in it, so I only push it off my face. "Are you two okay?" I ask loudly, my hearing still compromised.

"What?" Vienna yells, shoving a finger in one ear like she's trying to clear it. Instead of repeating myself, I give them a thumbs-up, to which she nods and Colton blinks.

Okay, we need to get him to a doctor fast. I grab my Glock and climb out of my car, wanting to question the man whose knee I destroyed. I look around and see Sage checking on the guy who tried to pull us out of the car. His wide, blank eyes stare at the sky, but Sage still puts a round between his eyes just like we were taught.

I look around and see Tristan doing the same with one of the others, but when I look toward the guy whose knee I destroyed, I find Xavier standing over him, his gun pointed at his body. Xavier is talking to him, his face furious, but I can't make out what they are saying. I stumble slightly, my body banged up a little more than I realized now that the adrenaline is wearing off, but I feel a hand on my arm as Sage steadies me.

"I've got you, love," he says, then he helps me over to where Xavier and the remaining alive combatant is. Before we can make it to them, though, there's a bang, and Xavier puts a bullet between the man's eyes.

"No. What the fuck?" I scream at him, yanking my arm from Sage and stomping over. "I wanted to fucking question him. You had no right to do that." I slap Xavier's chest, and he just glares down at me.

"He knew nothing. They were hired to ambush the limo, but they were told it was only going to be the two of you. They weren't expecting us to be here as well."

"Who hired him? Was it Lorenzo?" I demand, and he shrugs.

"He didn't say."

"Argh!" I stomp my foot like a toddler having a tantrum. "I would have been able to get that information out of him. I could have taken him back for interrogation." I'm so fucking pissed.

"Easy, Tori," Sage murmurs. "He was only protecting us. He didn't know. They don't lead the same kind of life we do."

I'm not so sure about that now. They are way too familiar and confident with weapons than the average college student, as well as the way Tristan was making sure they were well and truly dead without even hesitating. Then again, they did grow up rough, so I could understand the need to know how to protect themselves at all costs.

I heave out a sigh as Xavier pushes past me and stalks toward the vehicle to check on the other two. Tristan drags one of the other bodies over to this one and drops their legs.

"If we put them in a pile, it will be easier to clean up."

I wave a hand at him. "It's okay, I have a crew coming." I sag against a nearby tree and close my eyes, leaning my head back. My temples are throbbing, and my ribs ache something fierce.

"I'll go check on Cecil, but I doubt he survived," Sage tells me, and I sigh. Cecil has been our driver for years, and he even survived the bomb that took out Dad's limo, the destruction being contained to the passenger section.

"I'm going to dig around in pockets and find the keys for that vehicle," Tristan tells me, nodding at the SUV the armed men arrived in. "The limo is toast, and we need a way to get home, and that's as good as any."

"What about the drivers of the cars that hit us?" I ask, and he shakes his head.

"Both of them were knocked out when the airbags exploded, and Sage and I took care of them earlier," he tells me, tilting his head to the side. "You know, Xavier meant well," he explains, and I shrug, not willing to concede just yet.

"Let's get moving. I want to get home. This day ended up being a huge clusterfuck after such a great start." I can't help but sound annoyed, especially since I still need to head out late tonight, and by then, everything is going to hurt.

Maybe I'll have a smoke to ease some of the discomfort.

Chapter Twenty

It doesn't take long for the cleanup crew to arrive. They managed to avoid the roadblocks they confirmed were in place, keeping traffic from using the main road. They came through one of the side roads the two cars that T-boned us used. They also brought a couple of tow trucks with them to clear away the smashed cars and assured me they would dispose of the bodies. They are going to make sure Cecil's next of kin are notified of his death due to a car accident and secure his remains so they can mourn him whichever way they choose.

We finally make our way home in the combatants' vehicle. It's a squeeze with all six of us, but Vienna perches on Tristan's lap, fussing over Colton the whole way. We bandaged the gash on Xavier's arm, and I was right, it is going to need a couple of stitches, as is the cut over Colton's eyebrow. Sage drives us, careful not to attract the attention of an over enthusiastic cop. It would not be good to get pulled over in the condition we're all in. There would be questions we don't want to answer, not to mention the car is not ours.

The doctor is waiting for us when we return, and Suzy bustles the others off to get checked, leaving Sage and me alone.

"Ugh," I groan, leaning against the counter. "Well, today went to shit."

"Are you two okay? Should you see the doctor as well?" Ben asks, sounding concerned as he looks between us.

Sage waves him off. "A few bumps and bruises, but we came out the best. We were kind of sandwiched between the rest of them."

Ben frowns. "Really? That was lucky."

"No shit," I grumble. "I need a couple of ibupro-fen, a meal, and a hot shower, followed by a nap. I still have to go out again tonight." I slump against the counter, resting my head on the cool marble.

"Nope, don't stop, it will just be harder to get up." Sage grabs my shoulders and drags me off the chair. I stumble slightly, and he steadies me.

"I just want a break. When is it going to let up?" I whine, feeling tears well in my eyes. I've been strong for so long, but I think I'm about to finally break.

"Aww, baby. It's okay. I'm going to look after you. After your little breaking and entering adventure tonight, Vienna's going to make sure you're pampered until you're a squishy ball of mush, then this weekend, we're going to party like its 1999. By then, Lorenzo will be out of our hair, and there will be one less problem on our plate. Everything will get better," he promises, but I have trouble believing him. "Ben, my man, did Suzy prepare what I asked for?"

Ben smiles and nods at a basket I hadn't noticed sitting on the other counter near the sink. "Yup, everything you asked for is in there. Go. I'll tell the others you are resting after your ordeal if they ask, but I'm pretty sure Suzy is going to mother hen the shit out of them. They'll be so distracted, they won't even notice the two of you are missing."

"But Gio will be back soon. I need to ask him if he knows about that tunnel," I argue as Sage grabs my hand, takes the basket, and drags me toward the elevator.

"Fuck Gio. Ben, if he asks, tell him we are working tonight. Don't give him any details. Just shrug and pretend ignorance of our whereabouts," Sage instructs, and Ben gives him a jaunty salute, grinning like a loon.

Sage hits the button for the elevator, and the doors open. He scans his eye for the concealed level, and I feel it start to move.

"What are we doing?" I ask him, and he grins.

"We are having a picnic in my grow house. I'll roll you a joint that will take away all your aches and pains and then give you an orgasm that will make you so mellow and relaxed, you'll practically slide under the door of the warehouse we're breaking into tonight."

The doors open into the warehouse. We bypass the

empty space and head toward the corridor that leads to his grow house.

"Where do you think the door to that tunnel is?" I ask him, and he points at a door across the large space.

"Dean called and told me where it was, and he said one of our guys was going to secure a bar across it for now so nobody can open it. We have one of our contractors coming in tomorrow to lock it down. You will be the only person who can open it. Not even Gio will be coded to it."

I make a snap decision. "I'm not even going to tell Gio about it. I really don't trust him anymore, and he's distracted enough that it could put us and our operation in danger."

Sage opens the door to his warehouse, and the skunk smell of marijuana plants hits my nose. He inhales deeply and grins with pure joy as he leads me down a row of waist-high plants. The lights are bright. He runs on a sixteen and eight growth cycle. I installed solar panels on the roof of the mansion to counter the electricity bills.

He leads me down the back where there is row after row of mature plants, ready for harvest. Under the large bushes is a blanket with a bunch of cushions, surrounded by small electric tea lights.

"The team is picking this lot tomorrow, but I want you to see it in all its glory before they do." He places the picnic basket down next to the blanket. "And I promised you a picnic. I'm not topping the plants, but

I can at least play some music to accompany our dinner."

He pulls out his phone and swipes at the screen. A serene, instrumental piece fills the space, and he does a small twirl before gesturing toward the blanket.

"You're throne, my lady."

I smile, some of the exhaustion seeping away in the face of his joy. "It's no Taylor Swift or the Weekend, but my plants seem to like it just as much," he explains as I toe off my heels and lower myself onto the pile of cushions. I groan as my aches and pains make themselves known. His smile drops, and he holds up a finger.

"Give me a moment. I'm going to grab the right strain for you. We need something that is higher in CBD than THC so you get the pain relief, but retain the clarity you need for our nighttime escapades," he tells me before disappearing in the direction of the drying room.

Sage knows more about each strain of marijuana that he grows than I ever will, and if I let him, he will ramble on for hours about each and every one of the properties. To be honest, it actually doesn't sound too bad at the moment. It would take my mind off everything else.

It's not long before he skips back toward me, waving a jar of dried flowers. The label on it reads, "AC/DC."

I frown, pointing to it. "AC/DC? Like the band?"

He nods and drops down, opening the basket and

pulling out an herb grinder and packet of papers. "Yeah, this one will be exactly what you need. It will take away the pain but leave you mentally alert and your reflexes firing."

He places everything on the blanket in front of him before also pulling out a bottle of wine and a couple of glasses. He opens the bottle and pours me a glass, then passes it to me before he sets about preparing the joint. I lean back against the pillows and watch, completely mesmerized by the care he takes, his calming ritual lulling me into a relaxed state.

I take a sip of the red wine. Full bodied and tart, it perks me up as he runs his tongue over the paper before sealing the cone and rolling the end into a point.

"Voilà!" He pulls a lighter out of his pocket and lights it, dragging deeply before blowing out the thick smoke. "Yup, this is going to be just what you need. Here, take this while I get our food ready."

He passes it over, and I take it with my spare hand, putting it to my lips and taking my own deep drag of the skunky weed. I watch as he starts to unpack the picnic basket. He pulls out some foil wrapped packages, a couple of sealed bowls, and some utensils.

When he removes the lids, I see mac and cheese and what looks like a couple of small bowls of tomato soup. He unwraps the foiled packages, and I smile when I see the grilled cheese sandwiches. Sage had Suzy make all my favorite comfort foods. How can I do anything but love him? He passes me one of the bowls of soup before spooning some mac and cheese onto a paper plate, then he sets a grilled cheese on it as well. With a waiter-like flourish, he deposits the plate in front of me before picking up his own glass of wine and taking a large sip. I smoke a little more of the joint before handing it to him. Picking up my plate, I eat a few bites of the mac and cheese before dipping my grilled cheese into the bowl of soup. My stomach rumbles as the food hits my taste buds, and we quietly devour the meal between us, passing the joint back and forth before Sage finally puts it out in one of the plant pots.

"This was perfect," I tell him, feeling sleepy, relaxed, and pain free about half an hour later. We've talked about nothing important, avoiding everything that happened today and the subject of my brother. Instead, Sage has told me about his plans after he harvests this new batch and frees up some pots for a new crop. He's super excited about a new strain he's developing. Most of the details go over my head, but it's nice not to have to think too hard about anything for a moment.

He puts away the remnants of our picnic until only the almost empty bottle of wine and both glasses remain. Sage pushes the basket away and tops off our glasses with the remaining liquid before that too is added to the picnic basket.

He crawls over to me and takes my glass, putting them both off to the side out of reach before he pushes me back, and I flop into the pile of cushions, all boneless and relaxed.

"I'm going to give you an orgasm now, and then we will head upstairs where I'll run you a bath. I'll set the alarm, and we will sleep until we have to head back for our little investigation. I don't want you thinking about anything but what my tongue is doing to your pussy," he tells me, peeling off my bloodstained clothes.

A warm rush of affection flows over me. It is so fucking nice to be taken care of for a change. I feel light, and my mind is silenced of all the usual worries that live there rent free these days. I pull my top over my head and take off my bra before lounging back on my elbows and admiring him as he strips my panties down my legs, leaving me naked and exposed.

"I want you naked too," I purr as he pushes my legs open and runs a finger through my glistening folds.

He grins goofily and uses one hand to pull his shirt from his back, having already shed his jacket earlier. I watch with admiration as he gets to his feet and strips off his dress pants, taking his underwear with them. I groan with desire when I see the drop of precum on the tip of his hard cock when he palms it and strokes it a couple of times. I gesture for him to step closer so I can run my tongue over it, but he shakes his head and kneels between my legs.

"Nope, it's my turn to return the favor from the limo." He situates himself between my thighs, his shoulders pressing them wider as he runs his tongue through my folds. My head drops back in pleasure, and I stare up at the bright lights and the top of the plants that seem to bend in slightly like they are shielding us from the world. I groan loudly as he flicks his tongue over my throbbing clit, the ring in it giving the perfect amount of pressure as he slides a single digit deep into my core.

"You always taste so fucking good, sweet and all mine," he mumbles against my pussy, sending delicious vibrations through it. I straighten my arms to grab his head as I flop back on the cushions and grind my cunt into his face.

"Yes, just like that," I beg as he adds another finger, stretching me as his tongue dances across my clit, alternating between licking and sucking in the perfect rhythm.

He inhales deeply, and when I look down at him, his eyes are practically rolled back in his head. "Oh man, the smell of you combined with the smell of my plants just about has me coming on the spot. If only I could bottle it and wear it every day," he murmurs as he licks and sucks my clit, adding another finger to the ones already deep in my pussy.

My walls clench, and my head thrashes back and forth as he curls his fingers, plunging them in and out, hitting that magic spot inside me.

"Oh God, Sage, more," I cry out as the sound of his slurping hits my ears. His free hand kneads my ass, and his thumb teases my puckered hole, adding sparks to the fire building rapidly inside me.

My thighs tremble, and sweat pools between my breasts, the hot grow lights making the room humid and steamy as the overhead sprinklers turn on, misting the plants. I grip his hair tighter, grinding my cunt shamelessly into his face, and he moans, the vibrations sending jolts to my core. My toes curl, and my back arches, and just as I'm about to fall over the edge, he pulls back, leaving me wanting. I peel my eyes open and glare at him.

"Why did you stop?" I ask, but instead of replying, he flips me onto my stomach and drags my hips into the air.

He runs a hand down my sweaty back, and just when I think he's going to tease me a little more, he grabs my hips and slams his cock home.

"Fuck!" I scream as my pussy stretches around his girth, the sudden intrusion giving me the slight bite of pain I love. I moan, and my head hangs forward as he starts a punishing pace. I try to rise up on my hands and push back, but he shoves on my back, forcing my face into the pillows. Sage doesn't pull any punches, and his pace is brutal, pulling out to the tip before thrusting in hard, our skin making obscene slapping sounds in the mostly silent grow house.

All I can do is hang on for the ride. He slaps my ass before grabbing my hair and yanking my head back, biting my neck brutally before muttering, "Take it, Tori, just like that. Your cunt feels like a hot, tight velvet glove."

I try to push back to meet every brutal plunge, but

he keeps me pinned in place as his cock pistons in and out of my pussy, which is so wet, the squelching sounds rise above the quiet hiss of the sprinkler system.

"Harder," I beg. "I want to come. Please, make me come, Sage." My breathing is harsh, and the words shudder out of me, muffled by the pillows. Sage obliges, snapping his hips, his balls slapping against me with every stroke. A sharp slap to my ass cheek is what sends me over the edge. I wail as my pussy clamps down around his thick length, my walls spasming and body shaking as I cry out his name.

"Sage!"

It's enough to send Sage into his own orgasm. He groans and buries himself deep in my cunt, flooding me with his seed as he mutters words of praise, thrusting in and out to prolong my release as his hot cum scalds my insides. We both collapse, sticky and sated, with tiny drops of skunky water dripping over our sex heated bodies from the plants above us.

"So fucking good," I mumble, giving Sage a kiss before collapsing on his chest.

"And that's how you woo the fuck out of someone," he says, placing an arm over his eyes and smiling with satisfaction.

A little later, we head back upstairs, and I take a bath filled to the brim with boiling water and an abundance of bubbles. I try to convince Sage to join me, but he insists I relax, so instead, I watch him shower, the steamy glass enclosure providing entertaining flashes of him washing his gorgeous body.

Once I'm dry and dressed in my pajamas consisting of a camisole and a pair of panties, all my worries and concerns return. I can't stop seeing the blood all over Xavier's arm, Colton's eyebrow, and Vienna's panic as she tried to rouse him. I know I'm not going to get any sleep without checking on them before I go to bed.

"I'm just going to check on the others," I tell Sage, stopping my pacing and heading for the door.

He jumps up off the bed where he was reclining, scrolling through his phone, and grabs the other joints he brought back to our room.

"Good thinking. I was going to give them these, so we can go together." He takes my hand and leads me out of my room and down to theirs. I wouldn't be surprised to see them all in one after today. I glance briefly down the hallway. I've managed to avoid Gio so far. In fact, I don't even know if he's home. I'm surprised he wasn't banging on my door as soon as he heard what happened—or maybe he doesn't know, or he's still pissed at me after this morning's altercation. Whatever the reason, I'm grateful.

Sage knocks on the door as I bite my lip in anticipation. It takes a moment, but eventually, the door opens, and a sleepy-eyed Tristan peers at us.

"Oh my god, you guys were sleeping. I'm so sorry!" I'm horrified we woke them. Of course they are resting, it's been a clusterfuck of a day.

"No, it's okay, come in." He steps back and gestures for us to enter. The room is dark, with only a light from the bathroom illuminating it. The bed is a mess of limbs and bodies, and Xavier and Colton haven't even heard us enter. Both are out for the count on one side of the bed, slightly snuggled together. Vienna lies on the other side of the enormous bed with a space next to her. I guess that must have been Tristan's spot. There's also a rather large gap between each couple. They probably don't want to disturb the injured ones.

"Tori, Sage, we were so worried about you. You weren't checked over by the doctor. What if you aggravated your injuries from the last accident?" Vienna throws back the sheets and starts to get up, but Sage is quick to stop her, putting a hand on her chest.

"Stay, beautiful. Tori and I are fine. We're tougher than you think." He smirks at her, and she blinks.

I'm not surprised, because that smirk is mesmerizing.

"Are you sure?" Tristan approaches me, looking me up and down, his gaze lingering on my bare legs before returning to my face. He studies me closely. "Your head hit my knee pretty hard. Are you sure you don't have a concussion?"

I try to wave him off, but he won't be deterred, so instead I try to distract him. I step forward, pressing my body against his. He's shirtless and only wearing a pair of briefs, and there's a lot of bare skin that brushes against mine. A shiver runs down my spine, and his concern turns to something more as his lips curve up in a small smile of approval.

"I'm positive. I'm hardheaded, just ask anyone," I tell him, twining my arms around his neck. "How about you? How's your knee? Did you ice it?"

He scoffs but puts his hands on my waist. "Please, I'm tougher than that. You barely left a bruise."

"He iced it and bitched the whole time," Vienna shares, and Tristan glares at her. Colton grumbles and rolls over, and Sage holds his hand out to Vienna. "Let's go out on the balcony so we don't wake the others."

She frowns. "But we're locked in." The shutters are down over both the window and the balcony door.

He winks at her. "I've got the right touch." He leads her over to the security pad on that wall, places his hand against it, and puts in a code, and the shutters roll up. Sage pushes the doors open, then he and Vienna move through them.

I unwind my arms from Tristan's neck. "Come on, Sage has a smoke that will help you sleep." I hold out my hand, and he takes it and lets me drag him outside.

"Fine, but I want you on my lap so I can check you over," he bargains, and I smile.

"I'm okay with that."

The balcony winds all the way around the top level, allowing access from all the bedrooms. There are chairs spaced along its length, but only two in front of this room. They are both chaise lounges, so Sage takes one and pulls Vienna into his lap, and Tristan does the same for me.

I make myself comfortable between his legs, leaning back against his solid, warm chest. He wraps his arms around me when I shiver, this time from the cool night air.

"Did the doctor see the other two?" I ask as Sage lights up the joint before passing it to Vienna.

"Yeah. Colton has a concussion and needed two stitches in his eyebrow. It was quite deep. Xavi has five stitches in his arm and pulled a muscle in his shoulder from where he stopped me from flying through the cab," Tristan murmurs in my ear. "Vienna's okay. Colton took the brunt of the impact on that side and has bruises all over his body to show for it, but she feels guilty as fuck and is being maternal about it." He turns my head with one hand to look at the other two. Vienna passes the joint back to Sage and starts running her hands all over his body to check that he's telling the truth about being uninjured apart from aches and pains. I roll my eyes, because his reaction is classic Sage. He practically preens and purrs, leaning into her touch, the bulge in his briefs growing rapidly.

"Babe, if you wanted to get your hands all over me, you only had to ask."

He hauls her against his chest with his free hand and proceeds to kiss the shit out of her. I squirm in Tristan's lap, because they look so fucking sexy. "You would make her night if you suggested that the two of you sleep with us to reassure her," he murmurs quietly as Vienna and Sage break apart. He must not have been quiet enough, because Sage turns his attention away from the breathless goddess in his arms.

"That sounds like a pretty good idea." He looks to me for confirmation. I want to say yes, but we still have some business to attend to tonight.

"We have that thing," I remind him, and his face drops in disappointment, "but I can go on my own. It's fine."

He shakes his head. "Absolutely not. I'm coming with you."

"Oh, what are you doing?" Vienna asks, taking the joint from Sage and putting it to her lips. "Maybe we can help." She gestures to Tristan and herself before taking another drag, then holding it out to us.

Tristan takes it from her and puts it to his lips as I shake my head.

"Yeah, no, it's work stuff, but thanks for the offer." I try to let her down easily, but I can tell she's disappointed. "But maybe we can nap here for a few hours before we have to leave," I suggest, trying to soften the blow.

"Okay. I can compromise. That sounds nice." Her smile is bright, even if it doesn't reach her eyes. She does a good job of hiding her disappointment.

"And anyway, you don't want to have to wake up and find Sage sprawled across the whole bed. I swear, since we've been sleeping together, I wake up with more aches and pains than today's accident gave me," I joke, and he glares at me, but she laughs lightly, the rest of the disappointment fading from her eyes.

"Tris is the same, a complete bed hog. It's why we make him sleep on the outside."

Tristan grumbles behind me. Sage holds out his hand for a fist bump, and he quickly complies.

"Did you guys get some food?" I ask her. We were at our picnic a lot longer than I thought, and it was already dark by the time we emerged.

"Yes, Suzy fed us after the doctor left. She's the best. You are so lucky to have such an amazing family," Vienna says, sounding a bit envious.

"Yeah, we lucked out. My dad was amazing as well," I reply quietly, and Tristan's arm tightens around me, giving me a little squeeze as he passes me the joint. I take a drag, blowing out the smoke before asking, "Speaking of family, did Gio come home tonight?"

Vienna shakes her head. "No, he and Casey stayed in Suncity in your suite at the Lucky Diamond."

I breathe out a sigh of relief that I obviously don't hide too well.

"What's with you and Gio? I thought you guys were tight, but since we moved in, I sense some tension between you," Tristan asks casually, and I see Vienna's attention turn from Sage's creeping hands to me.

"Is it because of us?" she asks quietly, but I'm quick to shake my head.

"No, not at all. We were having issues long before you moved in." I don't tell them that I think the issues stem from his relationship with Casey and his interest in being more like them then running the family business. "Don't worry about us, it will all sort itself out eventually," I assure her, even though the reality is there's a good chance we might come to blows, and one of us may not survive.

We pass the joint around between us a little longer and talk about mundane things. Vienna is excited for our spa day and the party over the weekend, and it's nice to keep my mind occupied and not obsessing over tonight's job. Eventually, we decide to turn in. A few hours of rest will help keep my mind sharp, and if it's spent between a sexy man and woman, I'm not going to complain.

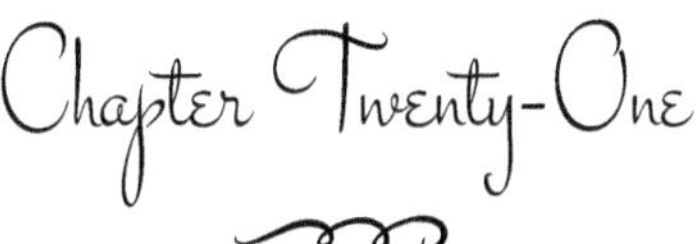

Chapter Twenty-One

"Are you ready?" I whisper to Sage as I pull the balaclava over my face. I tried to leave without him, but it was a little tricky. With Tristan on one side, Vienna on the other, and Sage next to her, I had to get away from three people without waking them, and I wasn't successful. I'm not complaining, though, because I got two delicious goodbye kisses from the ones who stayed behind. Colton and Xavier were still knocked out, the pain killers the doctor gave them doing their job.

"Let's do this," he confirms, his voice slightly muffled by his own balaclava.

We're both dressed in tight black clothes suitable for breaking and entering and scaling buildings. I decided a roof ingress was the best option once we dealt with the dogs and guards. The dogs were easy. I just stole some chuck from Suzy's fridge and stuck the sedatives in it. They wolfed it down, and we waited fifteen minutes for it to activate before we climbed the chain link fence. Thankfully it wasn't electrified, so it was one less thing to worry about. Then, it was just a matter of taking care of the guards. Eight in total all received a tranq dart to the neck. After that, we could have pretty much strolled into the building, but I didn't know who or how many were inside, so we climbed the fire escape to the roof and peered down through the skylights.

"Holy shit!" Sage swears as we take in the contents of the warehouse. Cages like dog kennels, but bigger, have been set up, and they are not empty. There appears to be about twenty in total, and at least three quarters have bodies slumped in either sleep or despair.

"Can you see any guards?" I ask him as my gaze scans the area we can see. It seems the majority of the space is just this one large room, but like ours, there appears to be a reception area and possibly some bathroom facilities on one side. There is also a large mezzanine level that circles the space. I can see two men using a money machine to count a pile of cash.

"Only the two there." He nods to the two I noticed.

"We need to go down there and see if the fed's sister is there. None of this is helpful to me unless she is."

He sighs. "It couldn't just be easy this one time."

"No rest for the wicked," I reply as we creep

toward the fire escape door. It doesn't seem to have any security on the outside, which is what I expected. I just hope there isn't a bar across the inside of it. I try the handle, and it turns easily and quietly.

"Thank fuck," Sage mutters. "I'm too sore to smash through a window and repel into the building."

"And it doesn't exactly scream subtle," I say sarcastically as the two of us slide through the door, our guns at the ready. The exit is behind some shelves, and neither of the men counting cash on this level have noticed us. We both lift our guns and aim, firing at the same time, and the darts hit the guards, who both shout in surprise, but the sedative is fast acting, so before either of them can react, they are out for the count.

"Grab the cash. We will make it look like a robbery so they aren't suspicious and pack up and shift their operation before the feds can raid it."

"If we take the money, I bet that will bring Lorenzo running to investigate too, which will make it all nice and easy for the feds to clean up," Sage says as he hurries over to the table and starts loading the cash into the backpack we brought our gear in.

While he's doing that, I look through the rest of the stash they have up here. There's a shipment of weapons, as well as some canisters of nasty looking chemicals. I wrinkle my nose in disgust. The Russos have never dabbled in chemical warfare. It's despicable.

There's also an entire shelf filled with little silver

foil packets in large bags. I'm pretty sure that's heroine or fentanyl. I'm tempted to take that too and ditch it, but it will add to the case against Lorenzo when the warehouse gets busted.

"I'm going to call Garcia as soon as we verify if his sister is here or not. Even if she isn't, this needs to be busted as soon as possible. Once the guards wake, they are going to tip off the bosses. All he's going to have to do is lie in wait and round them up when they arrive."

"You think Mario will come too?" Sage asks as he finishes his job, and we start to move quietly toward the stairs leading to the main floor.

"We could only be so lucky," I mutter, gesturing for him to be quiet in case there are any guards we missed down here.

The steps are creaky, and the lower we get, the more my stomach starts to roll. It smells bad, like unwashed bodies and fear. Keeping a sharp eye out, Sage and I creep around the cages. Most of the inhabitants are asleep or whacked-out on something, and no one really shows any interest in us, even if they do notice us pass by. I keep a keen eye out for the agent's sister. He sent me a photo of her not long after I promised to help him, and her face is practically burned into my memory.

We pass by one cage that has a woman rocking back and forth, muttering to herself, as tears stream down her cheeks. The sheer desperation on her face almost makes my cold dead heart give a shit—almost, but she's not who we're looking for. Garcia's sister has dark hair, and this one has matted blonde hair.

"Tori," Sage hisses from farther down. I hurry to catch up with him. I can't even promise the woman everything is going to be okay. I don't want anyone to be tipped off that a raid is coming. "Is this her?"

I get to a cage that has another woman in it. This one looks like she still has some fire left in her by the way she glares at us.

"My brother is going to kill you all," she spits, her eyes blazing with fury.

"Yeah, this is her." I recognize those whiskey brown eyes that are so much like her brother's. She even has the same nose as him. In fact, they could be twins, though she's a far more delicate version. "Are you Xiomara Garcia?" I ask quietly, and she spits at my feet.

"Charming," Sage drawls.

"Hang in there, Xiomara, Gabriel is coming." At my words, her eyes widen, and she jumps to her feet, stepping up to the bars and grabbing them.

"Who are you? Are you cops?" she whispers, looking around to make sure no one is within hearing distance.

Sage scoffs. "Not even close. We're more like the devil, but better the devil you know, am I right?" She frowns in confusion, and I pat part of her hand around the bar.

"Stay safe for a little while longer. Come on." I tug at Sage's shirt, and we move back the way we came. She calls out quietly for us to stop, but we don't. As much as I would like to take them all with me, they are Lorenzo's downfall, and I need that more than I need to breathe.

Now that I have confirmation, it's time to blow this joint. I don't want to risk staying any longer, even though the tranq darts should keep them out for at least another hour or so.

As we climb the stairs and head back through the fire escape, I pull out my phone and send a message to the number the agent gave me. It contains the address of the warehouse and the code word "Tamales," which is apparently Xiomara's favorite food.

They will put an agent on Lorenzo to know when he goes to the warehouse, and then the raid will happen, and Sage and I will be far away. I just need to practice my shocked expression when I find out my dear old uncle has been arrested. I also need to instruct the family lawyer not to represent him, so he is stuck with a public defender. I can only hope that someone will shank him in prison, saving me from having to order it.

"Well, that was a successful evening," Sage says as we get back to our car, which is parked in a discrete alley ten minutes away from the warehouse. "Wouldn't you like to be on scene when it all goes down? I want to see the look on Lorenzo's face when he realizes he's been busted."

"He's probably going to try to pin the blame on us.

Thank goodness we're the ones working with the feds. It will completely exonerate us."

"I bet he'll just about have a stroke when they tell him you're the one who tipped them off to his operation. I wonder if we can get Colton to hack into the surveillance so we can watch."

I stop dead. "Fuck, the surveillance. I didn't even think of that. I'm off my game. The accident today rattled me, and Gio and..." I trail off as Sage shakes his head.

"Don't stress. We're covered from head to toe, and they saw us steal the money. I would say it probably makes it more plausible that we were just thieves."

I feel some of the tension drain out of my body. "Maybe."

"Or we can wake Colton when we get home and get him to erase any trace of us. We have options."

"Okay, yeah, we could do that." The ride home is quiet but more relaxed than the ride to the warehouse. When we arrive at the house, it's still locked up tight, and there are a few hours of night left.

"Come on, princess. You need your beauty sleep if you're heading to the spa with Vienna in the morning," Sage says as the elevator travels up.

I groan and slump against the wall. "Ugh, it's going to suck," I mutter, but he shakes his head.

"No, it isn't. You're going to feel like a ball of mush with all of that tension draining out of you. It will be great, and you'll get to spend some more time with Vienna. It's a win-win."

He leads the way down the hallway to my room. We both pause in front of the door, looking toward the room the others are in. "I should probably wake Colton and get him to hack the warehouse surveillance feed, right?" Despite everything, I'm still nervous about my feelings for the others.

Before we can make a decision, the door opens, and Colton peers out, blinking at the bright light of the hallway. "I thought I heard someone out here." He rubs a hand across his naked chest. "You guys okay? Are you going to come back? Vienna says you were here earlier in the night but had to go out for work."

"Ah, yeah, we're good," I reply, distracted by his naked skin. These men really are a work of art, like someone sculpted them out of clay. Shaking my head, I move closer to him, feeling Sage at my back. "Um, I know it's late and you're probably still hurting, but I was wondering if it would be possible for you to help us out?"

Asking for any kind of help is difficult for me. I like to be able to do everything, but even I know hacking a surveillance feed is beyond my meagre hacking skills.

His eyes brighten, and he becomes more alert. "You want my help? Sure, what can I do for you?"

Sage groans and mutters, "So many things."

I roll my eyes at his reaction but focus on Colt. "Ah, so Sage and I may have done a little B and E this evening."

He becomes even more alert, his body tightening

with awareness. "Are you guys okay? You didn't get caught or hurt, did you?"

I wave him off. "No, nothing like that, but I'm embarrassed to admit I forgot about the surveillance cameras."

Before I even finish explaining, he spins around and reenters their room. Sage and I exchange a glance and follow him. He turns on one of the overhead lights and sits down at the small desk, then he opens up his laptop, and his fingers start flying across the keyboard.

"What's the address? I'll hack the feed and erase it."

"What's going on?" Xavier sits up in bed, and I see the other two stir as well.

"Just helping Tori and Sage out with something. Go back to sleep." Colton doesn't look away from the screen, his focus on the task at hand.

"Hi, how's your arm and shoulder?" I ask him when he winces, sitting up further.

"A little sore," he admits, and I walk over, grabbing the bottle of pain pills from the side table and tapping a couple into my palm before passing them to him.

"Here, take these. There is no point in being in pain if you can avoid it." I hand him the glass of water that is also there, and he doesn't hesitate to throw them back.

"Are you guys okay?" Vienna sniffs. "You don't smell smoky this time."

Sage chuckles. "Nothing quite as dramatic as

arson. Just liberating some enemies of something that doesn't belong to them," he says vaguely.

"What's the address?" Colton asks me, and as I rattle it off, Sage pulls the backpack from his shoulder with a cheeky grin.

"How about some role play? You can be Demi Moore, and I'll be Robert Redford, and I'll offer you money to sleep with your wife," he says to Tristan who frowns.

"I'm so much better looking than Woody Harrelson."

Sage starts pouring the cash onto the bed.

Vienna's eyes grow wide, but then she purses her lips. "So you think I'm a whore?"

He tosses the bag to the side when he's finished and puts a finger under her chin, lifting it so he can place a kiss on her lips.

"A very expensive one." He winks, and she rolls her eyes.

I shake my head at his antics as Tristan wrinkles his nose.

"Ugh, do you know how dirty money is?"

Sage toes his shoes off and leaps onto the bed, making money angels. Vienna giggles at his behavior and showers him with bills.

"Who cares? I've always wanted to roll around in a mountain of cash."

"Where did that come from?" Xavier looks at me, curiosity and wariness in his eyes.

"From someone who didn't need it." I shrug, and he frowns, but Colton requires my attention.

"Tori, what the fuck am I looking at?" His voice is hard, and I can tell he found the footage.

The others stop messing around on the bed as Xavier climbs off and peers over Colton's shoulder. I wince.

"You are looking at the holding cells of a future skin auction," I tell them bluntly.

Vienna gasps, and she and Tristan scramble off the bed to hurry over to have a look. She puts a hand over her mouth in shock, and Tristan swears up a storm.

"Well, that killed the mood," Sage grumbles and starts to gather the money off the bed. Thankfully it's only on the top covers, and the sheets beneath it are still clean.

"And you just left them there? How could you?" Vienna scolds, and I feel it stab through my heart.

"I don't need to explain myself to you," I tell her coldly, becoming the angel of death in an instant.

"But all those people," she argues, and Xavier puts his hand on her shoulder.

"Leave it, Vienna, I'm sure Tori has a reason."

She crosses her arms and turns her back on me as Colton continues to input things into his laptop. Suddenly, the screens flash and return to an image without Sage and me in it.

"I looped some earlier footage and spliced it into the gap where I removed the footage of the two of you. They won't know what happened or who it was," he tells me, not looking in my direction, and I release a small sigh of relief.

"Thank you," I reply, annoyed that I had to rely on him for his help, but grateful that he did it.

"Do you want to share what's going on?" Tristan prompts, and I cross my arms and shake my head.

"No, this is one of those things that I can't share with you. You need to decide whether you are okay with that and still want whatever this is." I gesture between us. "It's nonnegotiable."

There's a loaded silence, and I guess that tells me everything I need to know.

"Well, okay then. Thank you again. I need to head to bed." I turn my back on them and walk toward the door. I can feel everyone's eyes on me, and I hold my breath to see what Sage does.

"Goodnight," I hear him mutter, and again, another rush of air escapes me in my relief. He chose me. God, that feels good.

Before I can pull the door closed behind us, I hear Vienna cautiously call out, "Tori, are we still on for tomorrow?"

"Why don't you decide what your answer is going to be and let me know?" I reply without looking back, pulling the door closed.

It's not until we're in Sage's room and his arms are wrapped around me that I react to what happened. A small sob escapes my lips before I can stop it, and my chest aches with heartbreak.

"Fuck, I allowed myself to hope for the first time in

ages," I admit as he rubs a hand up and down my back in comfort.

"I know, but don't count them out just yet. I think you're going to be pleasantly surprised in the morning," he says reassuringly, but I'm not so sure. It's a big ask, and I wouldn't like to be put in the same situation.

"We'll see," I mutter before he steers me to the bed, helps me remove my clothes, and holds me as silent tears trail down my face. Damn it, I had been teasing Sage about catching feelings, but he wasn't the only one.

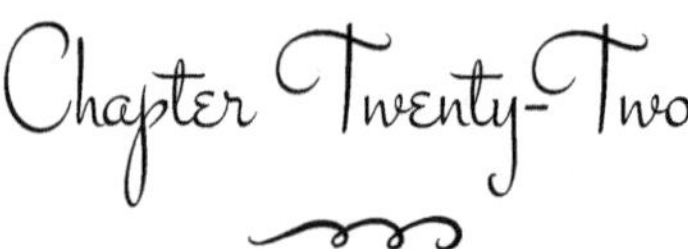

Chapter Twenty-Two

I dread getting up the next morning, and Sage has to physically force me out of bed, but just after my shower, I get a message from Agent Garcia that has me putting on the jets. I rush to get dressed and hurry downstairs. I'm not sure what Vienna has decided, so I wear my usual work uniform but take a change of clothes suitable for a spa visit on the off chance she hasn't had a change of heart.

"Whoa, where's the fire?" Ben asks as I barrel into the kitchen.

"Lorenzo is on his way to the warehouse. The feds are going to raid it soon, and I kind of want to watch from a distance to make sure he doesn't get away. Where's Sage?"

"In the dining room." Suzy points in that direction.

"Good luck, I hope they nail his ass to the wall," Ben calls as I hurry to find Sage.

"Sage, we have to go," I snap as I fling the door open.

Taking one look at my face, he jumps to his feet, rubbing his hands together. "Aww, this is going to be good. Karma, thy name is Tori."

Before we can leave, Vienna also jumps to her feet. Although I hadn't looked at anyone but Sage, I could feel them all watching me. "Tori, are we still on for today?"

I pause and turn to look at her. None of them are glaring at me with judgment, and Vienna wrings her hands in anticipation. "Are we good?" I ask calmly, and she nods.

"Yes, I apologize for getting upset last night. I'm sure you had a valid reason." The apology feels a little hollow, but she looks sincere enough. My gaze shifts to the guys, and they all nod but don't say a word.

I make a snap decision. "Do you want to join us? I would like to show you the reason I didn't do anything last night."

The four of them exchange loaded glances but quickly jump to their feet.

Xavier gestures. "Lead the way."

"But the limo was smashed. How are we going to get wherever we are going?" Tristan asks as I lead them to the elevator and down to the garage.

"Please," Sage scoffs. "Did you think that was our only vehicle?"

The elevator doors open, and there is a fleet of cars waiting for us. Gio's is obviously missing, but both my and Sage's personal vehicles are here, as well as Ben and Suzy's. Tristan's Maserati is also parked in one of the bays, as is a flashy BMW which I don't recognize, so I assume it belongs to one of them. Then there are the work vehicles. Each and every one of them is bullet-proof and have the same kind of reinforcement the limo had. It's why we didn't all end up as mangled piles of mush yesterday. I pick one of the SUVs big enough to seat all six of us.

I drive, and Xavier takes the passenger seat with the rest of them spreading out in the other two rows. No one talks until we're on the road.

"Where are we going?" Vienna asks, unable to stop her curiosity.

I point to the center console. "Can you all put your phones in there?" I ask them, and Xavier frowns.

"You don't trust us?"

"Trust is something that is earned, and I trust very few people. In fact, you can count on one hand the people I trust, and Gio and you four are not on that list." I don't bother mincing words. I still haven't heard from Mickey, and until I do and know they aren't hiding anything, I'm going to err on the side of caution.

"Fair enough," Colton replies, and when I glance in the rearview mirror, he's passing his and Tristan's phones forward to Sage, who takes them and Vienna's and puts them in the center console. Xavier's soon follows.

I take a deep breath and take my first step into

sharing something work related with them. Colton really came through for me last night, so it's the least I can do, especially now that everything is in play. "Right, so last night's B and E was courtesy of my dear uncle Lorenzo. I've long suspected he's working against us, possibly with a rival family, and I recently discovered I was right."

"We suspect Lorenzo is responsible for Stefano's early demise, an attempt to take his place as the eldest Russo and head of the family," Sage adds.

"He assumed two teenage kids would be pushovers?" Xavier questions, and I nod.

"Yes, despite knowing Dad was training us for our roles within the family. We believe we were supposed to be in the limo when it exploded as well."

"Oh my god!" Vienna gasps, and when I look in the mirror, she's grasping Sage's hand tightly.

"But then Gio and Tori cut a bloody swathe through the rival families, taking out anyone who looked at them wrong, as well as rejecting offers of marriage from alliances in the hope that they could just absorb the Russos into their own. In the end, everyone backed off, realizing these teenage kids weren't pushovers like they thought they were going to be." I can hear the love, admiration, and awe in Sage's voice and give him a small smile.

"Everyone backed off, and we made it clear to Lorenzo that he could either deal with the status quo or permanently disappear. He tucked tail and went back into his little rat hole, but both Gio and I knew that wouldn't be the end of it. We just never thought he would go so far as to partner with our biggest rival, who up until now, we've had a tentative truce with that my father negotiated. We aren't exactly sure what he promised, but it all goes out the window. They've declared war, and I don't plan on losing."

The car falls silent on my last comment as I pull into a parking lot in view of the warehouse, but not close enough for anyone to notice anything out of the ordinary, the other cars parked around us providing plenty of cover.

I turn off the car and tap my finger against the wheel, anticipation sending adrenaline firing through my body.

"So what is happening then?" Vienna breaks the silence, and I hold up a hand.

"Just watch. It should be any moment now. It would have taken Lorenzo half an hour to drive from Suncity, so by my calculations, he will be pulling up any minute."

"Something's happening to your uncle? Are you going to kill him?" Tristan has unfastened his seatbelt, and he leans through the front seats to look at me.

I smirk and shake my head. "Nope, something better, and he's never going to know I'm responsible."

"Here he comes." Sage points at the vehicle moving down the road, and I roll my eyes. My asshole of an uncle drives the most ostentatious bright green Lamborghini. "I wonder what's going to happen to the car when he's gone. Can I have it?"

"Sure, because that's just what you need, a car that goes from zero to a hundred in three point six seconds," I say sarcastically, not taking my eyes off it as it pulls up to the gates of the warehouse. A guard comes out with a snarling dog on a leash and peers in the window before gesturing for the gates to open, then Lorenzo drives through.

"The dogs seem to have recovered well," I remark absently to Sage as I watch my uncle get out of his car. I can tell by the way he's waving his arms around that he isn't happy.

"That's where you broke in last night?" Colton asks.

"Yup," Sage replies.

"All those women and men are in there?" Vienna asks, holding her breath.

Again, Sage answers. "Yup."

"What's going to happen to them?"

I turn to look at her, and she's wringing her hands, but instead of watching my uncle, she's looking at me.

I give her a gentle smile. "Hopefully they are all about to be liberated."

Just like that, the street falls into mayhem. Eight black government SUVs surround the warehouse, and a SWAT van pulls up, men and women in tactical gear pouring out, their guns held high. Although we can't hear anything, we can see they are yelling. Gunfire erupts, and the feds take cover behind their cars, but the guards are no match for the government personnel. The gunfire doesn't last long, and I see a few dead bodies lying on the ground as they get the gates open and make their way into the compound. I watch eagerly as they flood into the warehouse. More gunfire erupts, and Vienna lets out a little yelp and clutches Sage. He pats her absently, but like me, his eyes are glued to the action.

The gunfire stops, and the car is silent. Only the sound of our breathing can be heard as we watch with loaded anticipation. Eventually, people begin to pour out of the warehouse, and another set of vehicles, this time paramedics and ambulances, arrives in a blaze of sirens.

We watch as victim after victim is led out of the warehouse and shown to an ambulance to be checked by medics. Feds swarm them to question them, but I ignore all of that, my eyes locked on the warehouse door. Eventually, the thing I'd been waiting for happens. My uncle comes out, and while I didn't expect him to go down without a fight, I didn't expect him to be wheeled out on a gurney with medics surrounding him as they rush him to a vehicle.

"That's a lot of blood," Sage comments. You can't miss it. His shirt is gone, and there is blood smeared all over his chest as one of the medics straddles his torso, giving him compressions. I hold my breath as I wait for them to load him into the vehicle and take off, but instead, they stop, and the paramedic shakes his head, giving up on CPR.

"Well, isn't that a delightful sight?" I murmur as I

see Agent Garcia step out if the warehouse, a girl wrapped in a blanket in his arms.

"The death of your uncle?" Xavier asks, and I shrug.

"That among other things. Okay, are we ready to start our day? Should we have breakfast out? I suddenly feel like celebrating." I turn away from the action and start the car, driving away from the chaotic scene.

"Did you tip off the feds?" Colton asks, and I scoff.

"Me tip off the feds? Now why would I do a thing like that? An informant just happened to know all that was going down and told me. Had I wanted to protect my uncle, I could have warned him, but as it happened, that helped take him off the board permanently." I reach out and turn the radio on, blocking the chance for any more questions, and I start to sing along as we drive toward Suncity, brunch at the Lucky Diamond, and my relaxing spa day with Vienna, happier than I have been in ages.

⁓

I'm not sure what the guys do while Vienna and I are pampered and massaged into comas, but the four of them are waiting when we leave the spa. I had an amazing morning and feel light and airy after spending time with Vienna and just talking about girly shit. I don't remember a time when I had so much fun. There were no expectations, just casual and intimate conversation, and I learned so much about her. She really does love the boys more than life itself, and their bond is soul deep.

I also learned she's a sucker for children and small animals, and if she had her way, she would have a menagerie of animals and a whole truck load of kids. She laughed when I wrinkled my nose at that statement but didn't make me feel bad about my lack of maternal instincts. She asked me what I would do with my life if the choices hadn't been taken from me, and I didn't know the answer to that. We talked movies and fashion, and she gossiped about the people in her classes, but I refrained from asking the one question I really wanted to ask.

We are walking back through the hotel to meet the guys when I finally cave to my curiosity. I guess acting like a teenager has made me regress, because I really want to know the answer to this.

"Do you ever see Stacey?" I ask her quietly, and she wrinkles her nose.

"Yeah. She, the twins, and Nikki Steel hang around a lot of the same people we do. Stacey is constantly putting her hands all over the guys. I want to throat punch her," Vienna growls.

"I can teach you that if you want," I offer, enjoying the thought of Vienna doing that to the bitch.

She smirks. "Xavi already taught me. It's been easier to avoid her since we've been living at your place and don't hang out at all the college haunts." She pauses for a moment. "She's probably going to be there on Saturday. Will that be a problem for you?"

I scoff. "Stacey is but a blip in my memory. Seriously, the only thing you will have to worry about is me putting a bullet between her eyes at the party."

"You know you could leave your gun at home for a change," she suggests, and I visibly shudder, and she laughs.

"That isn't happening," I tell her as we approach the guys, who are sitting in a small lounge area in the foyer of the hotel. Before we get to them, she puts a hand out and stops me. I turn to face her, raising a questioning eyebrow.

She looks a little nervous, and it's kind of cute. She's usually so confident, so I wonder what is about to come out of her mouth.

"This was really nice, just you and me," Vienna says, giving me a sideways look. "I really, really want to hold your hand, but I know you don't want to be seen with us in public like that, so just imagine I am. Also, I'm sorry about last night. I was tired and emotional from worrying about the boys. I should have known you had a reason for leaving those people in that warehouse. Please forgive me."

I give her hand a squeeze, the most affection I can afford to show in such a public place. "It's okay. I probably would have felt the same if I had been in your shoes, and I like the idea of holding your hand, I'm just sorry I can't make it a reality."

She nods, and we continue toward the guys.

Sage catches sight of us first and jumps to his feet, a huge smile on his face. "Ah, my eyes! How can I look at such beauties of radiance without being struck dumb from the sight?"

I roll my eyes at his ridiculousness, but Vienna giggles and gives him a little kiss on the cheek before skipping around to the other three. I stay where I am. This is way too public for displays of affection, but I can't help feeling a little jealous. I want to do the same thing, but for their sake, I'll restrain myself.

"Hey, what do you want to do now? There are still a few hours of daylight left. We could go to the beach or the amusement center and go skating or bowling," Tristan suggests, and my heart starts to race. That actually sounds like fun, and now that Lorenzo is dead and I don't have such pressing issues, I could take a few days to have some. Before I can answer, though, I hear someone call my name, and I turn around to find Bryce heading toward me.

"Can I speak to you for a moment?"

I feel my bottom lip drop in a pout. "What's wrong?" I ask him, and he wrings his hands in worry, side-eyeing my guests before replying.

"One of our guests trashed their room, and we need someone to deal with it."

"Why? You're the manager. You deal with it," I tell him with a scowl. Dealing with unruly guests is most definitely not in my job description.

"He's demanding to see one of the owners," Bryce replies as something occurs to me.

"Is Gio here? I was under the impression he stayed here last night."

Bryce bites his lip before nodding. "Yes, he and his lady friend checked in last night and asked not to be disturbed."

I growl. "I don't fucking care. Disturb him. Don't even mention you saw me. It's time he started carrying a bit of his weight."

Bryce nods. "Okay, it's just that the room is Penelope's," he says quietly, and I frown before something occurs to me.

"Is her gentleman friend with her?" I ask, and once again, he nods. A wide smile crosses my lips. I guess Mario has heard of my uncle's untimely demise, but then I remember something else. "Does she have her little friend from the other day with them?" I ask, instantly worried about Addi, but I release a small sigh of relief when Bryce shakes his head.

"No, thank goodness."

"Is Penny okay? He didn't beat on her, did he?" My fingers itch to reach for my gun. Despite all the issues between us, I hate men who beat on those who are weaker than them.

"I think so. I considered calling the cops, but he calmed down and demanded to see one of you."

"Okay, well, you have your instructions. Go disturb the owner. Technically, this is his empire anyway," I say bitterly and turn my back on Bryce.

"I'm sorry," he mutters, sounding hurt before

hurrying away to do as instructed. I'll make it up to him later.

"Is everything okay?" Xavier asks, watching as Bryce departs. I force a smile onto my face and wave toward the exit.

"Come on, let's get out of here. We can decide what we want to do on the way."

I don't wait for them to respond and head in the direction of the valet. I hand him my keys and listen absently while the others decide what they'd like to do.

"Paintball," Colton suggests, and my ears perk up. "I bet Tori would love to get out some of that excess energy she built up while relaxing."

I spin and stare at him, feeling my mouth drop open. "How did you know I was feeling twitchy?" I ask him, admitting the truth. It's been a long time since I had idle hands, and I hadn't even realized I was starting to feel anxious. It's like I don't even know how to relax anymore. I've been busy since Dad died. I don't even remember the last time I took a day off.

He tilts his head. "Since I've known you, I've never seen you relax. Even in our... sessions, you're like this tightly wound bunch of energy, always moving and talking. Your brain doesn't ever switch off. Even when we are talking about something mundane, I can tell you have a million and one things going on inside your head."

Sage whistles quietly. "Damn, man, you really pay attention. Even stoned, she's always thinking. I've been trying to convince her to try some X with me, hoping it will help get her out of her head."

Colton shrugs. "I may be quiet, but I pay attention, and to be honest, Xavier is exactly the same. He has all this pent-up energy but holds onto it like he's an unlit ball of dynamite."

I'm still stunned when Sage chuckles. "Maybe we need to get them both on X and sit back and watch. I bet that would be something to see."

Just then, the valet returns with the car, saving me from answering.

"Right then, how about I drive?" Tristan takes the keys from the valet. "You can continue with the unplanned day off and be a passenger princess."

He doesn't wait for me to argue and jumps into the driver's seat, Sage taking the front passenger seat with Colton and Vienna hopping into the back, leaving me with my apparent emotional twin.

"After you." He gestures, and I shake my head and climb in.

I slide over, and he climbs in behind me, pulling the door shut. Instead of keeping to his side of the vehicle, he sits right next to me, his thigh warm against mine through our clothes. He picks up my hand and holds it, giving it a squeeze.

"We'll look after you, whether you want it or not," he tells me, his gaze serious as he stares into my eyes. "No matter what happens, know we will always put you first," he promises, and I can't help but believe him.

A rush of warmth flows through my body that has nothing to do with the temperature of the car. These people accept me for me, flaws and all, and I can't even begin to describe how fucking good that feels. They are not with me because I'm Tori Russo, enforcer of the Russo family, or because of what I can do for them. They just want me, Tori Russo, messed up in the head and emotionally stunted, but still worthy of affection and kindness.

Chapter Twenty-Three

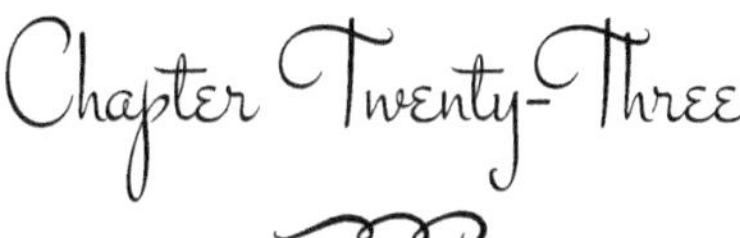

Paintball is exactly what I needed, and I'm in a super good mood when we arrive back at the estate. There's a strange car in the driveway, but we continue past it and park in the underground garage, using the elevator to head upstairs.

"You should have seen your face when I nailed you in that last game," Sage crows at Tristan, who grabs him around the neck in a headlock. The two of them wrestle as we get out of the elevator, their hands becoming more and more grabby as they wrestle. Eventually, they give up, and Tristan slams Sage against the kitchen wall, kissing him like he's the air he needs to breathe.

He pulls away, leaving Sage panting heavily, and winks at him. "Paintballing gets me all hot and bothered." He strolls off, and the rest of us laugh.

"Looks like he nailed you good this time," Colton teases, and Sage groans while Vienna and Xavier laugh.

I shake my head at their antics and continue out into the main living area to find out whose car is in our driveway. None of the others follow me, I guess they are going to wash all the paint smears off themselves. I'll clean up after I've sated my curiosity.

"Suzy? Ben? Whose car is in our driveway?" I call but come to an abrupt stop when I reach the lounge and find Agent Garcia and another FBI agent sitting on my couch. Ben has his arm around Suzy, comforting her, and she has tears streaming down her face. Oh, here we go. It's showtime.

"What's wrong? What happened?" I ask them, and Agent Garcia stands up.

"Ms. Russo, I'm Agent Gabriel Garcia, and this is my partner, Agent Fisher. I'm sorry to say that your uncle Lorenzo was killed in an FBI sting operation this morning. I was wondering if you could answer a few questions for us."

I slap a hand over my mouth and will shock into my eyes. "A sting operation? Oh my god. What did he do?"

"Ms. Russo, can you tell us your whereabouts today?"

"What? Why? You don't think I have anything to do with any of this, do you?" I ask. "I was at the Lucky Diamond all morning in the spa, and then as you can see, we were playing paintball this afternoon." I gesture to my paint smeared clothes. "What is this about? Why was my uncle involved in an FBI sting operation?"

"Ms. Russo, it seems that your uncle was involved

in a sex trafficking operation. We raided a warehouse this morning and uncovered about thirty people waiting to be auctioned and shipped to their buyers," Agent Garcia explains. I already know this, but we are putting on a good show for Fisher.

I widen my eyes in shock. "A sex trafficking operation? That's horrible. I had no idea."

"I bet," Fisher mutters under his breath sarcastically, and I harden my eyes and give him my dead stare.

"I know there are a lot of baseless rumors about my family in this state despite our legitimate business, but I can assure you that we would never stoop so low as to be human traffickers. Only scum of the earth deal in nonconsensual flesh."

"So you had nothing to do with your uncle's operation?"

I scoff. "My uncle and I were not on speaking terms. We avoided each other as much as possible. If you're expecting me to weep over his demise, then you would be sorely mistaken. I had nothing to do with his actions nor will I miss the bastard, but thank you for informing us. When will his body be released for burial?" I ask.

"This is an ongoing investigation, so until it's concluded, we will keep him on ice," Agent Garcia tells me.

"Just contact my office when he's ready to be released, and I will make arrangements. Can I help you with anything else?"

Agent Fisher opens his mouth to ask more questions, but Gabriel cuts him off. "No, we will contact you if we need to ask anything else."

"Well, in that case, Ben will see you out," I tell him, and he nods goodbye before following Ben out.

"We're watching you," Fisher hisses as he passes me, and I clutch my imaginary pearls, unable to stop myself from responding.

"Oh no, whatever will I do?" I say sarcastically, and he glares before stomping after the other two.

"Tori," Suzy scolds, the teary act drying up like a bar during summer break. "Don't poke at the vindictive FBI agent."

"I'm going to get cleaned up," I tell her as we walk back toward the kitchen.

"Did you have a good day?" she asks, threading her arm through mine.

"Actually, it was pretty awesome," I admit, and she beams at me.

"Oh, honey, I'm so glad to hear that. I'm so proud of you for letting them in. They are going to be so good for you."

"Yeah. I think you might be right," I admit. "I'm going to a party with them on Saturday night," I tell her, and she drops my arm and claps her hands together.

"Your first college party. I'm so excited for you. You're going to have so much fun."

I scoff. "I'm sure any college party, lame or not, will be better than any of the other formal ones I've been to recently. I'm so sick of socializing with people twice my age, not to mention they all have their heads up their asses."

Suzy laughs. "Unfortunately you'll probably find most college students are just as likely to have their heads up their asses as well, but at least they will be similar ages. You can drink and dance and maybe make out with your bunch of delicious paramours."

"Hopefully there will be a lot of all that," I tell her, feeling excited. "All right, I need to go get cleaned up. I'll see you at dinner."

"Are you going out tonight?" she asks before I depart, and I shake my head.

"Nope, I'm staying in. Maybe we'll watch a movie in the theatre room or something." I wave goodbye and head to my room via the stairs rather than the elevator. It means I approach my room from the other end of the corridor than I normally do, passing my secret room. My mind is running over all the movies we could watch tonight. There are so many I haven't seen, since watching movies moved way down on my priority list once Dad was gone. When I hear noises coming from the room the others are sleeping in. I slow down and peer inside, unable to stop my curiosity.

A silvery light is cast over the three of them, who are tangled in a frenzy of limbs and lust. The silk sheets beneath them are rumpled, and the air is thick with sweat and arousal. The wet towels on the floor tell me they got distracted after their shower.

Tristan is lying on his back with Vienna sitting on

his face, her breasts heaving as he licks her pussy. Xavier stands at the end of the bed with his cock in Vienna's mouth as he slowly flexes his hips back and forth, sliding in and out of her lips.

"Yeah, that's it. Suck it," he rumbles as he threads his fingers through her wet hair and holds her in place, pushing in deep and holding it there. Her eyes roll back, and her hands reach up to her breasts, tweaking her pretty pink nipples.

A movement off to the side has me stepping back so nobody notices me watching. Colton comes out of the bathroom, rubbing a towel over his naked body, and he tosses it on the floor with the others. "You started without me," he complains as he climbs up onto the bed and licks a long line up Tristan's cock. It's all I can do to muffle my moan and clench my thighs together, my core throbbing with need.

"Prep her ass for me," Xavier orders Colton, who shudders at the command and releases Tristan's cock before straddling his legs and biting Vienna's neck. He leans over and grabs a bottle of lube off the bed, coating his fingers before his hand disappears to do as Xavi ordered. Vienna moans, and I know that Colton has breached her tight ring and is stretching her.

"We're going to fill every one of your holes, and you're going to take us all like the needy slut you are," Xavier croons to Vienna as tears roll down her cheeks.

He pulls out, leaving her panting, and lifts her off Tristan's face. He sits up, and his mouth is covered with her glistening arousal. I almost groan with the need to lick it off him.

Colton does exactly that, leaning down and licking all of Vienna's juices off Tristan, his hand caressing Tristan's cock with firm strokes. Tristan groans, and Colton smirks at him.

"Don't stop," he mutters, but Colton moves, and Xavier lowers Vienna onto Tristan's hard length. The two of them moan as she slides down it, Tristan's fingers tweaking her pert nipples hard. She gasps and shudders as Xavier climbs up behind her, and I watch with interest as he slides his lube-covered cock into her ass. I'm envious, but I haven't done ass stuff, and I'm not sure if it's something that ever interested me, but now I am very curious.

"What a naughty little Peeping Tom." The voice in my ear has me shrieking and spinning around, but Sage muffles my shout with his hand and holds me in place, his other arm like a vise around my waist. "No, keep watching. God, it's live porn and beautiful." His words are husky in my ear, and his hand slips into my pants, dragging a finger through my dripping folds. "And you're so fucking wet."

He rolls a thumb over my clit as he slides two fingers into my channel. I turn my attention back to the sight before us. Colton is now standing in front of Vienna, his cock sliding into her mouth as the three of them move in sync.

"Look at you taking us all so beautifully." Xavier groans as he flexes his hips in tandem to Tristan.

"Imagine if Sage and Tori were with us too. She could suck on your tits while Sage fucks Colton's ass, or you could ride his cock while the three of us do this to Tori."

"Yes," Vienna pants, lifting her mouth off Colton for a moment. "I want that."

"So do we," Colton replies before sliding his cock back into her mouth.

The three of them are relentless, and Vienna's tits bounce wildly as the three of them fuck her, the bed frame thumping against the wall. The three men's groans of pleasure are obscene but so fucking sexy. I reach back and slide my hand into Sage's shorts, stroking his length in time to their sounds. He pumps in and out of my core in the same rhythm, and my orgasm barrels through my body.

We watch as Vienna's orgasm hits like a storm, her pussy and ass milking both men as she struggles to swallow Colton's cum. Some of it dribbles from the corner of her mouth as all three men fill her with their seed. In unison, Sage and I also come, muffling our groans so the others won't realize they are being watched. Sage's cum fills my hand as I gush all over his. I want to stay longer and observe them, but I know we've pushed it by staying too long, so I slide my hand out and shove his away, then I drag him back to our room. I'm not ashamed to admit that I tug him into the shower and fuck his brains out with the images of the four of them in the forefront of my mind. Hopefully next time, Sage and I can join them and make my and their fantasies come true.

Chapter Twenty-Four

The next morning, I wake up in the best mood. I kiss everyone goodbye and leave early, skipping breakfast. I have meetings all day and will eat at the office. Sage decides to stay home and work with his plants, and the others have college and will be taking their own cars, so I take my Charger, the music blaring and the sunroof open as I sing along to a song.

Gio's car still wasn't in the garage when I left, so I'm assuming he stayed at the Lucky Diamond again last night. I'm hoping to get a chance to see him today to tell him all about Lorenzo, but when I arrive and head up to the office, he isn't there. When I send him a message, I get no response, so I pick up my desk phone and call reception.

"Janice, it's Tori Russo. Is Gio still here, or has he checked out?" I ask her.

"Good morning, Ms. Russo. Mr. Russo left about

twenty minutes ago with his lady friend. I heard them talking about morning classes, if that's any help."

I thank the woman and hang up. Damn it. Oh well, I can tell him tonight, I guess.

My door bursts open, and Bryce storms in and throws himself into the chair in front of my desk. He scowls as he crosses his arms and glares at me.

"Everything okay?" I ask lightly, and his frown deepens.

"Fuck you, Tori. You left me to deal with that mess yesterday."

I raise an eyebrow at him. "Correct me if I'm wrong, but aren't you the operational manager of this resort?" I ask flatly, and he sighs.

"Yes, damn it. I'm sorry. Gio was an asshole to me, and then after talking to Mario in his room, he just moved him to the presidential suite below your penthouse and told me to let it go. When I asked him if we should bill him for the destruction, he told me that insurance would cover it."

"He did what?" I sit up straighter, bristling with annoyance.

"He just showed him to another suite and apologized for the inconvenience—he and the girl."

"Casey?" I ask, and he nods.

"Yes, they went in there together, and when they came out, she looked like she had been crying. Why would he take his girlfriend with him to deal with a client? And Penny had definitely been beat on. She has a huge black eye, and her face was red, and she was all hunched over, but she just followed behind like an obedient lap dog."

What the fuck is going on?

"Let me get this straight. You asked Gio to deal with Mario Maricuso after he lost his temper and trashed Penny's suite, but instead of calling the cops or asking them both to leave, he showed them to another suite and said everything was okay?"

"Yes," Bryce confirms. "Then Gio fucked off to his room and left me to deal with the cleanup and relocating the person who was booked into the suite he moved Mario into. I had to comp their whole stay when I had to downgrade them to a junior suite instead. Then he didn't reemerge again for the rest of the day and night, and then scurried out of here first thing this morning like his ass was on fire."

Something starts to tickle at the edges of my mind, but my seething anger is making it hard to form it into coherent ideas.

"Is Mario still here? I'll go speak to him." I stand up, but Bryce shakes his head.

"No, he left just before I came up here. He was on his phone and talking loudly, and I overheard him say everything was falling into place."

Damn it, just when I thought I was getting a break. I thought Lorenzo's death would put a kibosh on whatever Mario had planned, but I was obviously wrong.

"Is Penny still here?" I ask him, and he nods.

"She hadn't left when I was downstairs half an hour ago."

Again, I call reception. "Janice, it's Tori again. Is my stepmother still in the resort?"

"Oh, I'm sorry, Ms. Russo, she just left. She didn't look so good, and when I asked, she said she walked into the door of her suite, and she was going to the doctor to get checked out," Janice tells me, too discrete to gossip about how Penny looked like she had the crap beaten out of her.

"Thank you," I tell her before hanging up.

Fuck. What is going on? I pick up my cell and pull up the tracking app I installed. I tap on Gio's profile, expecting to see him at Suncity U, but instead, he's at home. I stand up. "I'm done with this shit. I'm heading home to deal with Gio," I tell Bryce, and his face pales.

"*Deal* with him deal with him?" he asks vaguely, crossing his neck with his finger.

I sigh. "I don't know. I guess it will depend on what he has to say. Have Susan reschedule all my meetings today. I doubt I will be back," I tell him, and as I pass him, he grabs my arm and gives it a squeeze.

"You're doing the right thing. Gio either has to get his head straight, or he has to disappear. This is not working, and you know the family supports you." He releases my arm and taps his hand where his tattoo is.

"How did it come to this, Bryce?" I ask, feeling defeated. "How did my family fall apart? If I do this, all that will be left is me. I'm the last of the Russo line.

Lorenzo is gone." Bryce's eyes widen, and I explain what happened yesterday, supposing that hearing of Lorenzo's death is what set Mario off. "With no Gio, there is no chance of the Russo name continuing. What will happen to the family? I don't want kids, so there is no chance of me popping out a blood Russo."

"Aww, Tori." He pulls me into his arms and hugs me tightly. "Don't worry about that now. Concentrate on things you can actually fix. Worry about the rest later. Maybe it won't come down to Gio's disappearance. Maybe he has a perfectly reasonable explanation for his actions."

I pull away and straighten my jacket, pulling myself together. "Hmm, it's going to have to be a fucking Hail Mary of an excuse."

I leave, brimming with anger and fear and heartbreak, but when I get to my car, the fluttering little note slipped under the wipers makes me pause. I pull it out and read it. Again, there is an address on it but no explanation. It's the same writing as the last one, and that led to the warehouse with the trafficking victims. Does this one lead to a missing victim? And who the fuck is leaving them?

I pocket the note and burn rubber out of the parking lot. I'm so mad and distracted that I make a split-second decision, and instead of risking an ambush like yesterday, I turn into the unused forest road that our secret tunnel leads to, using it to return to our place. I can't drive at breakneck speed like I want to, so

I'm just driving into the cave entrance when my phone rings. My car picks it up.

"Hey, Mickey, I'm just about to drive into the tunnel, so I might lose you," I say, happy to hear from my uncle.

"The escape tunnel? Good. As soon as you reach the underground bunker, call me. Make sure Sage, Ben, and Suzy are there. I have the results of those background checks, and you're all going to want to hear what we found." I hear the urgency in his voice, but before I can respond, I lose cell signal as the floor lowers.

Damn it. What could possibly be so urgent? My heart starts to beat even faster, my anger replaced by anxiety. I tap my finger on the wheel, desperate to get going, and when the elevator comes to a stop, I gun my car. It's not advisable to drive fast through these tunnels, since they are not all that wide, but I ignore that in my desire to call Mickey back. The normal twenty minute drive is over in just ten. My adrenaline is racing, my hands are shaking, and I've chewed through the skin on my lip when I peel to a stop in the bunker. I'm just hopping out of the car when Sage, Suzy, and Ben emerge from the grow rooms.

"You're here?" I hurry over to them. "I heard from Mickey."

"Yeah, that's why we're all here. He called me and told me to bring Suzy down here so he can talk to all of us."

Sage holds out his phone. "I missed a call from

him. My music was loud, so I didn't hear it," he explains.

I gesture to a small seating area we have down here for the workers' breaks. "I'll call him back and put him on speaker."

My phone beeps with an alert at the front gate. Before I can check the security screens, the alert disappears, like someone has already activated the gate.

"Is Gio here?" I ask Ben and Suzy, and Suzy nods.

"Yeah, he returned this morning with Casey. I said hello, but they rushed through the house like their pants were on fire. Casey looked like she was crying, and then when I followed them to see if they were alright, she was throwing up in one of the downstairs bathrooms. Gio told me to leave them alone. He said she just ate something that didn't agree with her, and he would look after her."

"Oh maybe he called the doctor to look at her then," I reply and forget about him for the moment and call my uncle back.

"Tori, thank God. Are the others with you?" Mickey sounds frantic.

"Yeah, I have you on speaker. Sage, Suzy, and Ben are here too."

"What about Gio?" he asks. "I tried to call him, but he rejected my call."

"He's looking after his sick girlfriend."

Mickey growls. "Casey King, right?"

"Yes," I reply, and we proceed to listen to everything Mickey has found about Casey and the other four. By the time we hang up, I'm completely speech-less and livid, and from the look on the others' faces, so are they.

"Well, fuck," Sage says, scrubbing his hand through his hair, his eyes shiny with sadness.

"I just can't believe it," Suzy sobs, and Ben gathers his wife in his arms and comforts her.

I stand up and pace back and forth for a moment before picking up one of the plastic chairs and hurling it through the space.

"Fuck!" The sound of it crashing against a wall and splintering into pieces echoes around the mostly empty warehouse. I'm glad no one else is scheduled to work today as I systematically lose my shit, throwing anything I can get my hands on before pulling out my gun and unloading the whole magazine into the concrete wall of the bunker, shards of the material blasting out with every impact. It's far enough away not to hurt anyone, so nobody says a word as I unleash my fury.

My ears are ringing, but my mind is clearer as I drop the magazine and grab another one from my corset and slam it home. I run over the events of the previous few days before looking up in horror.

"Pull up the gate footage," I tell Sage, gesturing at my phone as I hurry over to them. Suzy and Ben are practically catatonic with their shock, and Sage's hand trembles as he picks up my phone and shows the footage of the front gate. "Damn it."

"I think it's safe to assume that they are going to

hold Casey over Gio," Ben says flatly, and I nod as I try to come up with a plan. "And they've probably shared the fact that you two are together. You didn't flaunt it in front of Gio, but he isn't stupid."

I freeze, and my anger turns to panic. "They are going to use you against me," I announce, and Sage nods.

"Yeah, I would say it's probably a sure thing."

My mind whirls, trying to come up with a plan, but it's Suzy who starts to talk, and when she finishes, I stare at her in surprise.

"I had no idea you had it in you," I say, gaping at the woman.

She shrugs. "Before your mother, Ben and I were very close with your father." She blushes, and my mouth drops open. "We were very involved with the family."

I look at Ben, and he smiles sadly. "We didn't want you to think any less of your dad, but your lifestyle now mimics his when we were younger. Why do you think neither of us batted an eyelash and encouraged you to explore those relationships? It's also why your dad was so accepting when you told him you liked girls."

"Stefano was bi?" Sage sounds as stunned as I am.

"It doesn't matter now," Suzy snaps, trying to get us back on track. "Sage, go grab the rigged tactical vest from the locker. For this to work, you're going to have to die."

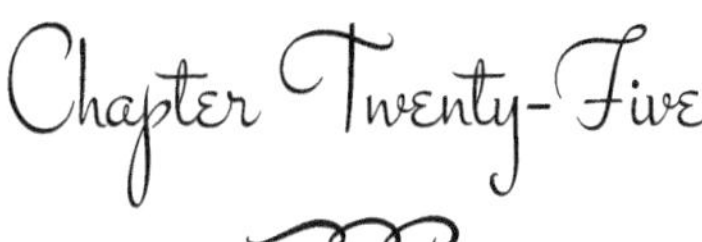

Chapter Twenty-Five

I am about to perform the most important show of my life.

When the elevator stops on the ground floor and the four of us get out, my broken heart is being held together with barbed wire, and I have the scary calm of the angel of death flowing through my veins. Suzy is carrying some grocery bags, since that's where they were returning from when Mickey called them and told them to wait for us.

We are discussing what's for dinner, acting like nothing is wrong, when Gio appears in the kitchen, looking pale and sweaty.

"Suzy, we have some guests for dinner. Please place four more settings at the table, and keep that in mind when you're preparing food."

"Gio," I snap, pretending to be oblivious. "It's a little late notice, don't you think?"

He turns to me and gives me a dead stare. It's like

all the light in his soul has faded. "Please join us in the lounge. Our guests would like to see you."

I feign a frown but nod. "Who is it? Why do they want to see me?" I argue.

"Because I said so," he snaps before turning his attention to Sage. "You too."

"But I was going to go play GTA," Sage whines convincingly. If we gave in too quickly, he would suspect something.

"Fine, let's just get this over with." I roll my eyes, and Gio glares at me before turning and leading the way from the kitchen.

Sage and I walk side by side, and he reaches out and gives my hand a little squeeze. Ben and Suzy stay quiet, knowing not to tip Gio off to anything that we have planned, but they will be waiting just in case we need backup. I don't doubt they will hover around the lounge in time for their cue.

"You didn't say who was here, Gio," I nag him, and I hear him sigh with exasperation, before holding the door open.

"Because if you knew, you wouldn't have come," he says sadly as Sage and I enter the lounge, and this time, I am truly shocked, so my reaction is actually genuine. I thought it was only Penny and Mario in the car, but I hadn't looked at the back seat, because sitting on the couch next to Casey, who looks as pale as Gio does, is a smirking Stacey.

"What the fuck are you doing here?" I demand as Mario stands up, as does the other man in the room. I recognize Stacey's father, who looks at me with great disdain.

"Watch your language," he snaps.

"Now, now, Gregor," Mario says jovially. "I'm sure Tori was just surprised to see her old school friend in her house, especially considering how badly their friendship ended."

Stacey scoffs. "Friendship, please. You paid me to be friends with her. I couldn't stand her. The gatekeeping bitch never thought I was good enough for her brother, otherwise I would have already had a ring on my finger."

Mario's smile turns brittle. "Yes, well, I certainly didn't get value for my money."

"Why are you here in my house? Gio, what's going on?" I demand, but before Gio can respond, Mario claps his hands together in an exaggerated manner.

"Why, we're here to celebrate the engagement of my niece to your brother, of course," he announces, gesturing to Casey and Gio in a way that I think he's hoping will shock me. He would have if it hadn't been for the phone call from Mickey in the nick of time.

I turn my attention to Gio, and he grimaces. "I didn't know they were related, I swear," he mutters quietly, and strangely enough, I believe him. I turn my attention to Casey, and she shrinks behind Gio, out of my line of sight.

"At least this one was successful where her cousin failed." Mario's smile is slimy, but it soon drops as I pull out my gun and aim it at Casey. Mario and Gregor shout, and Stacey scrambles back over the couch out of the way, but Gio jumps in front of her.

"Wait, Tori, wait. She's pregnant," he announces, and my trigger finger twitches ever so slightly when I feel Sage's hand on my back.

"Don't do it. You will regret it," he mutters, and I sigh and drop my gun.

"You stupid fucking idiot," I snap at Gio.

He nods and shrugs sadly. "I love her, and she loves me."

"Pfft, it's all fake. He put her up to it," I counter angrily, stabbing a finger in Mario's direction.

"No, Tori, it's not, I swear." Casey steps from behind Gio with a determined look on her face. "I do love him, I promise. I didn't want anyone to get hurt."

"Like I'd believe any words from your mouth," I sneer at her. "So what now?" I ask Gio, but he looks to Mario like he's deferring to him.

Mario's smirk has returned now that he knows I'm not going to put a bullet in Casey's skull... Yet! My mind whirls as I adjust my plans slightly.

"Well, I guess it depends on if you want your boy toy to live or not." He points at Sage who has moved around the couch and is opposite me now. He has a drink in his hand and has been quiet through this whole exchange.

"Go on," I encourage him, wanting to know what else he has schemed before I pull the pin on his plans.

"Well, everyone likes a double wedding. If you agree to marry my son, we will let your boy toy live."

My heart races as the four people I had been expecting to appear at any moment do so.

"Which one? You have three of them," I ask flatly, giving the four people who wormed their way into my heart and then ripped it to shreds like it was tissue paper a dead look.

Vienna has red eyes and looks like she has been crying, but the three boys have stoic looks on their faces. Gone are the college student outfits they were wearing when they left this morning, and all of them are wearing elegant suits, perfectly suitable for members of the Maricuso crime family.

We were played, and Gio and I waltzed neatly into the honey trap.

"That would be me," Xavier says, stepping in line with Mario who claps him on the back in greeting.

"Once the two of you are married into our family, we will absorb the Russo empire into the Maricuso's and rule the west coast like kings." Mario's delusions of grandeur reek of desperation. "After all, it's what your daddy promised me," he says with a growl.

Through all this, Penelope has been sitting quietly and wringing her hands, but at that, she looks up with guilt in her eyes. "It's true. I'm sorry, Tori. He was going to tell you on the day the limo exploded. He signed a marriage agreement promising you to Xavier. If you reneged, he would have forfeited this house."

I thought I had been hurt and blindsided before, but Penny's words almost stagger me.

"No, he promised me a choice," I argue, and she shrugs.

"I don't know what to tell you. He changed his mind."

"Because Mario told him that if he didn't sign the agreement, we would make war against him, and we had five other families in our pocket. When we won, he would see you passed around to each man who wanted to take a turn at the Russo family princess." Gregor chuckles and takes a sip of his whiskey, eyeing me like I'm a piece of meat. "Maybe I will have a turn before the wedding."

Xavier glares at Gregor, but Mario just chuckles. "You'll have to take that up with my son."

Gregor glares at Xavier who stares back with a look that says over his dead body. Well, isn't that a relief?

"And I get Tristan, don't I, Uncle Mario?" Stacey asks, pawing at the man in question who looks a little green and keeps trying to push her hands off him.

"We will see. It would make sense to marry him off in another alliance, but let's focus on this one first."

Stacey pouts, but Tristan's face stays blank. I guess hearing he's going to have an arranged marriage as well isn't news to him.

"No," I state flatly, my attention turning to Sage. "I love you," I tell him, and he nods, comprehension crossing his face.

Colton must realize what's about to happen, because he screams, "Tori, no!" as I lift my gun and put a bullet through Sage's heart. Everyone starts screaming as blood explodes from his chest, and he falls to the ground. Ben and Suzy come running at the sound of the gunshot.

"What did you do?" Suzy screams at me. Ben puts his hands on Sage's chest like he's trying to stop the blood from leaving his body. "Somebody call an ambulance," he cries.

Vienna screams, so Colton wraps his arms around her and carries her away from the sight. Tristan is muttering words of disbelief, and Xavier stares at me in complete shock.

"Tori, what the fuck?" Gio tries to push his way past Mario and Gregor to get to Sage, but they don't let him. Mario stares at Sage's body in surprise before an impressed smile comes to his face.

"Well, that was unexpected. Well played, Tori."

"He's not breathing," Suzy screams.

Ben leans back, his hands covered in blood, shaking his head. "It's too late, he's gone."

"What did you do?" Gio shouts, and I look him dead in the eye.

"What I had to, to survive."

Whoop! That's a doozy isn't it? Don't worry, I'm already working on the final one and hope to have it out in January, February at the latest. I really enjoyed getting back into Tori's world and I'm really happy with the way it played out. So hang tight, and the epic conclusion and all questions will be answered soon.

In the mean time why don't you check out one of my other series. You can find everything you need to know here.

www.lexiewinston.com

As always thank you to Jess at Elemental Editing. Working with you is a dream and I appreciate you putting up with me.

Thank you to both Tegan and Amanda, my awesome beta readers who give me valuable feedback and encourage me to keep going.

And thank you so very much to all of my readers who have stuck by me this year. Your patience during a trying time has been amazing and much appreciated. I'm well on the way to recovery and hopefully next year will be one of great creativity and production.

I love what I do, and probably would do it regardless if anyone read them or not, but you guys make it that much sweeter so thank you.

Until next time, happy reading
Xoxo

Lexie

Excerpt Unwilling Queen

Want to read something else from me? Here's a look at the first book of the Kingdoms Series.

Colbie

I shove my hands deeper into my pockets as I make my way down the cold, quiet streets toward my bakery. The thud of my sneakers echoes on the pavement. The days are getting shorter, and the temperature has really started to drop in the evenings, even if the days are still sunny. Soon enough, I'll need my hat and gloves as well as my warm winter jacket, but not yet.

The pale streetlights seem to flicker, the slight fog in the air giving my path a creepy vibe, but I don't hurry. I'm mostly safe in the neutral zone. Curfew dictates that everyone is indoors or returned to their own side by a specified time. Only those of us with special permission are permitted to be out after curfew. That doesn't mean people don't disobey the zones directive, but the punishment of imprisonment if caught seems to do its job in deterring both shifters and humans alike. It helps that the night watch are a visible presence as well, though none seem to be patrolling this particular area at the moment. Made up of highly trained shifter and human teams, the night watch is a formidable deterrent to anyone looking to flaunt the pack and human agreement. Of course, this only applies to the neutral zone, so those who want to party on into the night are free to do so in their home zones.

The yawn that leaves my mouth makes my jaw click, and despite the chill in the air, my mind is still foggy with sleep. I didn't get home until late, and with my early starts, I'm functioning on less sleep than normal. All the preparation in the lead-up to the shifter royal pack's retirement has sent many of the businesses in the neutral zone into a flurry, trying to use it as an excuse to boost sales—me included.

I have two recipes for a dedicated royal retirement cupcake special, as well as the cutest little marshmallow animals to float on top of coffee and hot chocolate. For the humans, I have a cupcake with a surprise filling, as well as one with "good luck" written on it, because of course all humans are praying that they become the next shifter king or queen. Well, most of them, because I'm certainly not. I am very happy with my life in the neutral zone, running my bakery, visiting with my mother, and occasionally hanging out with the few friends I have.

Living in the neutral zone and having to obey its curfew doesn't really lend itself to making friends or socializing. The neutral zone doesn't have a lot of permanent residents unless you own a business like my mother and I do, but it serves an important purpose.

It came into existence when the humans and shifters were at war. Both sides realized they couldn't go on like that any longer, so they called a ceasefire, and an amnesty was held to split Aramis into two territories, with a small neutral zone for trade and socialization. This agreement also caught the goddess Aramis's attention. The creator of both races didn't believe that would be enough to stop the antagonization, so she declared that the shifters would have a king or queen, who would rule for forty years before a new king or queen would be selected by her magic. This ensured that both races behaved, which they have.

The end of the current King Lucas's and his three queen consorts' rule is coming to an end, and everyone is eagerly awaiting the next step. Aramis not only selects the new royal, but she also marks a number of possible mate candidates from the shifter population, and then the king or queen will decide from those selected—hence the humans' excitement and my bakery's new desserts. Every human in the human zone of Aramis is on tenterhooks waiting to see if they get chosen.

The whole thing seems a little medieval to me. If and when I decide to marry, I want it to be someone I choose, not because someone has decreed it, but by all intents and purposes, the royals seem deliriously happy. Once they retire, they will become advisors to the new royals for the first few years. They will be known as the former king and queens, and any children from their unions will carry titles but have no ties to the crown.

Apart from that, I don't know a lot about shifters. I don't even really know how many types there are. I've occasionally seen some in shifted form, since they are allowed to wander around the neutral zone like that, but they mostly take their human form. The only way to tell a shifter from a human is by their eyes, which glow with an inner light, unlike that of a human.

I hurry across an intersection, not bothering to look either way. It's starting to drizzle, and I'd rather get to my shop without being soaked by the deceptively fine rain. Traffic isn't allowed in the neutral zone, apart from electric scooters and public transport specifically to prevent shifters from being hit by cars, so I don't have to wait for lights to change.

While adult shifters are usually pretty safe from that fate, they occasionally bring their children over in shifted form, and nobody wants to hit a shifter child.

Shifter children are considered precious, since their birth rate is low because they have such long lives, and harming a child, whether human or shifter, is considered a crime punishable by death.

I pull the key out of my pocket as I get closer, wanting to get out of the rain as quickly as possible. I turn down the alley that sits between my store and the one next to it—a quirky bookstore that caters to the romantics in both races. When Brock decided to open the Romance Nest, he and his partner Niles installed a cozy little downstairs reading room. People are encouraged to bring food and drinks and settle in to read their purchases. Luckily for me, instead of opening their own café to compete, we came up with an agreement to offer them a discount with proof of book purchase, and so far, it's been working well for both of us. Brock and Niles are shifters, but I don't know what type of shifter they are. It's rude to ask, and I'm not as close to them as I wish I was. They seem like such a sweet couple, and I think they would be fun to hang out with, but in the six months they have been open, I haven't worked up the guts to ask them.

As I put my key in the door leading to my kitchen, a noise at the end of the alley catches my attention. I turn to look, peering into the darkness. I wonder if it's just a rat shuffling around in the dumpster, but then a small, keening sound reaches my ears. I drop my keys back into my pocket and pull out my phone, turning on the flashlight so I can see as I step farther into the alley. There's nothing down here but a dumpster and a stack of cardboard boxes, but I keep going farther into the darkness, and I can't stop the surprised gasp that leaves my lips as the boxes tumble over, revealing the cause of the noise. A small black and orange tiger cub is curled up behind the pile, shaking like a leaf. I would bet my last dollar that this is no run-of-the-mill tiger cub, but what is a shifter child doing here in the dark early hours of the morning on its own?

"Oh, you poor, sweet thing. Where did you come from?" I crouch down and inch closer to it. It whimpers and shuffles backward under the boxes. I pause, not wanting to scare it, worried that it will make a run for it. I rack my brain for a solution. I'm not just going to turn my back on it and leave, but I also don't want to be scratched if they aren't happy with me picking them up. My eyes catch on one of the cardboard boxes, and I scrunch up my nose. I really don't want to catch them like a wild animal, but I have too much work to do today to have to worry about seeing a doctor if the cub injures me.

I purse my lips as I look between the box and the cub. How is this cub even here? I didn't see anyone on the walk from my apartment to the bakery. Not a single person was out on the streets, and certainly not a frantic shifter parent looking for their child. I'm surprised the streets aren't filled with worried shifters searching for this little one, curfew be damned.

Sighing, I reach for the box, knowing this is probably going to traumatize the child even more, but I slowly lift it and quickly bring it down over the shivering animal. A small, adorable snarl is muffled by the cardboard, and I feel them scrape at the walls of the box with their tiny sharp nails. Yup, glad I decided to protect myself. Looking down at my hands, I grimace, wishing it was cold enough for gloves. I know I'm probably not going to be able to get out of this without an injury or two, but I'm also not leaving the cub here. I slide my hand under, and in one quick movement, I flip the box. More snarling sounds, louder this time now that it's not muffled, and when I peer down, the cub is glaring up at me with bristled fur, but it has stopped fighting.

"Come on then, let's get you warmed up," I tell it and tuck the box under my arm, using my phone to light my way to the rear bakery door. I turn off the flashlight, shove my phone into my pocket, and retrieve my keys, opening the door to my second home. A rush of warm air brings the scent of yeast, flour, and yesterday's sweet treats with it. I don't bake a lot of bread, mostly just pastries and savory treats to have with coffee in the café, but I do make all the rolls we use, as well as bagels. I flick on the lights and slide the heavy box full of tiger cub onto the counter before turning the ovens on. It won't take long for the kitchen to heat up.

"Just stay there for a moment, and I'll find you something to eat," I tell the cub, who has settled and is now looking up at me with intelligent eyes. I'm not sure how old the child is, but it seems to understand me, so I'm praying it isn't an infant. Shifters are understandably tight-lipped about their children's development.

I slide my jacket off then hang it on the coat hook in my office, replacing it with a clean apron that covers my simple leggings and T-shirt. Work clothes aren't anything fancy for me. I'm just going to get dirty, and once I start prepping for the day, I won't be cold at all.

I pull out some towels I use when I want to shower before going home—my office has a small, attached bathroom—and then I return to the kitchen. The cub has done as I asked, staying in place. They are resting their head in their paws and waiting patiently. I put my hands on my hips and look down at them, smiling gently.

"Well then, I appreciate you listening to me. How about we dry you off and find you something to eat?" I suggest, and their ears twitch like they are listening to me. "But you need to keep your claws and teeth to yourself. I don't want to drop you by mistake if you hurt me, okay?" I ask, and the cub's little head tips to the side like they are acknowledging me.

I breathe out a sigh of relief and reach into the box, sliding my hands gently under the cub's tummy. It's not as rounded as I expected, and I frown. Surely a growing cub should be fed well to help with their growth. Slowly picking it up, I move it onto the towel I spread out on the bench, then I use the towel to vigorously dry them off. It yowls and squirms but keeps its claws and fangs to itself.

Once I'm happy it isn't going to shiver to death, I

pull away. "Right then, I'm sure you're probably hungry and thirsty. Let's get you something to eat. My name's Colbie, by the way. I guess you can't really tell me yours, so I'll just call you cub for now." The cub's eyes widen, and it quickly nods its head. I'm not sure if that's in acknowledgment of the name or wanting food, but I'm going to go with the latter.

"Can you shift?" I ask it, and it tucks its body in defensively, its tail sagging and its ears flattening against its head. "I'm going to take that as a no. How about I set you up a little nest and you can wait in there while I fix you some food?"

I take the other dry towels I have over to the side of the oven, which is starting to warm up nicely, and arrange them in a cozy little nest. "Right, so don't touch the metal, because it might be hot, but this should chase away the rest of the cold," I tell the cub gently, then I lift them up and transfer them to the pile of towels. Before I can pull my hand away, it bumps into it with its head, and a chuffing sound comes from its mouth. I give them a little pet on the top of their head, marveling at how soft it is. I expected the orange and black fur to be bristly, but it's not, it's like feather down. A little tongue swipes roughly across my wrist, and I smile. "What would you like to eat?"

Standing up, I go over to the industrial fridge and open it. I grab a bottle of milk and pour it into a little saucer before checking what other offerings I have that might be suitable for a tiger cub. There's a large roast beef I have been planning on cooking for rolls and sandwiches, but I'm happy to sacrifice it to the small creature, hoping it's old enough to be eating this kind of food.

Shrugging, I head back to the prep table and pull out a cutting board and knife before I cut off a chunk of the meat, dicing it into small, cub-sized pieces. I wrap the rest up and return it to the fridge before grabbing the offerings and placing them on the floor in front of the cub. It looks between me and the food with wide eyes. "Go on then. Eat up. I need to clean and start getting ready for the day." I turn around, but I smile when I hear the greedy sounds of the cub scarfing down its food. "Not too fast, you don't want to be sick," I caution, cleaning up the mess on the prep table and wiping the surface with cleaner so it's ready to go.

I need to think about calling the night watch to come and get the cub so they can find whom it belongs to, but first, I need to get my initial batch of muffins in the oven.

Available at Amazon or click the link below

<u>Buy it now</u>

www.ingramcontent.com/pod-product-compliance
Lightning Source LLC
Chambersburg PA
CBHW051241210726

48287CB00002B/349